Into the Dreamlands

Edited By Jason Andrew and Michael Dyer

Copyrights and Credits

Table of Contents

So Runs the World Away

by Caitlin R. Keirnan

"A falling star for your thoughts," she says, and Gable, the girl with foilsilver eyes and teeth like the last day of winter, points at the night sky draped high above Providence and the wide Seekonk River. Nightsecret New England sky, and a few miles farther north you have to call it the Pawtucket River, but down here, where it laps fishy against Swan Point and the steep cemetery slopes, down here it's still the Seekonk, and way over there are the orange, industrial lights of Phillipsdale. Dead Girl blinks once or twice to get the taste out of her mouth, and then she follows Gable's grimy finger all the way up to Heaven, and there's the briefest streak of white light drawn quick across the eastern sky.

"That's very nice, but they aren't really, you know," she says, and Gable makes a face, pale face squinched up like a very old woman, dried-apple face to say she doesn't understand, and "Aren't really *what?*" she asks.

"Stars," says Dead Girl. "They're only meteorites. Just chunks of rock and metal flying around through space and burning up if they get too close. But they aren't stars. Not if they fall like that."

"Or angels," Bobby whispers and then goes right back to eating from the handful of blackberries he's picked from the brambles

5

growing along the water's edge.

"I never said anything about angels," Gable growls at the boy, and he throws a blackberry at her. "There are *lots* of different words for angels."

"And for falling stars," Dead Girl says with a stony finality so they'll know that's all she wants to hear about it; meteorites that stop being meteors, Seekonk changing into Pawtucket, and in the end, it's nothing but the distance between this point and that. As arbitrary as any change, and so she presses her lips against the jogging lady's left wrist again. Not even the sheet-thin ghost of a pulse left in there, cooling meat against her teeth, flesh that might as well be clay except there are still a few red mouthfuls, and the sound of her busy lips isn't all that different from the sound of the waves against the shore.

"I know seven words for grey," Bobby says, talking through a mouthful of seeds and pulp and the dark juice dribbling down his bloodstained chin. "I got them out of a dictionary."

"You're a little faggot," Gable snarls at the boy, those narrow mercury eyes and her lower lip stuck way out like maybe someone's been beating her again, and Dead Girl knows she shouldn't have argued with Gable about falling stars and angels. *Next time*, she thinks, *I'll remember that. Next time, I'll smile and say whatever she wants me to say.* And when she's finally finished with the jogging lady, Dead Girl's the first one to slip quiet as a mousey in silk bedroom slippers across the mud and pebbles, and the river is as cold as the unfalling stars speckling the August night.

*   *   *

An hour and four minutes past midnight in the big house on Benefit Street, and the ghouls are still picking at the corpses in the basement. Dead Girl sits with Bobby on the stairs that lead back up to the music and conversation overhead, the electric lights and acridsweet clouds of opium smoke; down here there are only candles, and the air smells like bare dirt walls and mildew, like the embalmed meat spread out on the ghouls' long carving table. When they work like this, the ghouls stand up on their crooked hind legs and press their canine faces close together. The very thin one named Barnaby (his nervous ears alert to every footfall overhead, every creaking door, as if anyone Up There even cares what they're up to Down Here) picks up a rusty boning knife and uses it to lift a strip of dry flesh the colour of old chewing gum.

"That's the gastrocnemius," he says, and the yelloworange iris of his left eye drifts nervously towards the others, towards Madam Terpsichore, especially, who shakes her head and laughs the way that all ghouls laugh. *The way starving dogs would laugh*, Dead Girl thinks, *if they ever dared*, and she's starting to wish she and Bobby had gone down to Warwick with Gable and the Bailiff after all.

"No, that's the soleus, dear," Madam Terpsichore says and sneers at Barnaby, that practised curl of black lips to flash her jaundiced teeth like sharpened piano keys, a pinkred flick of her long tongue along the edge of her muzzle. "*That's* the gastrocnemius, there," she says. "You haven't been paying attention."

Barnaby frowns and scratches at his head. "Well, if we ever got anything fresh, maybe I could keep them straight," he grumbles, making excuses again, and Dead Girl knows the dissection is beginning to bore Bobby. He's staring over his shoulder at the basement door and the warm sliver of light getting in around the edges.

"Now, show me the lower terminus of the long peroneal," Madam Terpsichore says, her professorial litany and the impatient clatter of Barnaby digging about in his kit for a pair of poultry shears or an oyster fork, one or the other or something else entirely.

"You want to go back upstairs for a while?" Dead Girl asks the boy, and he shrugs, but doesn't take his eyes off the basement door, doesn't turn back around to watch the ghouls.

"Well, come on then," and she stands up, takes his hand, and that's when Madam Terpsichore finally notices them.

"Please don't go, dear," she says. "It's always better with an audience, and if Master Barnaby ever finds the proper instrument, there may be a flensing yet," and the other ghouls snicker and laugh.

"I don't think I like them very much," Bobby whispers very quietly, and Dead Girl only nods and leads him back up the stairs to the party.

Bobby says he wants something to drink, so they go to the kitchen first, to the noisy antique refrigerator, and he has a Coke, and Dead Girl takes out a Heineken for herself. One chilly applegreen bottle and she twists the cap off and sips the bitter German beer; she never liked the taste of beer, before, but sometimes it seems like there were an awful lot of things she didn't like before. The beer is very, very cold and washes away the last rags of the basement air lingering stale in her mouth like a dusty patch of mushrooms, basementdry earth and a billion microscopic spores looking for a place to grow.

"I don't think I like them at all," Bobby says, still whispering even though they're upstairs. Dead Girl starts to tell him that he doesn't have to whisper anymore, but then she remembers Barnaby, his inquisitive, dogcocked ears, and she doesn't say anything at all.

Almost everyone else is sitting together in the front parlour, the spacious, booklined room with its stained-glass lamp shades in all the sweet and sour colours of hard candy, sugarfiltered light that hurts her eyes. The first time she was allowed into the house on Benefit Street, Gable showed her all the lamps, all the books, all the rooms, like they were hers. Like she belonged here, instead of the muddy bottom of the Seekonk River, another pretty, broken thing in a house filled up with things that are pretty or broken or both. Filled up with antiques, and some of them breathe and some of them don't. Some, like Miss Josephine, have forgotten how or why to breathe, except to talk.

They sit around her in their black funeral clothes and the chairs carved in 1754 or 1773, rough circle of men and women that always makes Dead Girl think of ravens gathered around carrion, blackbirds about a raccoon's corpse, jostling each other for all the best bits; sharp beaks for her bright and sapphire eyes, for the porcelain tips of her fingers, or that silent, unbeating heart. *The empress as summer roadkill,*

Dead Girl thinks, and doesn't laugh out loud, even though she *wants* to, wants to laugh at these stiff and obsolescent beings, these tragic waxwork shades sipping absinthe and hanging on Miss Josephine's every word like gospel, like salvation. Better to slip in quiet, unnoticed, and find some place for her and Bobby to sit where they won't be in the way.

"Have you ever *seen* a firestorm, Signior Garzarek?" Miss Josephine asks, and she looks down at a book lying open in her lap, a green book like Dead Girl's green beer bottle.

"No, I never have," one of the waxworks says, tall man with slippery hair and ears that are too big for his head and almost come to points. "I dislike such things."

"But it was *beautiful*," Miss Josephine assures him, and then she pauses, still looking at the green book in her lap, and Dead Girl can tell from the way her eyes move back and forth, back and forth, that she's reading whatever's on the pages. "No, that's not the right word," she says. "That's not the right word at all."

"I was at Dresden," one of the women volunteers, and Miss Josephine looks up, blinks at the woman as if she can't quite remember what this particular waxwork is called.

"No, no, Addie, it wasn't like that. Oh, I'm sure Dresden was exquisite, too, yes. But this wasn't something man did. This was something that was *done* to men. And that's the thing that makes it truly transcendent, the thing that makes it . . ." and she trails off and glances back down at the book as if the word she's missing is in there somewhere.

"Well, then, read some of it to us," Signior Garzarek says and points a gloved hand at the green book, and Miss Josephine looks up at him with her bluebrilliant eyes, eyes that seem grateful and malicious at the same time.

"Are you sure?" she asks them all. "I wouldn't want to bore any of you."

"Please," says the man who hasn't taken off his bowler; Dead Girl thinks his name is Nathaniel. "We always like to hear you read."

"Well, only if you're sure," Miss Josephine says, and she sits up a little straighter on her divan, clears her throat, and fusses with the shiny folds of her black, satin skirt, the dress that only looks as old as the chairs, before she begins to read.

"'*That* was what came next — the fire,'" she says, and this is her reading voice now, and Dead Girl closes her eyes and listens. "'It shot up everywhere. The fierce wave of destruction had carried a flaming torch with it — agony, death and a flaming torch. It was just as if some fire demon was rushing from place to place with such a torch. Flames streamed out of half-shattered buildings all along Market Street.

"'I sat down on the sidewalk and picked the broken glass out of the soles of my feet and put on my clothes.

"'All wires down, all wires down!'"

And that's the way it goes for the next twenty minutes or so, the kindly half-dark behind Dead Girl's eyes and Miss Josephine reading from her green book while Bobby slurps at his Coke, and the waxwork ravens make no sound at all. She loves the rhythm of Miss

11

Josephine's reading voice, the cadence like rain on a hot day or ice cream, that sort of a voice. But it would be better if she were reading something else, "The Rime of the Ancient Mariner," maybe, or Keats or Tennyson. But this is better than nothing at all, so Dead Girl listens, content enough, and never mind that it's only earthquakes and conflagration, smoke and the screams of dying men and horses. It's the *sound* of the voice that matters, not the words or anything they mean, and if that's true for her, it's just as true for the silent waxworks in their stiff, colonial chairs.

When she's finished, Miss Josephine closes the book and smiles, showing them all the stingiest glimpse of her sharp white teeth.

"Superb," says Nathaniel, and "Oh yes, superb," says Addie Goodwine.

"You are indeed a wicked creature, Josephine," says the Signior, and he lights a fat cigar and exhales a billowing phantom from his mouth. "Such delicious perversity wrapped up in such a comely package."

"I was writing as James Russell Williams, then," Miss Josephine says proudly. "They even paid me."

Dead Girl opens her eyes, and Bobby's finished his Coke, is rolling the empty bottle back and forth across the rug like a wooden rolling pin on cookie dough. "Did you like it?" she asks him, and he shrugs.

"Not at all?"

"Well, it wasn't as bad as the ghouls," he says, but he doesn't look at her, hardly ever looks directly at her or anyone else these days.

A few more minutes and then Miss Josephine suddenly remembers something in another room that she wants the waxworks to see, something they *must* see, an urn or a brass sundial, the latest knick-knack hidden somewhere in the bowels of the great cluttered house. They follow her out of the parlour, into the hallway, chattering and trailing cigarette smoke, and if anyone even notices Bobby and Dead Girl sitting on the floor, they pretend that they haven't. Which is fine by Dead Girl; she dislikes them, the lifeless smell of them, the guarded desperation in their eyes.

Miss Josephine has left her book on the cranberry divan, and when the last of the vampires has gone, Dead Girl gets up and steps inside the circle of chairs, stands staring down at the cover.

"What does it say?" Bobby asks, and so she reads the title to him.

"*San Francisco's Horror of Earthquake, Fire, and Famine,*" she reads, and then Dead Girl picks the book up and shows him the cover, the letters stamped into the green cloth in faded gold ink. And underneath, a woman in dark-coloured robes, her feet in fire and water, chaos wrapped about her ankles, and she seems to be bowing to a shattered row of marble columns and a cornerstone with the words "In Memoriam of California's Dead — April 18th, 1906".

"That was a long time ago, wasn't it?" Bobby asks, and Dead Girl sets the book down again. "Not if you're Miss Josephine, it isn't," she says. *If you're Miss Josephine, that was only yesterday, the day before yesterday. If you're her* — but that's the sort of thought it's best not to finish, better if she'd never thought it at all.

13

"We don't have to go back to the basement, do we?" Bobby asks, and Dead Girl shakes her head. "Not if you don't want to," she says. And then she goes to the window and stares out at Benefit Street, at the passing cars and the living people with their smaller, petty reasons for hating time. In a moment, Bobby comes and stands beside her, and he holds her hand.

*　　*　　*

Dead Girl keeps her secrets in an old Hav-A-Tampa cigar box, the few she can't just keep inside her head, and she keeps the old cigar box on a shelf inside a mausoleum at Swan Point. This manicured hillside that rises up so sharp from the river's edge, steep and dead-adorned hill, green grass in the summer and the windrustling branches of the trees, and only Bobby knows about the box, and she thinks he'll keep it to himself. He rarely says anything to anyone, especially Gable; Dead Girl knows what Gable would do if she found out about the box, *thinks* she knows, and that's good enough, bad enough, that she keeps it hidden in the mausoleum.

The caretakers bricked up the front of the vault years and years ago, but they left a small cast-iron grate set into the masonry just below the marble keystone and the verdigris-streaked plaque with the name "Stanton" on it, though Dead Girl can't imagine why. Maybe it's there so the bugs can come in and out, or so all those dead Stantons can get a breath of fresh air now and then, though there's not even enough room for bats to squeeze through, or the swifts or rats. But still plenty of space between the bars of the grate for her and Bobby to slip inside whenever she wants to look at the things she keeps inside the old cigar box.

Nights like tonight, after the long parties, after Miss Josephine finally loses interest in her waxwork ravens and chases them all away (everyone except the ghouls, of course, who come and go as they please through the tunnels in the basement); still a coalgrey hour left until dawn, and she knows that Gable is probably already waiting for them in the river, but she can wait a few minutes more.

"She might come looking for us," Bobby says when they're inside the mausoleum, and he's standing on tip toes to see out but the grate is still a foot above his head.

"No, she won't," Dead Girl tells him, tells herself that it's true, that Gable's too glad to be back down there in the dark to be bothered. "She's probably already asleep by now."

"Maybe so," Bobby says, not sounding even the least bit convinced, and then he sits down on the concrete floor and watches Dead Girl with his quicksilver eyes, mirror eyes so full of light they'll still see when the last star in the whole goddamned universe has burned itself down to a spinning cinder.

"You let me worry about Gable," she says and opens the box to find that everything's still inside, just the way she left it. The newspaper clippings and a handful of coins, a pewter St. Christopher's medal and a doll's plastic right arm. Three keys and a ragged swatch of indigo velvet stained maroon around the edges. Things that mean nothing to anyone but Dead Girl; her puzzle, and no one else knows the way that all these pieces fit together. Or even *if* they all fit together; sometimes even she can't remember, but it makes her feel better to see them, anyway, to lay her white hands on these trinkets and scraps, to hold them.

Bobby is tapping his fingers restlessly against the floor, and when she looks at him he frowns and stares up at the ceiling. "Read me the one about Mercy," he says, and she looks back down at the Hav-A-Tampa box.

"It's getting late, Bobby. Someone might hear me."

And he doesn't ask her again, just keeps his eyes on the ceiling directly above her head and taps his fingers on the floor.

"It's not even a story," she says and fishes one of the newspaper clippings from the box. Nutbrown paper gone almost as brittle as she feels inside and the words printed there more than a century ago, and "It's almost like a story, when you read it," Bobby replies.

For a moment, Dead Girl stands very still, listening to the last of the night sounds fading slowly away and the stranger sounds that come just before sunrise; birds and the blind, burrowing progress of earthworms, insects and a ship's bell somewhere down in Providence Harbour, and Bobby's fingers drumming on the concrete. She thinks about Miss Josephine and the comfort in her voice, her ice-cream voice against every vacant moment of eternity. And, in a moment, she begins to read.

* * *

Letter from the *Pawtuxet Valley Gleaner*, dated March 1892:

"Exeter Hill"

Mr Editor,

As considerable notoriety has resulted from the exhuming of three bodies in Exeter cemetery on the 17th inst., I will give the main facts as I have received them for the benefit of such of your readers as "have not taken the papers" containing the same. To begin, we will say that our neighbor, a good and respectable citizen, George T. Brown, has been bereft of his wife and two grown-up daughters by consumption, the wife and mother about eight years ago, and the eldest daughter, Olive, two years or no later, while the other daughter, Mercy Lena, died about two months since, after nearly one year's illness from the same dread disease. About two years ago Mr. Brown's only son Edwin A., a young married man of good habits, began to give evidence of lung trouble, which increased, until in hopes of checking and curing the same, he was induced to visit the famous Colorado Springs, where his wife followed him later on and though for a time he seemed to improve, it soon became evident that there was no real benefit derived, and this coupled with a strong desire on the part of both husband and wife to see their Rhode Island friends, decided them to return east after an absence of about 18 months and are staying with Mrs. Brown's parents, Willet Himes. We are sorry to say that Eddie's health is not encouraging at this time. And now comes in the queer part, viz: The revival of a pagan or other superstition regarding the feeding of the dead upon a living relative where consumption was the cause of death and now bringing the living person soon into a similar condition, etc. and to avoid this result, according to the same high authority, the "vampire" in question which is said to inhabit the heart of a dead consumptive while any blood remains in that organ, must be cremated and the ashes carefully preserved and administered in some form to the living victim, when a speedy cure may (un) reasonably be expected. I will here say that the husband and father of the deceased ones, from the first, disclaimed any faith at all in the vampire theory but being urged, he allowed other, if not wiser, counsel to prevail, and on the 17th inst., as before stated the three bodies alluded to were exhumed and then examined by Doctor Metcalt of Wickford (under protest, as it were, being an unbeliever). The two bodies longest buried were found decayed and bloodless, while the last one who has been only about two months buried showed some blood in the heart as a matter of course, and as the doctor expected but to carry out what was a forgone conclusion, the heart and lungs of the last named (M. Lena) were then and there duly cremated, but deponent saith not how the ashes were disposed of. Not many persons were present, Mr. Brown being among the absent ones. While we do not blame any one for these proceedings as they were intended without doubt to relieve the anxiety of the living, still, it seems incredible that any one can attach the least importance to the subject, being so entirely incompatible with reason and conflicts also with scripture, which requires us "to give a reason for the hope that is in us," or the why and wherefore which

18

certainly cannot be done as applied to the foregoing.

*   *   *

With the silt and fish shit settling gentle on her eyelids and her lungs filled up with cold river water, Dead Girl sleeps, the sootblack ooze for her blanket, her cocoon, and Bobby safe in her arms. Gable is there, too, lying somewhere nearby, coiled like an eel in the roots of a drowned willow.

And in her dreams Dead Girl counts the boats passing overhead, their prows to split the daydrenched sky, their wakes the roil and swirl of thunderstorm clouds. Crabs and tiny snails nest in her hair, and her wet thoughts slip by as smooth and capricious as the Seekonk, one instant or memory flowing seamlessly into the next. And *this* moment, this one here, is the last night that she was still a living girl. Last frosty night before Halloween, and she's stoned and sneaking into Swan Point Cemetery with a boy named Adrian that she only met a few hours ago in the loud and smoky confusion of a Throwing Muses show, Adrian Mobley and his long yellow hair like strands of the sun or purest spun gold.

Adrian won't or can't stop giggling, a joke or just all the pot they've been smoking, and she leads him straight down Holly Avenue, the long paved drive to carry them across The Old Road and into the vast maze of the cemetery's slate and granite intestines. Headstones and more ambitious monuments lined up neat or scattered wild among the trees, reflecting pools to catch and hold the high white moon, and

19

she's only having a little trouble finding her way in the dark.

"*Shut up*," she hisses, casts anxious serpent sounds from her chapped lips, across her chattering teeth, and "Someone's going to fucking hear us," she says. She can see her breath, her soul escaping mouthful by steaming mouthful.

Then Adrian puts his arm around her, sweater wool and warm flesh around warm flesh, and he whispers something in her ear, something she should have always remembered but doesn't. Something forgotten, the way she's forgotten the smell of a late summer afternoon and sunlight on sand, and he kisses her.

And for a kiss she shows him the place where Lovecraft is buried, the quiet place she comes when she only wants to be alone, no company but her thoughts and the considerate, sleeping bodies underground. The Phillips family obelisk and then his own little headstone; she takes a plastic cigarette lighter from the front pocket of her jeans and holds the flame close to the ground so that Adrian can read the marker: August 20, 1890 — March 15, 1937, "I am Providence," and she shows him all the offerings that odd pilgrims leave behind. A handful of pencils and one rusty screw, two nickels, a small rubber octopus, and a handwritten letter folded neat and weighted with a rock so the wind won't blow it away. The letter begins "Dear Howard," but she doesn't read any farther, nothing there written for her, and then Adrian tries to kiss her again.

"No, wait. You haven't seen the tree," she says, wriggling free of Adrian Mobley's skinny arms, dragging him roughly away from the obelisk; two steps, three, and they're both swallowed by the shadow of an enormous, ancient birch, this tree that must have been old when her great grandfather was a boy. Its sprawling branches are still shaggy with autumnpainted leaves, its roots like the scabby knuckles of some skybound giant, clutching at the earth for fear that he will fall and tumble forever towards the stars.

"Yeah, so it's a tree," Adrian mumbles, not understanding, not even trying to understand, and now she knows that it was a mistake to bring him here.

"People have carved things," she says and strikes the lighter again, holds the flickering blueorange flame so that Adrian can see all the pocket-knife graffiti worked into the smooth, pale bark of the tree. The unpronounceable names of dark, fictitious gods and entire passages from Lovecraft, razor steel for ink to tattoo these occult wounds and lonely messages to a dead man, and she runs an index finger across a scar in the shape of a tentacle-headed fish.

"Isn't it beautiful?" she whispers, and that's when Dead Girl sees the eyes watching them from the lowest limbs of the tree, *their* shimmering, silver eyes like spiteful coins hanging in the night, like strange fruit, and "This shit isn't the way it happened at all," Gable says. "These aren't even *your* memories. This is just some bitch we killed."

"Oh, I think she knows that," the Bailiff laughs, and it's worse than the ghouls snickering for Madam Terpsichore.

"I only wanted him to see the tree," Dead Girl says. "I wanted to show him something carved into the Lovecraft tree."

"Liar," Gable sneers, and that makes the Bailiff laugh again. He squats in the dust and fallen leaves and begins to pick something stringy from his teeth.

And she would run, but the river has almost washed the world away, nothing left now but the tree and the moon and the thing that clambers down its trunk on spiderlong legs and arms the colour of chalk dust.

Is that a Death? and are there two?

"We know you would forget us," Gable says, "If we ever let you. You would pretend you were an innocent, a *victim*." Her dry tongue feels as rough as sandpaper against Dead Girl's wrist, dead cat's tongue, and above them the constellations swirl in a mad kaleidoscope dance about the moon; the tree moans and raises its swaying branches to Heaven, praying for dawn, for light and mercy from everything it's seen and will ever see again.

Is Death that woman's mate?

And at the muddy bottom of the Seekonk River, in the lee of the Henderson Bridge, Dead Girl's eyelids flutter as she stirs uneasily, frightening fish, fighting sleep and her dreams. But the night is still hours away, waiting on the far side of the scalding day, and so she holds Bobby tighter, and he sighs and makes a small, lost sound that the river snatches and drags away towards the sea.

*   *   *

Dead Girl sits alone on the floor in the parlour of the house on Benefit Street, alone because Gable has Bobby with her tonight; Dead

Girl drinks her Heineken and watches the yellow and aubergine circles that their voices trace in the stagnant, smoky air, and she tries to recall what it was like before she knew the colours of sound.

Miss Josephine raises the carafe and carefully pours tap water over the sugar cube on her slotted spoon; the water and dissolved sugar sink to the bottom of her glass and at once the liqueur begins to louche, the clear and emerald bright mix of alcohol and herbs clouding quickly to a milky, opaque green.

"Oh, of course," she says to the attentive circle of waxwork ravens. "I remember Mercy Brown, and Nellie Vaughn, too, and that man in Connecticut. What was his name?"

"William Rose," Signior Garzarek suggests, but Miss Josephine frowns and shakes her head. "No, no. Not Rose. He was that peculiar fellow in Peace Dale, remember? No, the man in Connecticut had a different name."

"They were maniacs, every one of them," Addie Goodwine says nervously and sips from her own glass of absinthe. "Cutting the hearts and livers out of corpses and burning them, eating the ashes. It's ridiculous. It's even worse than what *they* do," and she points confidentially at the floor.

"Of course it is, dear," Miss Josephine says.

"But the little Vaughn girl, Nellie, I understand she's still something of a sensation among the local high school crowd," Signior Garzarek says and smiles, dabs at his wet red lips with a lace handkerchief. "They do love their ghost stories, don't you know. They must find the epitaph on her tombstone an endless source of delight."

"What does it say?" Addie asks, and when Miss Josephine turns and stares at her, Addie Goodwine flinches and almost drops her glass.

"You really should get out more often, dear," Miss Josephine says, and "Yes," Addie stammers. "Yes, I know. I should."

The waxwork named Nathaniel fumbles with the brim of his black bowler and, "I remember," he says. "'I am watching and waiting for you.' That's what it says, isn't it?"

"Delightful, I tell you," Signior Garzarek chuckles, and then he drains his glass and reaches for the absinthe bottle on its silver serving tray.

*   *   *

"What do you see out there?"

The boy that Dead Girl calls Bobby is standing at the window in Miss Josephine's parlour, standing there with the sash up and snow blowing in, a small drift of snow at his bare feet, and he turns around when she says his name.

"There was a bear on the street," he says and puts the glass paperweight in her hands, the glass dome filled with water, and when she shakes it all the tiny white flakes inside swirl around and around. A miniature blizzard trapped in her palm, plastic snow to settle slow across the frozen field, the barn, the dark and winterbare line of trees in the distance.

"I saw a bear," he says again, more insistent than before, and points at the open window.

"You did *not* see a bear," Dead Girl says, but she doesn't look to see for herself, doesn't take her silver eyes off the paperweight; she'd almost forgotten about the barn, that day and the storm, January or February or March, more years ago than she'd have ever guessed, and the wind howling like hungry wolves.

"I *did*," Bobby says indignantly. "I saw a big black bear dancing in the street. I know a bear when I see one."

And Dead Girl closes her eyes and lets the globe fall from her fingers, lets it roll from her hand, and she knows that when it hits the floor it will shatter into a thousand pieces. World shatter, watersky shatter to bleed Heaven away across the floor, and so there isn't much time if she's going to make it all the way to the barn.

"I think it knew our names," the boy says, and he sounds afraid, but when she looks back, she can't see him anymore. Nothing behind her now but the little stone wall to divide this field from the next, the slate and sandstone boulders already half buried by the storm, and the wind pricks her skin with icing needle teeth. The snow spirals down from the leaden clouds, and the wind sends it spinning and dancing in dervish crystal curtains.

"We forget for a reason, child" the Bailiff says, his rustcrimson voice woven tight between the air and every snowflake. "Time is too heavy to carry so much of it strung about our necks."

"I don't hear you," she lies, and it doesn't matter anyway, whatever he says, because Dead Girl is already at the barn door; both the doors left standing open, and her father will be angry, will be furious if he finds out. The horses could catch cold, he will say to her. The cows, he will say, the cows are already giving sour milk, as it is.

Shut the doors and don't look inside. Shut the doors and run all the way home.

"It fell from the sky," he said, the night before. "It fell screaming from a clear blue sky. No one's gone looking for it. I don't reckon they will."

"It was only a bird," her mother said.

"No," her father said. "It wasn't a bird."

Shut the doors and run . . .

But she doesn't do either, because that isn't the way this happened, the way it *happens,* and the naked thing crouched there in the straw and the blood looks up at her with Gable's pretty face. Takes its mouth away from the mare's mangled throat, and blood spills out between clenched teeth and runs down its chin.

"The bear was singing our names."

And then the paperweight hits the floor and bursts in a sudden, merciful spray of glass and water that tears the winter day apart around her. "Wake up," Miss Josephine says, spits out impatient words that smell like anise and dust, and she shakes Dead Girl again.

"I expect Madam Terpsichore is finishing up downstairs. And the Bailiff will be back soon. You can't sleep here."

Dead Girl blinks and squints past Miss Josephine and all the colorful, candyshaded lamps. And the summer night outside the parlour window, the night that carries her rotten soul beneath its tongue, stares back with eyes as black and secret as the bottom of a river.

*   *   *

In the basement, Madam Terpsichore, lady of rib spreaders and carving knives, has already gone, has crept away down one of the damp and brickthroated tunnels with her snuffling entourage in tow. Their bellies full and all their entrail curiosities sated for another night, and only Barnaby is left behind to tidy up; part of his modest punishment for slicing too deeply through a sclera and ruining a violet eye meant for some graveyard potentate or another, the precious vitreous humour spilled by his hand, and there's a fresh notch in his left ear where Madam Terpsichore bit him for ruining such a delicacy. Dead Girl is sitting on an old produce crate, watching while he scrubs bile from the stainless steel tabletop.

"I'm not very good with dreams, I'm afraid," he says to her and wrinkles his wet black nose.

"Or eyes," Dead Girl says, and Barnaby nods his head.

"Or eyes," he agrees.

"I just thought you might listen, that's all. It's not the sort of thing I can tell Gable, and Bobby, well—"

"He's a sweet child, though," Barnaby says, and then he frowns and scrubs harder at a stubborn smear the colour of scorched chestnuts.

"But I can't tell anyone else," Dead Girl says; she sighs, and Barnaby dips his pig-bristle brush into a pail of soapy water and goes

27

back to work on the stain.

"I don't suppose I can do *very* much damage, if all I do is listen," and the ghoul smiles a crooked smile for her and touches a claw to the bloody place where Madam Terpsichore nicked the base of his right ear with her sharp incisors.

"Thank you, Barnaby," she says and draws a thoughtless half circle on the dirt floor with the scuffed toe of one shoe. "It isn't a very long dream. It won't take but a minute," and what she tells him, then, isn't the dream of Adrian Mobley and the Lovecraft tree, and it isn't the barn and the blizzard, the white thing waiting for her inside the barn. This is another dream, a moonless night at Swan Point, and someone's built a great, roaring bonfire near the river's edge. Dead Girl's watching the flames reflected in the water, the air heavy with wood smoke and the hungry sound of fire; and Bobby and Gable are lying on the rocky beach, laid out neat as an undertaker's work, their arms at their sides, pennies on their eyes. And they're both slit open from collarbones to crotch, stem to stern, ragged Y-incisions, and their innards glint wetly in the light of the bonfire.

"No, I don't think it was me," Dead Girl says, even though it isn't true, and she draws another half circle on the floor to keep the first one company. Barnaby has stopped scrubbing at the table and is watching her uneasily with his distrustful scavenger eyes.

"Their hearts are lying there together on a boulder," and she's speaking very quietly now, almost whispering as if she's afraid someone upstairs might be listening, too, and Barnaby perks up his ears and leans towards her. Their hearts on a stone, and their livers,

28

too, and she burns the organs in a brass bowl until there's nothing left but a handful of greasy ashes.

"I think I eat them," Dead Girl says. "But there are blackbirds then, a whole flock of blackbirds, and all I can hear are their wings. Their wings bruise the sky."

And Barnaby shakes his head, makes a rumbling, anxious sound deep in his throat, and he starts scrubbing at the table again. "I should learn to quit while I'm only a little ways behind," he snorts. "I should learn what's none of my goddamn business."

"Why, Barnaby? What does it mean?" and at first he doesn't answer her, only grumbles to himself and the pig-bristle brush flies back and forth across the surgical table even though there are no stains left to scrub, nothing but a few soap suds and the candlelight reflected in the scratched and dented silver surface.

"The Bailiff would have my balls in a bottle of brine if I told you that," he says. "Go away. Go back upstairs where you belong and leave me alone. I'm busy."

"But you do know, don't you? I heard a story, Barnaby, about another dead girl named Mercy Brown. They burned *her* heart — "

And the ghoul opens his jaws wide and roars like a caged lion, hurls his brush at Dead Girl, but it sails over her head and smashes into a shelf of Ball mason jars behind her. Broken glass and the sudden stink of vinegar and pickled kidneys, and she runs for the stairs.

"Go pester someone else, *corpse*," Barnaby snarls at her back. "Tell your blasphemous dreams to those effete cadavers upstairs. Ask one of *those* snotty fuckers to cross him," and then he throws something else, something shiny and sharp that whizzes past her face and sticks in the wall. Dead Girl takes the stairs two at a time, slams the basement door behind her and turns the lock. And if anyone's heard, if Miss Josephine or Signior Garzarek or anyone else even notices her reckless dash out the front doors and down the steps of the big old house on Benefit Street, they know better than Barnaby and keep it to themselves.

*   *   *

In the east, there's the thinnest bluewhite sliver of dawn to mark the horizon, the light a pearl would make, and Bobby hands Dead Girl another stone. "That should be enough," she says, and so he sits down in the grass at the edge of the narrow beach to watch as she stuffs this last rock inside the hole where Gable's heart used to be. Twelve big rocks shoved inside her now, granite-cobble viscera to carry the vampire's body straight to the bottom of the Seekonk, and this time that's where it will stay. Dead Girl has a fat roll of grey duct tape to seal the wound.

"Will they come after us?" Bobby asks, and the question takes her by surprise, not the sort of thing she would ever have expected from him. She stops wrapping Gable's abdomen with the duct tape and stares silently at him for a moment, but he doesn't look back at her, keeps his eyes on that distant, jagged rind of daylight.

"They might," she tells him. "I don't know for sure. Are you afraid, Bobby?"

"I'll miss Miss Josephine," he says. "I'll miss the way she read us stories," and Dead Girl nods her head, and "Yes," she says. "Me too. But I'll always read you stories," and he smiles when she says that.

When Dead Girl is finally finished, they push Gable's body out into the water and follow it all the way down, wedge it tight between the roots of the sunken willow tree below Henderson Bridge. And then Bobby nestles close to Dead Girl, and in a moment he's asleep, lost in his own dreams, and she closes her eyes and waits for the world to turn itself around again.

The Book of Dreams

by Louise Bohmer

On my forty-fifth birthday my mother fell dead at the table. One moment she stood holding her old Polaroid, ready to take a picture of me unwrapping my present. The next instant found her falling to the cracked linoleum, pulling her plate of cake with her as she crumpled. As the gold-rimmed china smashed, bits of frosted chocolate and glass embedded themselves in Mama's drab gray braid.

I stumbled from my chair in my rush to get to her. Dropping to my knees I cradled Mama's head in my hands, careful not to move her too much. Her fragile hands fluttered over my face and she smiled.

"I am so sorry I hurt you." She coughed. "I was younger then-- foolish. I am coming home now, sister."

"Shhh," I chided her for wasting precious breath. "I'm going to call Doc Gibson now, Mama ..." But my words died when I looked at her face. Her eyes had lost their focus, and I felt her body give one last spasm as my mother passed.

*   *   *

I held Mama like that, on the floor, for a while, crying like an abandoned child and wondering what I should do next. I thought about calling Doc Gibson in town, but then he'd want to call my sister Gertie, and I wasn't ready to face her. Not when the grief was so fresh. Gertie never got along with Mama and she terrorized me as a child, citing I was our parents' good little favorite. She'd left the farm for the bright and brassy world of Toronto as soon as she turned sixteen, and she hadn't returned since Papa died six years ago.

After the sobbing settled, I crawled back to the table and hauled myself up into one of the rail back, wooden chairs. With bleary eyes I looked down at the half unwrapped present Mama had so carefully taped for me, adding a satin bow of my favorite color--deep blue. I pushed the torn white gift-paper, sprinkled with blue roses that matched the bow, off the top of my gift. Blinking hard, I read the title etched in gold across the cover of the book within: *Interpreting Your Dreams*, by an author I was not familiar with. I picked up the heavy, hard back tome and found another smaller, soft cover book beneath it.

"*Ancient Folktales of Ireland*," I read aloud, and then looked to my mother's corpse sprawled unceremoniously on the kitchen floor.

"You knew me so well, Mama." I looked away from her, pulling my gaze back to the books on the cracked, melamine tabletop. "What will I do without you?"

*   *   *

I thought that without Mama, there was nothing left for me. And my older sister, Gertie, was sure to take the farm from me when she learned of Mama's passing. That big shot lawyer husband of hers

33

would find a way to have me declared mad, I was sure of it, like he had tried with our mother, so he and Gertie could have the farm just after the cancer took Papa. I'd been there to fight then for Mama's rights, but who would fight for me?

After much deliberation, I decided to bury Mama in the root cellar. I carried her down through the outside entrance, careful not to fall while I maneuvered down the few stairs into the dank room.

I had pondered laying her to rest in Papa's now forgotten flower patch. In life they'd loved that little spot of garden so much, and worked it together as their getaway--shared relaxation. But I couldn't bear to part with Mama, and I wanted her as close to me as she could possibly be, so I chose the cool, preserving earth of the cellar, and I would bury her deep.

Strange I know--perhaps some would call me morbid. But I never claimed my mind worked by conventional terms. Neither did Mama's. Perhaps that is why she and I always got along so well, bonded so deeply. Our madness was shared, as was our scorn from Gertie, over all those years.

* * *

As I readied for bed with the rising of the moon, I went over Mama's final words to me--how odd they were--once again.

I am so sorry I hurt you ...

Doc Gibson reckoned Mama's madness was on account of an early onset of Alzheimer's. He reasoned she'd had it since her late thirties.

I knew that was possible, but it didn't explain a lot of things from my childhood--things I had seen alone and with Mama. Mama never had a proper examination for her "condition", and I always concealed mine very well. When she was young, and Doc Hartley was still in town, it was bad nerves. Me--I was just the quiet, withdrawn child while Gertie was the social butterfly.

I pulled back the fresh sheets and folded them over the patchwork quilt on Mama's bed. Tonight I would sleep in her room, before I washed the linens and lost the last physical traces of her left in the simple double bed--a few strands of grey hair, the smell of her lavender soap.

Settling beneath the cozy blankets with the book of Irish folktales Mama had given me earlier, I opened the glossy soft cover and tried to focus on the words.

I was younger then--foolish.

Something crashed downstairs and then I heard the rapid thud of footfalls. Suddenly I was a child again tucked tight in Mama's bed with Gertie. Mama held us close to her and hushed us. Papa had ventured to the city to sell livestock at the big auction there. He went twice a year. And every time he left us ladies alone--as he used to call us, affectionately—the strange noises came back, wafting upstairs and awakening the three of us from our deep sleep.

Holding my breath, I shut the book and laid it on my lap while I listened. Every nerve in my body grew taut as I waited for the tinkle of breaking glass, or the wail of shrill laughter.

Nothing. Silence reigned.

Letting out the stagnant breath held in my lungs, I gulped in fresh air coming from the breeze that drifted in the open window. The night was pleasantly cool for late August. I chided myself for hearing phantom noises and for being such a fool, and then went back to my book.

Only the book was gone. Or rather, it had been replaced by the larger, hardcover tome on interpreting dreams. I stared down at the burgundy dust jacket with its gold-lettering. My mouth gaped as I ran a trembling hand down the book's spine.

I am coming home now, sister …

As a scratching came at the window sill, Mama's final words rang in my head like a tolling church bell. My head snapped up and I focused on the fluttering lace sheers.

A hand, bone-white with long yellowed claws, curled over the wooden ledge. I watched another soon join it and, as I swallowed over the hard lump of fright choking me, I knew this was my final descent into lunacy. I would soon join Mama in the hereafter, and that both terrified and comforted me. I would finally lay eyes on whatever had terrorized our nights without Papa--the unseen ones Gertie claimed never to hear. The ones I had heard Mama and Gertie argue about in hushed whispers, just before Gertie left the farm for the city.

I closed my eyes tight and then looked back to the hands on the ledge. They were gone and I blinked hard, twice, to make sure I was not imagining their absence. Perhaps I had been saved for tonight.

And then I heard the voice, soft and deep and masculine, come from behind me.

"You need not fear me. Have you opened the book of dreams yet?"

I jumped and a small scream escaped me. The beast stood at my bedside now, towering over me and smiling down at me. Its amber eyes were like an owl's eyes, set in a long face with sharp features. His naked body was obviously male and covered in a fine, white down. I looked away in embarrassment and focused on his wings--luminous, they also resembled the regal span of an owl.

You do not remember me?" He tilted his head like a bird, too. "Ahh, but then you were very young when you left. No more than a babe."

"Who ... who are you?"

He sat on the edge of the bed and I could feel the coolness seeping from his skin into the sheets, touching my leg with a frosty bite that wafted off his body. "I am Isaiah." He looked deep into my eyes and paused. "Your betrothed. I've come to take you home."

"Home?" I knew I'd gone insane now, and I wondered if I had died of heartbreak in my sleep--perhaps this strange birdman was an angel?

He nodded. "But first, there are reunions to be made and truths to be told. Time for you to wake up, Gwenyth." He reached out and stroked my face and I shivered. His hands were like smooth stone. "Time for you to leave this bad dream you've been trapped in for so very long."

"I ... I," Tears fell before I realized I was crying. "I don't understand."

"You will." He blinked slowly--long white lashes brushed his ivory cheeks. "Open the book."

And I did.

*   *   *

We were flying, but I couldn't see where we were going. When Isaiah instructed me to open the book on dreaming, he covered my eyes with his hand as I flipped back the cover. In an instant I felt the bed fall away from us, and he wrapped his arms about my waist, carrying me high in the air within his strong grip. As we sailed upward, I grew sick from the unexpected change in my surroundings. Dizziness overcame me and I struggled not to faint. As we soared, the crisp night air against my face helped to keep me alert--aware.

The clean fragrance of evergreens mixed with the wind and stroked my face. I inhaled deeply as we touched down in what I suspected was the six acre patch of woods behind our farm. One of my favorite places to escape as a child, but Mama severely forbade me to venture into the thick forest alone--even as an adult she dissuaded me from the woods. Still, some mornings, now and then, I would sneak into the clearing I had found just a few feet past the entrance through the old fir and pine.

Strange things happened in that clearing. Things that I could never explain, and when Isaiah removed his hands from my face, I was not surprised to find myself beneath the heavy canopy of pine, a flat circular earthen floor stretched out before me. Only this time I was not alone. Along with Isaiah--who stood behind me, hand still wrapped about my waist--there were watchers in the woods, observing me from the edges of the clearing. I could feel them even if I could not see them.

"Step forward, Gwenyth." The voice was deep but feminine, and there was something strange to its lilt. Something otherworldly.

I looked over my shoulder to Isaiah and he nodded encouragingly. Dropping my head and folding my hands at my waist, I took a step ahead on legs that felt too weak too carry me.

A woman stepped from the shadows cast by the pine fronds. The moonlight held her in an ethereal glow, but there was something else too, about her. A bluish hue that seemed to illuminate her lithe form. As my eyes lighted upon her face something familiar tugged in my belly. I knew this lady of the woods--knew her well--and I felt an odd joy at seeing her again, yet I could not remember her.

I must be dreaming... I shook my head as she floated toward me. *Or perhaps I really am dead.*

Others drifted from the shadows with her. Dressed in tatters of gossamer, their skin glimmering, they looked like tranquil ghosts as they glided closer.

And then among them I saw her; Mama. She looked different now, younger. I ran to her phantom; she smiled serenely and held out her arms to me. But as I drew closer her smile grew sad, and she stopped me with an outstretched, luminescent hand.

Music, high and eerie and sweet, filled the clearing as Mama stopped my approach. A collection of woodwinds I could not readily identify, punctuated by the bellow of a low, deep horn that trailed off only to sound again after a brief pause. The mixture created a melody that raised the fine hairs on the back of my neck.

The dark woman who first stepped from the covering of trees floated up behind my mother. Mother jumped and looked behind her, then drifted to the side meekly, letting the phantom take her place before me.

"Come join us, Gwenyth." The dark woman held a long-fingered transparent hand out to me. "Time for you to join us once again, after so much time away. Time for us to dance you awake, my daughter."

I darted a glance at my mother and frowned. "Mama ...?" I clutched at the wisps of fabric at her waist and she dropped her head.

"No child, not anymore." Mama raised her head and there were tears falling from her now-black eyes. "In truth you were never mine, Gwenyth, but I wanted a female child so very much ..." She looked away and dashed the tears from her cheeks with a brusque hand. "Females are prized by our kind, just as males are prized by the humans."

"What are you talking about?" I was frantic now as I looked from Mama to the wood woman.

"Come child. We will show you. Strip the glamour away from your eyes so you may remember. We will dance you awake, to your true self." The dark lady took my hand as the other phantom forms gathered into two lines--ladies opposite the gentlemen.

The haunting music picked up tempo, and the dark lady led me in a strange and intricate jig. I tried to find Mama in the throng of see-through faces. But the dancers whirled faster and faster about me, blurring in a shimmering smear of color and moonlight. My face grew hot and my heart thumped hard in my chest. I could scarcely breathe, as the dark lady let go of my hand and let them take me deeper into the dance. I felt as if I were falling, and then it was as if my heart burst in my chest, and I felt it beat no more.

I was waking up …

$$* \quad * \quad *$$

Harmony ruled the day, and she was a wood woman of the highest respected order. It wasn't fair that her nighttime sister, Eris, should birth the prized girl child. Eris represented strife and discord, and belong to the lowly Unseelie Court. She didn't deserve such a child-- such a gift!

But Titiana ruled that the two faerie courts should practice harmony amongst themselves, if concord was to balance with discord in the universe, and the marriage of Harmony's adopted son, Isaiah, to her sister's newly born babe, was contracted.

"But I will not have it," she hissed down at the fair fae child cradled in her arms. "Filthy Unseelie. Peace among us is not worth the price of mingling with them. And peace among us does not guarantee peace throughout the universe. I should know such things; it is my job."

The overgrown forest snatched at her ethereal body, and Harmony skirted a snapped pine branch that jutted out dangerously toward the girl child's head.

That is when the scream ripped through the quiet dawn. Harmony muttered a charm quickly, and cloaked herself and Gwyn in a concealing glamour. She crept over the forest's edge and out into the field of wheat that belonged to a farm family that neighbored their forest.

The laughter of a child caught her attention, and Harmony swerved to the right, careful not to drop the still-forming fae infant nestled in her arms. The wheat rustled far ahead of them and parted. Someone fled through the tall golden stalks, toward a sprawling, white farmhouse that overlooked the field.

Like a ghost, Harmony's willowy form floated through the field, keeping watchful while Gwyn cooed and squealed. Harmony shushed the child and pulled her brown cloak tighter around them.

The blood came suddenly. One moment the rows of straight standing wheat were high and slightly slanted in the wind, the next they were trampled in an erratic circle. Splashes of blood stained the ripening stalks like deep, rich smears of paint.

Her years of life far surpassed a human's years, and Harmony had seen this sort of carnage from humankind before, but something about the scene before her disturbed her--unsettled her. Still, in a strange way, the bodies that lay broken before her were like a gift from something beyond her. Harmony would require human forms for herself and Gwyn if they were to hide, at least for awhile, in this world.

Right now, she had no plans beyond concealing her faerie form, and the girl child, in the skin of a mortal. Possession was her only other option, but these two slain bodies--mother and babe--seemed to call out to her. They had a story to tell. Harmony could hear their spirits whisper "Murder" as she knelt down beside them to listen closer.

Harmony felt the cold brush of a spirit at her back, and she knew the dead mother stood over her. Gently, she placed Gwyn on a patch of ground left untainted by the massacre before them. Harmony rose and turned to address the ghost at her back.

"You require a body." The dead woman spoke. "My body, and the body of my child."

Harmony nodded, and her heart cringed when tears fell through the woman's face.

"If I let you have them, hide yourself and the babe within," her voice broke and the phantom sobbed, tears washing the blood from her scratched cheeks. "If I let you take us, use our bodies as a refuge, will you do something for me?"

Harmony took the specter's hand and squeezed it. "Of course."

*   *   *

Where was I? I tried to get up, tried to open my eyes, but it was as if I were blind and paralyzed. *Was I dead?*

"No child, you are not dead." It was the voice of the dark lady; the strange shade from the dance who claimed to be my true mother. Eris.

43

Suddenly, I remembered the visions. The things I had seen when I had fainted amidst the dance. My mother running through the forest-- but she was not my mother, not then, not yet.

Blood, blood everywhere. A mother and child lie dead in the middle of Papa's wheat field. Harmony, stands over the dead pair. A young elemental child is cradled in her arms.

I stoop down to the bodies and I look at their mangled faces. My pulse quickens and I fight back the vomit that burns in my throat. The slain mother is my mother; the child is a much younger version of myself.

Standing up, my eyes scan the wheat field for the maniac who has committed this slaughter. When I see the truth, when I see the axe in her hands, my stomach rebels and I can hold back the sickness no longer.

Gertie runs toward the house. Papa is on one of his trips to the auction in the city, with our livestock. Gertie's white frilly dress is stained with large, shiny patches of blood, as are her hands and face-- even her knee-stockings. She can't be more than twelve years old.

Dropping the axe in the dirt as she breaks through the edge of the field, she laughs wildly, greatly pleased with herself--mad with triumph. She thinks that Mama and I are gone--the two women she viewed as bitter competition for Papa's affections.

*   *   *

Harmony made a promise to a dead woman, now I, Gwyn, must fulfill that promise, before I return to my home, my world, my people.

Before I am allowed to awaken fully from this lifelong "dream", old debts must be settled. The balance of concord and discord must be restored.

I have emptied three gas cans upstairs--two on the main floor of our old farmhouse. Early this morning, after I came to from my visit to the forest, revived from the night of dancing, I found Isaiah waiting for me inside, in my bedroom, with final instructions.

Gertie, my older sister--or, the woman I once thought of as my sister, I suppose--never wanted a sibling. She was an only child until the age of ten and Papa spoiled her. Mama chided him for his lavish gifts to the girl, in the early days, when the farm was young and profitable and Papa was healthy. But Papa dismissed her, saying it would do no harm--cause no jealousy when other young 'uns were born.

But Papa never saw Gertie's spiteful side. She used to beat me and Mama, both with fists and words.

The breeze blows my faded ginger hair against my face, as I wait on the front porch for Gertie to arrive. I watch dusk move in, and the sun slipping low over the prairie horizon. In the pocket of my bib-apron, I play with Papa's old Zippo lighter. He treasured the lighter, given to him by Gertie's fancy lawyer man on one of our visits to Toronto.

Aunt Harmony made a mistake when she thieved me from my mother's breast, but the universe has a way of showing us our mistakes in the strangest of ways, and righting our wrongs. The human body Harmony sought refuge in, the dead woman whom she made a deal with, possessed a diseased mind. Schizophrenia. Harmony's fae soul was tainted by the illness, and wasted within her disguise, trapped in her own form of madness as she hid from persecution. Her refuge became her punishment.

Gertie's immaculate, black Model-T appears around the corner in the long dirt road that leads to the farm. She sounded very angry when I phoned her this morning, citing that a trip to the farm would take her most of the day. And screaming down the crackling phone line at me, demanding to know just what I thought she'd do with the kids, and why couldn't I ever fix a mess myself? I remained calm, as I always did, through her tirade.

But for all her wrongs, Harmony was forgiven by the fae. Her deed, although spiteful, was forgivable. Gertie's crime went unresolved, and spirits need their rest.

So, tonight, I right this final wrong, and fulfill the promise my Aunt Harmony, my captor although I never knew it, made to a dead woman so long ago.

Gertie pulls into the driveway and dust puffs up from her whitewall tires. She steps out of the vehicle in a huff, glaring at me as she adjusts her black wide-brimmed hat.

"What the hell is so bad you can't handle it yourself, Gwenyth?" She fishes a cigarette out of a slim, gold case and lights it. "I swear I don't know how you and Mama survive out here now that Papa is gone."

"Mama is dead," I tell her in a flat voice. Her eyes get big and she smiles before she catches herself and can fake grief.

"When?" Dabbing at her eyes with a silk handkerchief, Gertie forces a sniff even though no tears fall.

"I don't know exactly." I walk closer to the stairs that lead up to the porch. "I've been away, dancing."

She frowns at me. "What the hell you taking 'bout, little sis? You are just as crazy as Mama always was, I swear. Think it's about time you saw someone for that screwy head of yours. Me and Paul could— -"

I step down to the dirt and put a finger against her painted lips, silencing her. "I know. I know about everything. About the murder." She drops her cigarette in surprise.

"What are you …?" She pivots and walks up the three stairs leading to the porch, slowly distancing herself from me.

"What you must've thought when Mama and I walked in with Papa that day, when he got home from the city. Good thing you'd cleaned yourself up by then, or imagine the explaining you'd have had to do. The lies you would have had to tell, not that you weren't use to that."

Lunging forward, she slaps me across the face. Smiling, I do nothing to retaliate. Her abuse means nothing to me now. I know who I truly am, and Gertie can hurt me no longer.

"What did you think, hmm?" I follow her up the steps and she backs toward the open screen door. "Did you think we were ghosts returned to haunt you for what you did?" I curl my hand around her throat gently and whisper in her ear, "Well, in a way you were right. We weren't human."

Gertie pushes me back and, as she tries to flee into the house, she slips in a puddle of gasoline and the heel on one of her grey dress pumps breaks. I hear another snap as she meets the hard wooden slats, and her leg twists painfully beneath her.

"Concord and discord always find a way to right themselves in the universe," I say to her, ignoring her whimpers for help as I pull Papa's lighter from my apron pocket. "I know who I am now, Gertie. You have no power over me anymore. This life with you, on this dying farm, has been nothing more than a bad dream, and now I'm waking up."

I open the Zippo and strike a flame. Gertie is aware of the pungent gas fumes, and she looks around her at the iridescent puddle soaking into her smart suit, shining in the dying light of the sun. She begs me not to touch the flame to the old, rotting wood.

"I'm going home." I stoop over, my eyes never breaking their hold over hers, as I touch the flame to the soaked boards.

Fleeing the house as the flames quickly take hold, consuming the porch and eating their way through the door, I laugh as I run through the field. Gertie's screams punctuate my mirth.

I am free. And at the tree line, as the moon just begins to rise over the furry pine tops, I see mother and Aunt Harmony waiting for me. Isaiah is with them, and they have come to take me home.--to dance me awake.

I take in one last breath as I draw near to them, preparing to shed this body that does not belong to me. Then to the side, something catches my eye. I stop and turn.

A young child and her mother stand and watch me. They smile warmly. I look to those who wait for me at the tree line and Eris and Harmony nod me on. I approach the dead mother and child.

"Thank you." The woman cries as she takes my hand and kisses it. "We can rest now."

The child I know well. I was her once and she was I, or so I thought for many years. The little one holds a large book out to me.

"This is for you. The white lady says it is a key." She points to where Aunt Harmony stands, smiling affectionately at me, with apology in her sloe-black eyes.

"Thank you." I bend and kiss the child goodbye and take the tome she offers. Looking down at the cover, I see it is the book of dreams; the book mother gave me for my forty-fifth birthday. Turning back to the forest, I open its pages.

Before the Fall

by Bev Vincent

The tremendous impact from the explosion pushes Dan forward with the relentlessness of a tidal wave. His arms and legs splay outward.

When gravity regains hold of him, he tucks into a tight ball and tumbles to the ground. His helmet flies into the nearby bushes, but somehow he maintains a grip on his rifle. After he stops rolling, he flattens his body against the ground, orients himself and surveys his surroundings for the enemy while waiting for the ringing in his ears to stop. He tastes blood in his mouth and realizes he bit his tongue.

The tank is less than a hundred yards away, the machine-gunner silhouetted against the burning buildings behind him.

The acrid scents of cordite and burned gunpowder fill the air. A gentle breeze blows left to right. Dan takes the extra second necessary to compensate, to ensure his aim is true. The muscles in his finger grow rigid then relax as he squeezes the trigger.

The gunner stiffens, arches his back, slumps.

Taking advantage of a lull in firing, Dan scrambles to his feet and throws himself into the thick clump of bushes nearby. His foot hits something solid—his helmet.

A jet of flame spews from the tank's turret gun. The vehicle recoils. The blast is too close for comfort. One hand clutches his helmet to his head. He hugs himself with the other arm as shrapnel and debris rain down around him.

Overhead, a fighter jet flashes past. It launches a missile that destroys the bunker he recently vacated.

Not normally in the habit of praying, he utters a silent request to a faceless, nameless deity to guide the path of his one remaining hand grenade. He wonders what kind of god would respond to such a ghastly prayer. He unclips the fist-sized explosive from his belt and watches the tank lumber closer.

When it is near enough that he can count the individual bogey wheels enclosed by the track, he pulls the pin and lobs the grenade in a high arc. Time stands still as it descends toward the enemy vehicle.

Compared to the percussion caused by the missile, the blast is disappointingly small, but Dan is heartened when the track on the side closest to him unravels. The tank jerks awkwardly to the right and grinds to a halt.

Even disabled, the tank presents an ongoing threat. Dan clutches his rifle and slinks through the woods in search of the remains of his company. In the distance, lights and flames flicker. He crouches to make a smaller target of his body. As he creeps through the brush, he winces at each twig snap.

Without warning, the cold, hard circle of a gun barrel materializes against his back, poking him in the spine. A voice utters words he does not understand but he is familiar with the language nonetheless. The mere sound of its guttural diction sends adrenaline and hatred through his veins.

Dan inhales sharply then holds his breath. His rifle is at his side, in his left hand. Under the cover of darkness, he slowly reaches his right hand forward to grip the barrel, then jams the butt back as hard as he can manage. He's rewarded with a solid impact and a grunt of surprise. The small, deadly circle disappears from his back. He whirls around, finishing the job with his bayonet.

A commotion breaks out in the brush to his left. The sounds of several people rapidly approaching fill the night. They're coming from the wrong direction to be members of his company. Not wanting to meet up with his fallen enemy's comrades, Dan swivels and breaks into a run. Branches whip and scratch at his face, sting, draw blood.

A bullet sends splinters of bark and wood from a tree trunk three inches from his head. Dan ducks instinctively but does not ease his pace.

Ahead, he sees a clearing. Crossing it in the daylight would be foolhardy, but now it promises the opportunity to put some distance between him and his pursuers. He bursts through the last cluster of trees and launches himself into a mad dash across the field.

After the third step, his right foot encounters nothing but air. His forward momentum makes it impossible to stop and he is falling, falling, falling . . .

*   *   *

Dan awoke with a start and tried to make sense of the darkness. "What?" he said stupidly. The word echoed in his mind as he tried to figure out where he was.

His bedroom.

Hot blood rushed through his veins, but now that he knew where he was, his muscles relaxed. He let his head fall back onto the pillow and listened to the pulse pounding in his head. The dream seemed so real. Just before he hit bottom, he had been jerked awake, saved by that strange guardian who keeps dreamers from dying.

Slow, deep breaths. That was what he needed to quell his throbbing head. In, hold, out. Again. He wiped sweat from his brow and dried his hand on the sheet.

This was the third time in as many nights that he had been jolted out of a vivid dream by the sickening sensation of falling. Each time he awakened drenched in sweat.

His breathing slowed to a normal rate, then deepened to a steady rhythm as he re-entered the world of dreams.

*　　*　　*

He climbs the broad cement steps leading to the entrance of his office building, a tall monument to modern architecture. Together with its brother edifices, it reaches to the clouds, threatening to block out the sunlight with an impenetrable wall of concrete, steel and mirrored glass.

He encounters a surge of people leaving the building as he enters. His watch reads 8:05 AM. He's late for work, but only by a few minutes. He opens his mouth to ask a question, but he can't speak and can't get anyone to explain where they're going.

He continues on his way to his office. He has a job to do.

In the lobby, people mill around aimlessly, reminding him of a ballroom dance scene from an old movie. He pushes his way through the crowd toward the elevator, which magically opens the moment before his finger comes into contact with the call button.

The elevator is empty. He presses the button for the 38th floor, which glows at his touch, as does every other button above it. This puzzles him, but as long as the floor indicators below 38 don't light up, he doesn't care. He moves to the back of the car where he can watch the floor display without straining his neck.

1 . . . 2 . . . 3 . . . 4 . . . 5 . . .

At first, the floor numbers flicker on and off in the display at a regular pace, like a heartbeat. After the car reaches the tenth floor, it takes longer for each new number to appear. By the thirtieth floor, the elevator has slowed to a crawl.

31 . . . 32 . . . . . . 33 . . . . 34 . . . . 35.

He taps his foot. Clenches his fists. Urges the car up the remaining floors.

36.

The elevator inches its way upward. Dan has no outlet for his building anger. He flexes his fingers and clenches his fists again. Glances at his watch. It's still 8:05.

37.

Only one more floor to go. If he could get out of the elevator and push it upward, he would.

Finally the 37 disappears.

Dan waits.

Nothing.

The number 38 appears briefly in the display, as faint as a ghost.

Without warning, the car reverses direction.

Plummets downward.

Dan becomes weightless. He watches with horror and futility as the numbers descend in a blur. Floating several inches off the ground, he can't reach the emergency stop button.

Air whistles outside the elevator car, like a shriek of terror.

When the counter reaches single digits, Dan knows the elevator can't possibly stop at ground level. He flails his arms, trying to find some way to brace himself against impact, but he's still floating. The display reaches 1, continues to zero and then into negative digits.

The car continues to descend, more leisurely now, drifting down, down, down . . .

*   *   *

Damn!

Dan shook his head. His heart was pounding again, like someone was beating his chest with a sledgehammer. Every ounce of energy was drained from his body. Tremors claimed his arms and legs.

As he had in the dream, he clenched his fists to calm his shaking body. Took slow, deep breaths. When he felt in control again, he sat up in the darkness and peered at his clock. 5:42. Just over an hour before he had to get up.

He lowered his head onto the pillow, which was damp with sweat, but all traces of sleep were gone. He poked his leg from under the covers to cool his body. A moment later, he rolled onto his stomach and sighed. After several minutes in this position, his outstretched arms went to sleep. Unable to move them, he had to thrash around like an enraged sea lion to flip onto his back and allow blood to return to the numb limbs.

When the pins and needles abated, he rolled onto his side, though he knew that getting any more sleep was a lost cause. Even so, he stayed in bed for another half hour, trying to solve the puzzle of sleep as if it were a logic problem.

Finally, he admitted defeat and got up. Showered. Shaved. Dressed.

At the kitchen table, he drank coffee and stared vacantly at the newspaper, trying to make sense of the headlines. He tried not to think about Moira or the things she'd said to him when she left. The angry, hurtful things, all of which he deserved. He'd let her down.

Betrayed her.

He was lucky she hadn't made him leave instead. Luckier that she hadn't yet found some way to retaliate.

More coffee. The newspaper still didn't make sense, and the crossword puzzle looked like it was written in a foreign language. He tried the number puzzle, but realized a few minutes later that he'd entered the same digit in all the empty squares.

On the bus that took him from the suburbs into the city, businessmen and women talked on cell phones, typed on notebook computers and wrote e-mails on handheld devices. Dan stared out the window in a trance, seeing only a blur as billboards, malls and used car lots sailed past.

Drowsiness descended upon him halfway through the morning. At ten-thirty it felt like he'd been awake for days. His tired eyes drooped and closed on him when he let down his guard. Each time he yawned, the woman at the desk across the hall yawned in response.

He ran into Becky in the break room shortly after two o'clock. By then he'd had so much coffee he was jittery and making frequent trips to the men's room. Any coworker observing him would be led to believe he had a drug problem.

"You okay?" Becky asked.

Dan's mouth and lips went dry. He remembered how nervous he was the first time they were together. How excitement and anticipation had allowed him to push all other thoughts aside. "Bad night," he said. "Didn't get much sleep."

"When can I see you again?"

His breath grew shallow. The room felt warm and airless. "Maybe in a few days. This weekend?"

She glanced around to make sure they were unobserved before closing the distance and resting her arms on his shoulders. Her body heat radiated toward him in waves. He tried to meet her direct gaze, but his eyelids were so heavy that he couldn't stop blinking.

"We'll get through this. Together."

Dan nodded. Her breasts brushed his chest. Static filled the air between them. He didn't trust his bleary mind to say much. "I'll call you. Saturday." Her brow flattened and her lips pursed slightly. He knew that look, but he couldn't kiss her. Not here. Afraid someone would see them in this compromising position, he backed away from her. The last thing he needed was office gossip that ended up as supporting testimony in a divorce hearing. He'd lose the house for sure, and everything else.

He tried to smile, but his face felt tight, as if it were coated with a layer of plastic. Becky's eyes narrowed. He felt her watching him all the way out the door and down the hall as he returned to his office.

The next three hours seemed to last days. He changed the wording in a report he was supposed to have finished by Friday, only to change it back to its original form the next time he read through it.

He fell asleep on the bus ride home. The old lady sitting beside him jostled him awake with her elbow and wrinkled her nose at him when he leaned against her. He clutched the hand rest closest to the aisle and struggled to stay awake for the rest of the trip.

He was almost too tired to eat, but made a bowl of soup anyway. If he didn't have something, hunger would waken him in the middle of the night. He picked up the newspaper, which was on the table where he'd left it at breakfast. After a few moments of trying and failing to make sense of the Bizarro comic, he threw it in the recycle bin.

Though tempted to go to bed at seven thirty, he knew that if he did, he'd wake up too early. He forced himself to sit through three sitcoms and the first half of a drama. The plot seemed so convoluted that he felt like he was studying for an exam, trying to figure it all out. Finally he gave up and turned off the television.

Undressed, switched off the light and crawled between the cool sheets.

Lay on his back.

Turned on his side.

Rolled onto his back again.

Waited for sleep to carry him off to unknown worlds.

And waited.

Familiar sounds assailed him from all sides. The wall clock in the living room bellowed ticks and tocks. The purring refrigerator almost lulled him to sleep, but then the ice machine went through its noisy cycle, bringing him back to the surface of consciousness.

He counted sheep. Imagined vast flowery fields. Tried not to remember the look on Moira's face when she found out. Blanked his mind and allowed no thoughts to enter. Fantasized about Becky and him, naked, alone on a blanket on a beach with tropical waves crashing against the shore. Masturbated.

Fatigue finally emerged from hiding, tucked Dan under its arm and stole him away to the underworld.

*   *   *

Somehow, his target makes him.

Dan has been tailing him for nearly five blocks, waiting for him to contact his dealer, when the scrawny character bolts into a dark alley.

Dan clutches at his hip to make sure his gun is secure but unclipped. He takes off after the perpetrator, colliding with a trashcan as he rounds the corner. Clanging reverberates through the alley. He curses between clenched teeth.

Ahead, he makes out the shape of the culprit as he swings up onto a dangling fire escape ladder with the grace of a gymnast.

Seconds later, Dan reaches the ladder and hoists himself up. His body feels like it weighs a ton. His arm muscles burn from the strain.

"You! Halt or I'll shoot," he yells.

The sharp report of a gun is his only reply. A bullet ricochets off the handrail beside his head. The man is now two flights above him. Without slowing his pace, Dan gropes at his waist, feels the rubber handgrip, and produces an impressively large revolver.

He takes aim, but the moment the man is lined up in his sights he disappears around the corner. Dan fires anyway, to throw a scare into the lowlife. Maybe force him to make a mistake.

The dealer clambers over the edge of the roof onto the building's rampart. Dan climbs the last few steps cautiously. He checks to make sure there's a round in the gun's chamber.

He presses his body against the wall.

Eases up the final three steps.

As he pokes his head above the edge of the roof, the first thing he sees is the zigzag tread of the sole of a boot swinging toward his face. He flinches instinctively, but the boot connects solidly with his forehead, sending him backward. Inertia keeps him moving when he hits the railing, up and over. And down, down, down . . .

*   *   *

Goddamn it!

Dan sat up quickly, his head throbbing as if he'd actually been struck. He shivered in counter beat to the pounding of his heart.

Though exhausted, he didn't want to go back to sleep. He couldn't stand the thought of another dream like that. His nerves could only take so much. He crawled out of bed, bare feet sinking into the carpet. The alarm clock taunted him with the time: 1:35 AM.

He needed fresh air.

He donned a pair of pants and tee shirt, then grabbed his jacket from the back of the kitchen chair near the door. He slipped his bare feet into a pair of work boots and left the laces untied.

At the bottom of the front steps, he paused, trying to decide whether to go left or right. He flipped a mental coin; left lost.

Right led him toward the river. He trudged along the sidewalk, shuffling his loose boots against the concrete.

Streetlights illuminated his path. For the first few minutes, everything was silent. The only traffic sounds came from a main thoroughfare in the other direction, a susurrus of rubber against pavement nearly half a mile away. If he hadn't been afraid of falling asleep, Dan might have been tempted to lie down in the middle of the street, just because he could.

A few minutes later, a car approached, blaring its horn and weaving wildly. Dan turned to watch, then darted into the vegetation beside the path when it seemed like the vehicle might hit him. The front tire rubbed against the curb a few inches away.

He emerged from the bushes, brushed himself off and shot his middle finger after the receding vehicle. Loud, seemingly angry voices wafted back to him as it swerved around a corner. Tires and brakes squealed as the car skidded to a halt. A door slammed. More squealing tires. The sound of the car motor receded.

Dan's muscles tingled with adrenaline. His shoulders ached from tension. He sighed deeply and continued on his way.

The river ran under a high bridge a mile from his apartment. Partway across, he leaned on the chest-high rail and stared into the mesmerizing water. A gentle breeze blew left to right. He cast his gaze upward at the generous spread of stars strewn across the sky and picked out familiar constellations. The Man in the Moon grinned back at him. The moon's silvery light cast a peaceful aura over the water's surface.

Other than the calming sound of the water chasing itself up the river, all was silent again. He couldn't resist the temptation to rest his head on his arms against the railing and doze. He was so exhausted that at first there were no dreams.

He was standing on a bridge, leaning up against a steel railing, resting his weary mind. Approaching footsteps shuffled against the sidewalk behind him, but he was too exhausted to care who else might be out at this time of night.

The footsteps stopped. Someone else admiring this peaceful night, he dream-thought.

Two hands grabbed him by the ankles. The railing became a

fulcrum. The unseen attacker pivoted Dan's body over the edge. His right boot fell off. For a moment he was suspended. The rushing water below roared in his ears. He tried to twist and grab the rail, but it eluded his grasp.

The fingers gripping his ankles loosened. The hands offered a final push outward.

And he was falling . . . falling . . . falling . . . and wishing the strange guardian who keeps dreamers from dying would scare him awake.

Terrified that he already was.

The Dreaming Mind Knows

by Larisa Walk

She could tell when the subconscious, the dreaming mind, woke. The outward signs of it--a single hair falling; the pupils widening for a brief moment--were among the most obvious. To her. *The dreaming mind always knows*, her mother had told her, and Daria saw it in the girl across the table from her now. Directed by the girl's subconscious, Daria's hands spread cards on the table. *In fortunetelling, the dreaming mind of the one for whom it's told makes you choose the right cards.* Daria's mother had told her that too.

"See, Irina," Daria told the girl--her closest friend in this small Siberian college, which the two of them had been attending for a year now. "This is you." Daria pointed at the queen of diamonds with an index finger. She frowned at the chipped red paint on her nail. "An unmarried woman."

"But I thought the queen of diamonds meant a blonde woman," Irina said.

"No, just an unmarried one."

"Where did you learn all that, Daria?"

Daria studied her friend for a moment. The snowstorm outside the dorm room window at her back sounded like the far-off keening of hired funeral criers. A draft of cold air from the window brushed at her neck. Daria shivered. Sure, the official communist party line preached acceptance for every nationality in the Soviet Union. Propaganda posters with attractive people in their national costumes screamed "brotherhood of nations, equality" from buildings and school textbooks. In reality, if you were Russian, the degree of acceptance improved. But Irina was her friend.

"My mom's a gypsy," Daria said and felt relieved to see no aversion in Irina's eyes. "She can fortune-tell even with the cards that people played with. It always comes true." Daria chuckled. "And every time she does it, she gets hungrier than a pack of wolves. I've seen her eat four bowls of borscht at a sitting. She says dealing with the subconscious drains her energy."

Daria pulled the king of diamonds from the deck of cards and put it below the queen of diamonds. "This is an unmarried man in your life." Daria didn't raise her eyes. She could sense Irina's tension. There was only one unmarried man in Irina's life--her boyfriend Sergey--and Daria hesitated to tell her what she saw in the cards.

Irina's chair scraped on the wooden floor whose once glossy brown paint sported many scars. Her fingers drummed on the table. *The dreaming mind always knows.*

"He may leave your side," Daria said. "For a while," she added a small lie to soften the coming blow. She sensed that she could close her eyes and name the next two cards she would pull from the deck. This scared her: She'd never experienced anything like this before.

"Leave?" Irina's voice shook. "Well, Sergey did say he was thinking about going to see his parents..."

Daria glanced at her. Irina's pupils widened again--the subconscious mind at work. Daria pulled out two cards from the deck without looking. Jack and eight of spades, she thought. She glanced at the cards. The jack and eight of spades softly scraped against the scarred surface of the table as she put them face up between the queen and king of diamonds. Hunger, like she hadn't eaten in two days, suddenly hit Daria. Her mouth filled with saliva at the stray smell of frying sausages that drifted in from somewhere in the dorm.

"What are these two?" Irina's hand twisted the button that hung loosely on her blue flannel robe with its washed out pattern of pink and white flowers.

Daria's fingertips felt cold. How had she known about the jack and eight of spades? She sighed, wishing she hadn't let Irina talk her into this card reading. She knew how much it would hurt her friend. But Daria wanted her to hurt too, just a little, because Irina wouldn't listen to reason about Sergey. Perhaps she would see that reason in the cards now.

"The jack and eight of spades together between two people mean trouble between those people. Especially if they are lovers." A breakup, Daria thought, but didn't say it. Irina's button made a click-click-click sound when it fell on the table, bounced and then rolled across its surface past a cigarette burn, between two tea-stained glasses.

The next day everyone but Daria went to school. She felt edgy, like maybe the flu was coming on or something. Her body ached. She stayed in bed, but every time she drifted off to sleep the same dream woke her: Sergey reaching for something in his pocket, his eyes full of hatred and fear; Irina raising a hammer to strike at Daria, her face pale as new snow and twisted with rage.

After three or four rounds of the dream, Daria gave up on sleeping. The bed's sagging wire mesh creaked under her weight as she climbed out of it, groaning from the aches and pains like an arthritic old woman. Outside, as if in answer to her, the wind moaned. It pelted the large dorm room windows with dry snow. The glass panes rattled.

A sharp, sudden pang of hunger felt like a stab into her midriff. Uneasy, shaking with an almost unbearable need for food, Daria threw on a flannel robe over her nightgown and ran to the front of the room. Two battered wardrobes, one stained in light oak color and the other in walnut, divided the room into two sections. The front section served as a kitchen, dining, study and a general hanging out area. The back was a bedroom for six girls.

Daria plugged in the hotplate that sat on one of the two shoved together mismatched tables. The shorter table had folded pieces of notebook paper under its rusting legs.

Daria's hands shook as she took an egg from the box that sat on the windowsill--the nearest thing to a refrigerator they had. The space in between the windowpanes served as a freezer in winter. But the mesh bag that hung there was getting pretty slim--no one had gone home since the end of the previous semester to scrounge food from their parents. So, dinners lately had been potatoes and canned stuff more often than not.

Daria hit the top of the egg with a knife, made a hole in it, and drank the contents in two gulps. She took out three more eggs and cracked them into a dented frying pan on the hotplate. The crackling eggs and the whining wind outside made an off-key duet that for some reason annoyed Daria.

After she had her fill of food, Daria's aches and pains drifted away. But not the uneasiness. To keep herself busy, Daria dressed into sweat pants and a sweater, put on make up and went about tidying the room.

She'd just finished mopping, when someone knocked on the door. Made of two sheets of much patched up plywood, the door was hollow inside. If someone knocked hard enough, it always sounded like they were trying to break it down. "Open up, Dasha," Sergey's voice called out from the corridor. "I know you're in there. I need to talk to you."

Daria rolled her eyes and made a face. "What do you want?"

"Come on, Dasha, open up. I told you, I need to talk." He was the only one that called her Dasha, no matter how many times she told him she'd grown out of Dasha when she turned fifteen and that now she was Daria. On top of that, he acted like he thought she should be grateful for his attention.

Daria put on a smooth face and unlocked the door. A whiff of cat urine drifted in from the corridor. Without waiting for an invitation, Sergey pushed past her, leaving tracks of dirty melting snow on the floor she'd just finished mopping.

"Can't you wipe your damn feet? I just finished mopping!" Daria snapped.

Sergey gave her one of his white-toothed smiles that he probably thought ingratiated him to women and plopped himself into a chair by the two tables. "Brrr," he said and took off his fur hat that sported a crust of snow. "It's good for a woman to do domestic stuff. Besides, if you girls don't practice it in the dorm now and then, you'll forget how to do it right when you're married." That grin full of perfect white teeth again. The first time he'd given it to Daria--before she learned what a son-of-a-bitch he was--she nearly swooned. Now his Don Giovanni smiles only irritated her. She wondered what Irina saw in him aside from his looks.

"What do you want?" Daria repeated. If he wasn't Irina's boyfriend, she wouldn't have let him in at all. Now she hoped that he'd say his piece and go away.

"Irisha,"--a pet name he used for Irina, which, for some reason, didn't irritate her at all--"told me that you're a gypsy. Or at least half of one." He unbuttoned his sheepskin coat and leaned back in the chair.

Daria pulled out a chair across from him and sat down. "And what of it?"

Sergey's eyes flicked to the frying pan with traces of eggs stuck to its bottom. He frowned. "You know, you really should wash cookware after you use it."

"Is that all you came to say?" Daria's hands on top of the table fisted. "In case you haven't noticed, I'm not Irina. So, quit ordering me around."

"Oh, Dasha." He smiled, put his hands on top of hers and began stroking her fingers. "Don't get upset."

Daria yanked her hands away. The memory of the recurring dream she'd had in the morning surfaced: Sergey reaching into his pocket for something. "You gonna tell me what you came here for or do I've to wait till next winter?"

"I just wanted to ask you to tell me my fortune, that's all. Dasha."

"Daria," Daria said. "My name is Daria."

He shrugged and gave her a patronizing grin. "Can you read my hand? Do Irisha and I have a wedding in our future? Babies?" She was sure that marrying Irina was the last thing on his mind. She wondered why he was asking her, then.

Ignoring his hand that he'd put on the table palm up, Daria said, "Not with that size four bra you got in your right pocket." She had no idea why she said it, but at that moment she knew it was true.

Sergey's face paled. "How'd-- how'd you know?"

It was Daria's turn to smile. She knew how superstitious he was. Perhaps she could do something with that. "I'm half gypsy, remember?"

He stuck his hand in the right pocked of his coat and pulled out a white bra. An uneasy laugh bubbled up from his throat. "Ah, I just bought it for Irisha, a little present."

Daria leaned back in her chair. "Hardly. She wears size two, not four." He glanced at her quickly. Hatred and fear, just like in the dream. He fumbled for the label. Number four stamped in gray was visible on it, even from where Daria sat. "So, did I pass your test?"

He tucked the bra back in his pocket. "Test?"

"Mhmm, you came here to test my witching powers, didn't you?"

"No, no... Um... Daria. I just wanted you to tell me my fortune, that's all." He still looked pale. He rose from his chair and reached for his hat. Droplets of water covered its mink fur. Daria thought he'd shake them off right on her clean floor, but he just held onto it, edging toward the door.

Daria smirked. "By the way. I can do other things besides mind reading," she lied. "So, if I hear about you disrespecting Irina..." Sergey bolted for the door.

In the late afternoon, when Daria was nailing old woolen blankets to the windows to keep cold drafts from blowing snow inside, Irina burst into the room in tears. Snowflakes were melting on her rabbit fur hat. "He broke up with me," she shouted through the sobs. "It's all your fault. You knew he was going to, didn't you? Didn't you?" She stood in the middle of the room, white-knuckled hands gripping her worn briefcase.

Daria set aside the hammer and nails. "Only from the cards." She wondered if she should've lied to Irina about what she'd seen in the cards.

"You lying witch. He told you he was going to dump me and to make it look like you saw it in the cards. He admitted as much." Irina ran up to Daria and grabbed her by the sweater. Pain twisted Irina's face. Her mascara ran down her cheeks.

"No, Irina, no, he didn't. He's lying. You know how I dislike Sergey. Why would I do anything for him?" Daria said, but what she thought was, *this might be for the best*. Everyone in the dorm but Irina knows that he'd been cheating on her and using her to help him boost his grades.

"Liar," Irina shouted, jerking Daria by the sweater.

Daria stood half a head taller than Irina, but anger gave Irina strength. Irina began to shake. Her eyes looked wild. She scanned the room as if looking for something. Her gaze settled on the hammer. "You just wanted him for yourself, didn't you?" Irina lunged for the hammer. When she spun around to face Daria, she held the hammer high in her trembling hand. "Admit it or I'll... I'll..."

"Irina, come on, don't do this." Daria held her hands in front of her in a *be reasonable, I'm unarmed gesture*. She began backing away from Irina.

Irina's whole body shook as though with chills. Anger lay on her face like a pallid mask. She kept coming at Daria with the single-minded determination of a train. Small girl, but rage and the hammer gave her dangerous strength. And she was blocking Daria's only exit.

"You envied me, didn't you?" Irina was breathing hard. Sweat glistened on her forehead. "You always wanted... wanted... him... Sergey, for yourself." Irina seemed to be having difficulty choosing words. The pallor of her skin made Daria wince.

Daria said nothing, sensing that no words from her would change anything. She backed into one of the beds, climbed on it and jumped off on the other side. Still Irina came after her. Something about her rage didn't seem real to Daria. Irina was one of those people that kept their anger to themselves. If she ever even got really angry.

As Daria climbed over yet another bed, a word surfaced in her thoughts. *Juice.* It seemed stupid at a moment like this, but she recognized it for what it was: her subconscious, her dreaming mind talking. Or maybe it was Irina's talking to hers.

No more beds to climb over. Daria pressed her back to the wall. On each side of her the metal bars of the footboards of two beds caged her in. The only way out was now through Irina.

And Irina kept coming. The hammer held high, she staggered toward Daria. "You think... you think..." Irina's speech seemed a little slurred. She stopped in front of Daria and her eyes turned vacant. Or maybe they'd been like that before, but Daria's attention had stayed on the hammer, not on Irina's face.

She seemed unsure what to do next. She tried to take a swing with the hammer, but her hand dropped and the tool clattered to the floor. Irina swayed and crumpled down next to the hammer.

Without another thought, Daria stepped over her friend and rushed to the kitchen/dining/study/hangout room. She grabbed an open jar of birch juice. The clear liquid slopped over her hand. Daria ran back to Irina with the jar, the birch juice dripping from her hand. She lifted Irina's head. "Drink this. You need it," she ordered.

For a tense moment Irina's blue eyes looked up at Daria without comprehension. Then Irina parted her lips and Daria brought the jar to her mouth. The juice spilled on Irina's face and into her mouth; it trickled down her neck and dripped on the floor. She swallowed, almost choked, coughed, and swallowed again. After she drank about a half of the remaining juice, she lay back down on the floor, panting.

In a few minutes Irina's breathing slowed and she sat up with Daria's help. "Feeling better?" Daria said.

"Yes." Irina stared at her own hands. Long silence hung above them. Daria tensed, wondering if she should run for the door before Irina grabbed the hammer again. Irina said, "How did you know?"

"Know what?" Daria studied her friend's sweat-stained face. Irina still hadn't raised her eyes.

"That I needed juice?"

Daria frowned. "I don't know. Guess the same way I know things when I do card readings."

"I never told anyone." Irina raised her eyes for a brief moment before lowering them to her hands again. In them Daria caught a glimpse of embarrassment and pain. Daria said nothing. If Irina wanted her to know she would tell her. "They recently diagnosed me with a tumor in my pancreas."

Daria gasped. "Oh, no." She threw her arms around Irina. To her relief, Irina didn't pull away.

"It's not cancer," Irina said. "But it makes me have low blood sugars. I haven't eaten anything since breakfast. And then this thing with Sergey on top of that... Well, you know the rest." Irina pulled herself up by hanging on to the footboard of the nearest bed. "But you knew, somehow."

Daria nodded. "Mom said that her seer stuff started coming in when she was about nineteen too. It kind of scares me."

"I'm sorry, Daria." Irina wiped the tears from her cheeks with the palms of her hands. "So, then you really did know that he was going to dump me from the cards." It sounded like a statement, not a question.

"Yes," Daria whispered.

Irina drew her into a hug. Her body shaking from sobs, she said, "Can you charm him back to me? Don't you gypsies do that sort of thing?"

"No, I can't," Daria told her, but she wondered if that was true. After all, she was now nineteen.

Lala Salama

by Gill Ainsworth

Ess heard an intake of breath, and her hand froze in mid air only inches from the chameleon. "Blast," she whispered, as she turned towards Neema, who had suddenly appeared in the kitchen doorway. *I thought she was cleaning the lounge.*

Wide-eyed and staring, Neema's face was pale beneath her black skin. "Bad magic, Madam," she muttered. "Very bad magic... Don't touch..." Tears began running down her cheeks.

"Neema," Ess said in a friendly but commanding tone, "how are we going to get it outside? It can't stay in here, and you won't touch it." She turned back to the chameleon, wondering what had enticed it into the house. There were few insects; the fly mesh saw to that.

As if in recognition of her interest, the reptile swivelled a bulging eye to stare at her. Its lime-green body was a perfect match for the walls. "Don't watch," Ess said. "I'm going to take it into the back garden where it belongs." She waited for Neema to turn away, then gently gathered the creature into her hands, enjoying the touch of its cool dry skin and prickly claws. It rocked, schizophrenic-like, as she carried it towards the screen door. Squinting in the bright Kenyan sunlight, she headed for a bougainvillea bush, deliberately ignoring Kazungu, the gardener. He would be as terrified as his wife.

76

"Bad magic, Madam," Kazungu said, once the chameleon was rocking itself on a thorny branch. "You must see Mganga."

I've had my share of bad magic, Ess thought, one hand stroking her stomach, she bent towards the purple bush. The scentless infertile flowers always invoked the memory of her trip to Nairobi and the operation to unblock her fallopian tubes. But, in itself, the memory wasn't traumatic; she almost relished it each time it came to her. It meant closure, an acceptance of fate and infertility. Especially now she and Michael had agreed to adopt a local child. An AIDS orphan. *God knows, there're enough of them.* She smiled and looked up at Kazungu. "I don't need to see a witch doctor."

Kazungu groaned, and Ess knew she'd said the wrong thing. Ready to offer solace to him, she took a step forwards. But now, visibly shaking, Kazungu was backing towards the jacaranda tree as if she were contaminated with some dreadful disease. "Bad magic, Madam. You must see Mganga. Undo bad magic."

Forcing a serious expression onto her face, Ess decided to bluff it out. "Tell you what, Kazungu. If bad things start happening to me, I'll visit your Mganga." She turned, pre-empting any discussion Kazungu might want to initiate, and headed for the house. As she walked, her hand went back to her belly.

The screen door swung shut behind her, and Michael appeared from the direction of the front stoep. "What're you doing home?" she said, and then she gasped. Blood and red African dust streaked his face. "Oh God! What's happened? Are you hurt?" She pushed him towards the sofa. "Sit down. Let me look at you."

Michael's hand went to his mouth, and then he seemed to realise his nails were as filthy as his face. He forced a smile. "One of the gamekeepers was mauled by a lioness. I closed the park early."

"Is he all right?"

"Not really." He shook his head. "Well, it could've been worse I suppose, but he won't be siring any more children." Michael wiped a hand across his grimy forehead, then took a handkerchief from his safari-suit pocket and dabbed at his hairline.

"Poor fellow," she said, as she took in his blood-soaked clothes and bloodied body. Even the ginger hairs on his legs were matted down, the surreal halo-effect they normally produced no longer apparent. *What if Michael were seriously hurt? What would I do then?*

"He's sixty-seven, Ess. With five children and eighteen grandchildren at the last count, I don't think infertility will bother him. Just the... well, you know." Again, he went to bite a nail, then remembered the blood and grime.

He was worried; Ess could tell. His nail-chewing habit always became worse at such times.

"It was his own fault. Showing off. Got out of the jeep to take a picture for tourists. Bam! She had him by the short and curlies. Literally. His second in command had to fire a tranq dart."

"Should I visit him in hospital? You know, as the bwana's wife."

Michael shook his head. "I wouldn't if I were you. It'd add insult to injury if a woman--especially the bwana's woman--turned up. He'll live. Best leave him be."

"I suppose." Ess turned to their minibar. "Just don't tell Neema or Kazungu about it. Want a beer?" She reached for a Tusker.

Michael nodded. "Why shouldn't I tell them?"

"I touched a chameleon."

"In front of Neema? Why?"

"I had no choice. Stupid thing was in the kitchen and you know what Neema's like. We wouldn't get another meal if she had to share her space with *bad magic*." Ess passed him the Tusker.

"I'll keep schtum." Beer in hand, Michael stood. "I've got to wash this filth off. I'll take this with me into the shower." He stooped to plant a kiss on her forehead, but Ess ducked away.

"No thanks," she said. "I prefer my husband clean."

Ess climbed into bed and snuggled against Michael's shoulder. "I can't understand what a chameleon was doing in the kitchen," she said, as she ran her fingers through his hair. "How did it get past the screen door? Why did it bother? Even the geckoes don't stay when they find nothing to eat. Neema says it's a bad omen."

Michael clasped the hand stroking his head and pulled it down to his chest, entwining his fingers in hers. She twiddled with his wedding ring, twisting it round on his third finger, and he sighed. "They go on instinct, Ess. You know that. I wouldn't worry. Okay, it gave Neema a scare, but I'm sure she's forgotten about it by now." He undid his hand from hers and moved it towards her breasts.

A shiver ran the length of her spine, and her nipples hardened. What did a chameleon matter when she had Michael? She closed her eyes, desperately wanting his hand to move down towards her thighs. It did.

After they'd made love, she kissed him on the cheek, then patted the mosquito net until there were no gaps between it and the bed. Finally, she manoeuvred herself into a foetal position. "Lala salama," she whispered.

"You have sweet dreams, too," he replied, his voice already groggy with sleep. Soon his breathing became heavy, and little snorting noises filled the room. For a while, Ess lay there listening, then her body began to grow heavy and sink into the mattress, and sleep overcame her.

Sweat glistened on Michael's shoulders and dampened his hair, making it look brown rather than rusty blond. Ess ran her hands through the long curly locks, crunching crystals of salt beneath her fingernails. She leant forward, licked his forehead, enjoying the taste. *I need salt. Hot. Tropical hot. Must have salt.*

She licked some more. But her craving wasn't satiated. His hair, now dripping with the liquid, was too tempting. She knelt, one knee either side of his naked sleeping body, and ran her tongue from his crotch to his chin, then up even further to his hairline. Each hair was like a straw, delivering the intoxicating saline mixture. She sucked, gagged on the gushing liquid, sucked again. But still it wasn't enough. If she tore out his hair, chewed it, she'd get the nourishment she craved.

It came out in chunks. Huge chunks. And each left raw flesh. Flesh oozing blood. She sucked that, too. Blood was salty. Blood was delicious.

Finally satisfied, she stared at her handiwork. Skin hung like torn nubuck leather. Tanned and soft. And very dead. She screamed.

"Ess. Calm down, Ess. It's all right; I'm here." Michael was stroking her cheek.

Ess blinked in the darkened room and then shuddered, trying to shake away the image of Michael's bloodied head. Slowly, the gossamer pyramid of the mosquito net came into focus, and, framed against it, Michael's face. She put a hand up to his forehead. Smooth, unblemished. "I thought I'd killed you," she said, and began sobbing.

The blue line crept across the pregnancy-test-kit window. Solid, definable. But it couldn't be true, surely? The consultant in Nairobi had told Ess she'd never conceive. Ess giggled. Somehow, one of Michael's little spermatozoa had managed to navigate a blocked fallopian tube. And somehow the fertilised egg had made its way to her uterus. Incredible but true.

That night of the chameleon, she thought. *And that awful dream. My body knew even then.*

"Women have the strangest dreams when they're carrying." It was her mother's voice, dredged up from the past. "When I was carrying you, Ess, I dreamt I gave birth to a litter of kittens. It was dreadful." She had laughed. "But when you popped out, there you were, my perfect bouncing baby."

81

Yeah, Mum. And you had some strange ideas, as well. Like naming me Esther. She could believe her mother's dream hypothesis though. In her whole thirty-two years of life, she had never had such an awful dream.

"Hey! I'm pregnant!" She grinned. "I can't wait to tell Michael."

But first she must ask how the mauled gamekeeper was. The last time she'd enquired, they had been worried about the possibility of gangrene. Ess grimaced. The thought of parts stinking, turning black and then dropping off wasn't pretty.

"He's on the mend," Michael said, as he reclined on the sofa, one hand clutching a glass of Tusker, the other proffering a fingernail to his teeth. "They've saved his penis, but his scrotum is a thing of the past." For a moment, he chewed a nail. "Not to worry," he said, now examining the ragged edge. "His wife isn't."

"I'm glad--" Ess picked up her own drink and went to kneel at Michael's feet "--because I've got something to tell you. Sooner or later your staff will find out, so I wanted to check first. I don't want to rub salt into open wounds." Ess shuddered. Why had she used the word *salt?* And now she found herself examining his hairline. Although he hadn't mentioned it, she was convinced it had receded slightly. Forcing the memories of her nightmare aside, she set her glass on the parquet floor and clasped his left hand in hers. All five nails were chewed. "Michael," she began, and then she stopped.

Maybe he won't be pleased. It'll mean shelving our plans to adopt. He'll never agree to adoption now I'm pregnant. Especially an AIDS orphan. Too much risk to our baby.

"Well?" Michael prompted. "I'm dying to know how this affects my staff."

"Only the gamekeeper who was mauled. And you, of course. Sit down, have a drink, as they say. You might need it." She looked at him, trying to anticipate his reactions.

"Well?" he asked again.

"I'm pregnant."

"You're what?" He dumped his beer on the occasional table next to his chair. "Ess, don't mess me about! It isn't funny."

"No, really, I am."

"Seriously?"

She nodded. "Yes, seriously. I really am pregnant. We're going to have a baby!"

He scrutinised her face for a moment, and then he leapt from the sofa and knelt by her side, squeezed her in a bear hug. Almost immediately, he jumped up again, a worried look on his face.

He doesn't want the baby! Ess's stomach lurched in dread.

"Damn! I've spilt your drink," he said, and then he stared at her. "You shouldn't be drinking. You're pregnant. Wow! You're pregnant! We're having a baby!" He lifted her off her feet and swung her round in the air.

Ess kissed his forehead. "Yes, we're having a baby. And the odd G and T before dinner won't hurt. Which reminds me--" she glanced in the direction of the kitchen "--it'll be ready any minute. We'd best get ourselves into the dining room before Neema gets angry. I'll ask her to wash the floor whilst we're eating." Ess took his hand and led him to the table where Neema was waiting to serve the food.

"Madam," Neema said, her expression even more concerned than Michael's had been a moment earlier. "I'm sorry to overhear what you were saying; I didn't mean to listen, but now I know, I must say something of grave importance." She smoothed her skirt against her ample thighs and took a deep breath. "I must tell you not to have the baby, Madam."

Hardly able to believe what she'd heard, Ess stared open-mouthed at her maid.

"You must not have it. Bad magic, Madam. The chameleon."

"Oh, is that all." Ess laughed and put her arm round Neema's waist. "I understand your worry. I do. Really. But I don't think any harm will come to my child." She smiled, deciding this was the right moment to pull the Christian card. It tempered superstition. "God is good, Neema. God is kind."

Neema shook her head, and her cheeks wobbled from side to side. "God *is* good, Madam. But He can't undo what has been done." She pulled away from Ess. "I will clean the floor after I have served your food, Madam, Bwana." With that, she turned her back and headed for the kitchen. "But, Madam," she called over her shoulder, "if you have any bad dreams..."

"What did she mean by that?" Michael asked.

Ess shrugged. But her scalp-eating nightmare resurfaced and, in spite of the air conditioning, a cold sweat formed all over her body.

After they'd eaten Neema's speciality, an East African curry with bananas and coconut, they retired to the stoep with their drinks. Crickets and tree frogs filled the night with their chirruping, and a gentle breeze wafted across the lawn, bending the blades of grass to its will. Tomorrow, Kazungu would cut the lawn. And the day after that it would need cutting again. Everything grew rapidly in Kenya, especially grass.

Michael slapped an invisible mosquito on his arm, and Ess made a mental note to ask the doctor whether she should change her anti-malarial medication now she was pregnant.

"What *did* Neema mean about dreams?" Michael's right hand was only inches away from his eyes, as he scrutinised it for signs of a direct mosquito kill. "Damn! I'd be hard pushed to see an elephant in the light this bulb's kicking out. Why does the voltage always drop in the evenings?"

"I don't know to the first question, and because everyone's got their air conditioners running and they're cooking dinner to the second." Ess began chewing on her bottom lip.

"Come on, you know something. I can tell when you're fibbing." He winked, and pointed at her mouth.

Making a conscious effort to leave her lip alone, she stared at his face. His forehead shone in the moonlight, and her gaze slid to his receding hairline. "I was thinking. I nibble me when I think. You're the one who self-mutilates when worried. Just look at your nails."

"Okay, so I bite my nails. But Neema doesn't make glib comments. Something's bugging her."

"She's still worked up about the chameleon, I guess. But, look, don't worry. First thing tomorrow I'll make a doctor's appointment. Get all the antenatal stuff organised."

Michael held Ess's hand, and cold gel oozed over her tummy. Then the radiographer slid the probe across her abdomen, and Ess tried not to tense her muscles. "Here," he said in a clipped Afrikaans accent, as he twiddled with knobs on his monitor, "is the heart." He moved the probe down an inch or two. "And this is the bladder. The poor kid needs a wee." He tapped the screen. "See the black area? Fluid--urine--shows up as black on ultrasound. Do you want to know the sex?" He looked at Ess as if she were the only other person present.

She chewed her lip, glanced at Michael who nodded, so she smiled up at the radiographer. "Yes please."

"Okay. Don't go buying pink paint for the nursery, but it looks like a girl. I can't be a hundred percent certain, but there doesn't seem to be anything--" He moved the probe again. "No, I'm pretty sure it's a girl. But, as I said, stick to yellow." He winked. "Just to be on the safe side."

Ess sat up and wiped her tummy with a piece of blue roll. "Thanks," she said, as she zipped up her shorts and made herself presentable.

"I'm glad it's a girl," Michael said to her when they were halfway down the hospital corridor, leading to the exit. His face told a different story.

"It might be a boy. You heard him."

"And I'll love a boy just as much." Michael squeezed her hand, and his wedding ring dug into her finger.

Ess wiggled her hand into a more comfortable position. "Have you told your gamekeeper about my pregnancy yet?"

Michael nodded.

"What did he say?"

"He said, 'Asifiwe Bwana! You know how to use your manhood. I am very pleased for you and the Madam.'"

"Praise the Lord? Goodness. Do we deserve such an accolade for partaking of marital sex?" Ess grinned. "Well, over the top or not, at least he's happy that you're using your tackle. How's his? Or shouldn't I ask?"

"Fighting fit and ready for muster, so it seems. And, whilst we're on about it, how about an early night?" He slapped her on the backside, then turned and kissed her. "I'm so glad we're having a baby," he said, once their lips had parted. "And I don't care what sex it is. Boy, girl, whatever. I'm thrilled."

"You sure?"

He nodded.

"Then what about names? I was thinking of Mwaura for a girl. It's pretty, don't you think?"

"It's a Kikuyu name."

"So?"

"I don't know." He nibbled at the nail on his ring finger for a moment, and then he shrugged. "It might upset Neema and Kazungu. They're Giriama."

Ess sighed. "They have friends from the Kikuyu tribe. They won't mind."

"Look, Ess--" Michael took a deep breath "--you heard what the radiographer fellow said. We don't even know for sure that it's going to be a girl. Let's leave it for the time being."

Ess lay in bed listening to Michael's snorting sleep-sounds and the backdrop of rain hissing through the air. Together, they drowned out the air conditioner's hum. She envied his ability to shut off his consciousness. Her mind always went into hyperdrive after love making. Especially when the sex had been exceptional. And it had been. But now, sad black faces of orphaned children floated in front of her closed eyelids. They were all boys, and they all wanted to be gamekeepers. She wanted to give Michael a boy. All that pink. It wasn't for the tough, nail-biting Michael that had been looking forward to taking his adopted son on safari. And Michael could teach the child so much. How to use binoculars properly, how to sight a rifle so the tranquiliser dart would go straight into muscle and cause minimal upset to the animal. A girl would be equally keen given Michael as a teacher, but he wouldn't see it that way. Eventually, she drifted off to sleep, her mind still miserable with thoughts of disappointing the one person in her life she truly loved.

It wasn't salt she craved. Not this time. What Ess needed was his manhood. His masculinity. His penis. She was a lioness; a lioness desperate for the taste of man. And this man was naked.

Dripping saliva, she straddled him, her engorged belly almost touching his navel. But, just as she was about to pounce, one of his fingers slipped into his mouth. His teeth began gnawing at the nail. It distracted her. Suddenly she didn't want his manhood. She wanted that hand. That finger. The one with a gold band on it. She bit down, and it came off with a snap. She spat out the ring, swallowed the digit. Blood gushed. She ignored the blood. She had what she wanted. She drifted from REM sleep into that of a woman satiated in all ways.

Bleary-eyed and drained by her bad dream, Ess felt her way into the kitchen.

"Coffee?" Michael asked.

"Thanks." She took the mug from him, sniffing at the revitalising aroma carried in the steam. "I had an awful--" She blinked. Blinked again. It was a hangover from the bad dream. Michael wasn't really wearing his wedding ring on his little finger. He couldn't be. If she focused properly, his ring would be back on the correct finger. She blinked a third time, and the ring stayed on his little finger. Then she collapsed onto the tiled floor.

"Madam, you are all right?"

Ess opened her eyes. Neema's face was as white as any black skin was capable of being. "I'm fine." She smiled. "At least I will be in a minute when I've got my bearings."

"I was so worried, I..." Michael's voice. Ess moved her head to see where it had come from. There he was, chewing at a fingernail. But not the one on his ring finger. That finger was missing.

"Your hand!"

"What?" Michael examined both hands. "Which one?"

"Michael! Your ring finger!" Ess thumped the floor with her fist. "What's happened to your ring finger?"

"Ess? What're you on about. I lost it. Remember?" He put his arms round her, pulled her into a sitting position.

Ess shook her head. "No. No. You didn't."

"The accident. Gangrene. It was amputated shortly after we married. Neema. Tell her."

But Neema was backing towards a corner. "So sorry, Madam. Sorry. My husband, Kazungu, he will take you to see Mganga. You must go quickly."

Ess pushed Michael away and stood. "Come and see!" she shouted, and grabbed his arm, dragged him to their bedroom.

"Look!" She yanked off the bedcover. "If I hadn't bitten off your finger, why is there--" She ran a hand over the white sheet. *I'm going mad! This wasn't an innocuous dream about kittens!* She thumped the mattress. *His finger is a stub. No scab. No bandage. A healed wound.*

I toyed with his ring the other night and it was on his third finger. I know it was. Ess curled up on the bed and sobbed.

"Ess." Michael ran his four remaining digits through her hair. "Ess, calm down. It's just a bed."

A bed. Yes. Just a bed with a rumpled white sheet from a good night's sex. No blood. No sign of mutilation.

"Ess. It's all right, Ess." Now Michael was stroking her cheek with his left hand. The one missing a finger. "We all forget things sometimes. It was a long time ago that I lost it." He bent and planted a kiss on her forehead. "I don't miss the finger, so why should you bother thinking about it?"

Ess sat up. "It isn't that, Michael." She took a deep breath. "Or it is. Last night... in my sleep... I ate your finger!"

Michael laughed. "Ess. It was a dream." He patted her slightly rounded stomach. "You haven't been sleeping properly. You're tired. That's all."

"It's more than that. Yesterday you had a ring finger. Last night I dreamt I ate it. Today it's gone!"

Michael shook his head. "Ess, you drove me to the hospital every day to have the scab picked off. Remember?"

"I remember eating it." She shuddered at the memory of it slithering down her throat.

"No, Ess. A baboon sank its teeth into me. They were worried about gangrene, and there was a shortage of antibiotics at the time. That's why I had to go through the daily scab-picking ordeal. Forceps, one tiny bit at a time. Keep the wound in contact with air so gangrene wouldn't set in." Again, she felt his hand against her cheek. "Didn't work though. I lost it anyway. Then we had to go to Nairobi to get the ring re-sized."

"No! It isn't true."

91

"It is, Ess. Look." He held his stump in front of her eyes. The wound was clean, neat. A thin white line marked where they had folded his skin over the stub to cover the bone.

Ess chewed her bottom lip until she tasted blood. Then she looked up at Michael. "Tell Neema to organise a visit to the Mganga."

He smiled, but, as he bit the nail of his little finger, the look in his eyes told her things she didn't want to hear: *humour her; the poor woman is having a bad time with her hormones.*

"Madam, God *is* good. God looks after His flock. But God can't be everywhere at all times. He sometimes forgets His African flock."

Rueing her decision to visit the Mganga, Ess wafted her hand in front of her face to chase off the flies. It had been a weak moment when she'd asked to see him, a mistake. Although the bones draped round his neck and the red and green cloth wrapped round his waist made him look like any other Giriama tribesman, there was an intensity in his gaze that scared her. It was as if he saw evil inside her. She moved her gaze away from his face and concentrated on the diamond-shaped shadows her hat cast upon the red ground on which they sat cross legged. Then his fly swatter flicked across the diamonds, forcing her to look back up at him.

He cleared his throat. "Madam," he said, "I tell you a true story. It will demonstrate to you how The Lord sometimes forgets about Africa. The land of famine and drought. The home of the black man, as he was destined to be. I hope it will help you understand the grave nature of your situation." Again, he swatted at the flies, attempting to drink the beads of sweat on his face.

"The Lord created the world in six days. And he created all men equal and black. On the seventh day He rested. During His rest, He imparted a job of much importance to the animals of the savannah."

A trickle of sweat snaked down Ess's cleavage. She pressed her dress onto it to soak up the fluid.

"This job was to tell His people about a magic pool of water He had created. It would make all men pure and white as well as equal." Another swat. The fly perched near one of his eyes didn't budge.

"To Europe, The Lord sent the impala. She ran swiftly and, when she got to the great lands, she told man that there was a pool in which he must bathe, and she gave him directions. The people of Europe heeded her advice and ran as fast as the impala, reaching the deep cool water in a very short time. They swam, they laughed, they had fun. And they came out white.

"To China He sent the giraffe, and to India, the elephant, and so it went. Each animal being slower than the one before. And, as each of mankind arrived at this pool, they found less and less water. But sufficient to whiten their skin a little." The Mganga swished his fly swat again, and the flies scattered only to land immediately.

"But, to Africa, He sent the chameleon. It is a slow creature, the chameleon, often stopping to rock and think about what colour it should be. By the time the African people arrived, there was no pool. Only a very small puddle. You see--" he held up his palms to demonstrate "--all we Africans could wet in the Lord's pool of water were the palms of our hands and the soles of our feet. We are black, Madam. Black because of the badness of the chameleon."

Ess shuddered. To her mind, the story was akin to that of Adam and Eve, or Noah and his ark, but the intensity in the Mganga's face told her he believed every word.

"The chameleon is bad. It is Black Magic, Madam. And that is not all. It can suck out a man's soul through his mouth." He prodded her abdomen with his fly swat, and Ess flinched. "You were lucky, Madam. It could have whipped out its tongue to cover your face. Then you would be dead and in eternal damnation." For a moment, his gaze drifted into the distance, and then he refocused on her face. "But your situation is still grave. Very grave."

Ess glanced down at the red dusty ground, then looked up again. "It didn't. I still have a soul. And I don't believe an ignorant reptile can hurt me."

"You are lucky; I have already imparted that to you. It is the life inside you that is suffering."

"The doctor looked at my baby through my tummy. It is happy and normal. Asifiwe Bwana!"

"You may praise The Lord, but He cannot alter this, Madam. I have told you that." For the first time, Ess noticed anger in the Mganga's voice. He swatted at flies again, taking his vengeance out on the insects. "The Lord will thank you if you kill it," he said in a gentle tone, which contrasted surprisingly with his previous anger.

Ess stood. "Kill my baby! For what?" She dropped a couple of shillings at his feet, and then stomped across the dirt track to her car and Kazungu who was waiting to drive her home. As she climbed into the vehicle she shouted, "To keep you and your stupid superstitions in business?" She slammed the door.

"Madam," Kazungu said, as he put the car into first gear, "you should show Mganga respect. He is a very wise man."

Ess didn't answer, and it wasn't until Kazungu had returned her to the house that he spoke again. "This is a bad place," he said, directing his words to Neema who was waiting on the stoep.

For a moment, Neema stared at her husband, and then she vanished into the house. Ess went to the minibar and poured herself a gin and tonic. It had been a tough day.

"Madam?" Neema, eyes downcast, had appeared in the lounge. "I am sorry, Madam, but we can no longer sleep in this house." She wiped her hands against her dress, smoothing the fabric. "Kazungu's brother will accommodate us. Dinner is in the fridge, and I will be back tomorrow to clean and cook for you again, and Kazungu will keep the garden looking very good. But we can't stay. Bad magic is too strong." She left.

Ess poured herself another gin and added sufficient tonic to make it up to a pint. She took it onto the stoep and sat, enjoying her baby's kicking inside her. All was quiet in the afternoon heat. Crickets and frogs would be hiding amongst the long grass, and, in the game park, lions would be lazily swatting flies with their tails as Michael co-ordinated hunts for the big five on his walkie-talkie. Everything in Africa was as it should be. Except that a chameleon rocked by her feet. It was a muddy-brown, the same colour as the stoep tiles that

Neema would have polished that morning. Ess sipped her drink and, slowly, the sun moved towards the horizon. Then, one minute it was squatting there and the next it was gone. Darkness ensued and the insects began their chorus.

"What're you doing out here?"

Ess started, surprised to hear Michael's voice. "Thinking."

"Yeah?"

She massaged her expanding waistline. "I've got my next scan in three weeks time."

"I know. I've booked the day off work."

"And Neema and Kazungu have left."

"Left?"

"I'm bad magic." Ess bit her lip, and then the tears came. A stumpy finger caressed the moisture into her cheek.

The probe spread the gel across Ess's abdomen, and she tried not to tense.

"It's cold. I'm sorry," the radiographer said, her voice soft and soothing.

Ess gazed up at the woman's face and smiled. She had nice eyes. Brown, almond shaped, friendly. Ess was tempted to ask if she minded being a light-tan colour, if she ever thought about blaming a giraffe for not being European-white, but she didn't. Apart from sounding a bit odd, it could be interpreted as racist, and Ess hated those who made such ignorant comments.

"Did they tell you what sex the baby is?" the radiographer asked.

"Yes," Michael said. "A girl."

"Oh, really? Then this chappie must have been hiding his willie. He's definitely a boy. See?" She enlarged the image on the screen, and Ess could make out a vague shadow between the baby's legs. "In fact, I'm so sure of it that I'm going to tell you to get decorating the nursery blue." She smiled.

"You're sure? I mean, really? A boy!" Michael was almost dancing on the spot.

"A very well-endowed boy if our machine is properly calibrated."

"Ess, we're having a son!" He hugged her shoulders--the only part of her he could grasp without interfering with the ultrasound scan. "Oh wow! In less than three months we're going to have a little boy! I can teach him how to stalk game. Where to find the big five. This is amazing!"

Ess gently removed his arms and began wiping up the sticky gel. "I'm glad you're pleased."

"I am. Oh, I am!" He looked at the radiographer. "But why did they think it was a girl before?"

The woman smiled. "An easy mistake. Sometimes, if you get the wrong angle, or it's hiding, you know." She smiled again. "I expect you were told not to go out and buy pink. That's because ninety-nine times out of a hundred we can't be sure."

"But this time you are?" Michael asked, as Ess got off the bed and pulled down her dress to make herself decent.

"Hundred percent. Go and buy blue paint, blue everything. And congratulations!"

As they walked along the same corridor that they had kissed in after the previous scan, there was a spring in Michael's step. "I'm going to give him a toy tranquiliser gun when he's five, teach him how to hold it properly. By the time he's ten, he'll be out stalking animals with me. We need a strong-sounding name. How about Matthew?"

"Perhaps," was all Ess could manage.

When they got home, they took their drinks onto the stoep, sat silently, listening to the cacophony of insect life.

"Neema won't look at me," Ess said. "She won't even stay in the same room as me. It's like I've got leprosy. Only I don't need to ring a bell to warn people."

"She'll come round after the baby's born, when she sees it's a normal healthy child."

"Will she?"

"Yes. And so will Kazungu." He laughed. "It's superstition. Easily hyped up and easily forgotten."

"I used to say that." Hard as she found it, Ess bit back her tears.

"Ess..." He was standing behind her; she hadn't realised he'd moved from his chair. "I love you, Ess. And you did the right thing, removing the chameleon. I can't believe all this has stemmed from one stupid incident less than seven months ago."

"Stupid? I could have picked it up with a stick. I didn't."

"No, because you're you, and you didn't want to hurt it." He left her side, wandered into the garden. When he returned, he held a branch of jacaranda and three spurs of bougainvillea. "For you," he said, and gave them to her.

98

She smelt his offerings. Beautiful. Jacaranda made up for everything the bougainvillea lacked. Together they were perfection. One with no scent and an abundance of colours: red, orange, purple. The other, a creamy white with a scent as intoxicating as anything Chanel might conceive. "Thank you," she said. A simple phrase meaning everything.

Sweat poured from Ess, and pain anchored her to the bed.

"Come on, push," the midwife was saying. "I can see the head. Such a lot of red hair. This one is a true child of African soil. Push, push, push. That's it. You're doing fantastically."

Michael mopped her forehead, his uncontrollable stub tickling as his hand moved across her face.

"You must pant now. Let the baby come in its own time."

Ess tried to obey, but the urge was too great.

"Oh, goodness!" the midwife shouted, and the baby seemed to land in her arms as if she were the backstop in a game of rounders. "Asifiwe Bwana! You have a son!" But there was a note in her voice that Ess didn't like. It told her something was wrong.

"We've made a little boy! We've done it!" Michael winked at Ess, and, despite her misgivings, she felt a warm glow spread through her.

Turning towards the midwife, Michael reached out with both hands. "Can I hold--" He stopped, his face ashen beneath his tan. "Oh my God! Ess!"

"Let me have him." Ess pulled the baby from the midwife's grasp. The umbilicus slithered across her stomach, as she lifted him closer to her face. "Our son," she said, staring at the finger nestled against the scrotum. Wispy red hairs curled around the dent where a wedding ring had once been. "Lala salama," she whispered. "Sweet dreams, my darling." Then she kissed him gently on the forehead. As tears ran down her cheeks, she placed a hand over his nose and mouth and waited for him to turn blue. They would adopt an AIDS orphan. A little girl.

boyfriend.com

by Amy J.Benesch

Janet looked up from her computer and groaned. It was raining, which meant the commute back to Long Island would be even more miserable than usual. Avoiding the rush hour crush was easy when you worked until nine or ten at night, which is what Janet usually did. But Kerry complained that Janet had been ignoring her since becoming Senior Manager at the accounting firm. Janet realized that if she wanted to hold on to Kerry's friendship, she'd have to make an effort to do things with her, which is why she agreed to pizza and a movie tonight. She shut down her computer, grabbed a *New York Times* in a woefully inadequate attempt to stave off the raindrops, and shoved her way into the mass of wet, angry suits.

An hour and a half later, drenched to the skin, she flung open the door to her apartment, tore off her running shoes, tossed her briefcase and the mail onto the kitchen table, peeled off her suit, blouse, and pantyhose, and wrapped herself in her ratty, blue flannel robe. She looked at the couch longingly.

Don't, she told herself. There's no time.

I'm just going to rest, she promised. I won't go there. Really I won't.

She collapsed onto the sofa, pulled the throw over her feet and before she could say, well, maybe just for a few minutes, she was back.

She looked down her arms at the sweep of green velvet. But there was no time to admire her finery. Tom was waiting. She looked around carefully to make sure no one was watching, then snuck away from her ladies-in waiting, down the broad expanse of lawn towards the forbidden woods. She ran until she came to a dense hedge of roses. She was breathing heavily, whether from exertion, or excitement, she couldn't say.

She heard something crashing on the other side of the hedge. She ran in the direction of the sound. It wasn't Tom who came trotting out to greet her, but his horse. Janet stamped her foot. Where was he? She tried peeking through the thicket of roses, but all she got was a pricked finger.

Janet lifted her bleeding thumb to her mouth, but before it reached her lips she felt a set of fingers closing over her wrist. Her thumb went, not into her own mouth, but into the mouth of her lover.

"Where did you come from?" she gasped. "I didn't hear you."

Tom didn't answer her. He never did. He simply pulled her towards him. She quickly forgot what it was she had asked.

After they made love, and were lying on Tom's cloak, Janet remembered all of her questions: Where do you come from? Why don't you ever speak? Are you human? Can I take you back with me to my apartment in the 21st century? Can I come live with you here? Do you love me?

She was trying to decide which question to ask first when a horrible jangling sound assaulted her ears, making it impossible for her to form a thought. It repeated over and over again, a grating, insistent ring, not the gentle clang of the bells she was used to. She commanded herself to ignore it. If she let it permeate her consciousness, she would lose him again. She had waited too long for their reunion to allow this caterwauling to come between them.

The ringing stopped, but was followed by a clicking sound. Someone called her name. Don't answer, she told herself.

She looked into Tom's eyes. "There's something I must ask you," she said.

"Janet, are you there?"

"Don't go," Janet cried out, but it was too late; her eyes had opened. She pushed herself off the sofa and grabbed the phone. "I'm here," she said breathlessly.

"What were you doing, running a marathon?" It was Kerry, of course.

"No." Janet said, slowly. She felt her hair. It was still wet. She shivered. "I was dreaming."

"Don't tell me you were dreaming about 'him' again."

"I'm afraid I was."

"Well, do you want to go back to sleep, or to the movies, like we planned?"

"Let's go to the movies. He never appears twice in one day. I'll be at your place in twenty minutes."

"I'm almost ready," Kerry called to Janet from the bathroom. "I just have to blow my hair dry. Miss Kitty will entertain you."

Miss Kitty gave Janet a bored look and returned to her self-cleaning regime. Janet looked around the apartment. Something seemed different. Had Kerry done another needlepoint? No, it was a photograph on the mantle. Janet was sure she'd never seen it before. She picked it up. A fifty-something man, standing in front of a small plane, grinned at her.

"Who's this?" Janet asked when Kerry emerged from the bathroom.

"Oh, that's Peter," Kerry answered. "We'd better hurry if we want to see the movie before we eat. Whose car should we take?"

"Yours. I need gas. Who's Peter?"

"My boyfriend," Kerry said. "What time did you say the movie started?"

"Seven. Your what?"

"My boyfriend. We'll be OK if there's no line. Come on."

"Since when do you have a boyfriend?"

Kerry shrugged. "Since last week, I guess. I'll tell you about it on the way over."

Janet could tell Kerry didn't want to talk about it, but they had been friends too long for her to care what Kerry wanted. "Talk," she said, when they got in the car.

"Well," Kerry said, easing onto the parkway, "you know that family wedding I'm going to in June?"

Janet nodded. "The one you've been dreading. Did you find a dress to wear?"

"I found something better - a boyfriend to talk about. His name is Peter; he's a businessman, and he flies his own plane. We met a few months ago. He's really sorry he can't come to the wedding - prior commitments - but I have a picture, want to see?"

"You're bringing a framed photograph to the wedding?"

"I have a wallet-sized picture, too."

"Forgive me for asking, but does Peter really exist?"

"Oh, sure. He *exists*."

"Where did you meet him?"

"Just between you and me, I didn't. I bought him for $12.95 at Boyfriend dot-com. But it's three weeks until the wedding - plenty of time for me to figure out where I met him. This is good. Keep asking me questions, so I can be prepared."

"Boyfriend dot-com?"

"No, not that one. I'm not going to tell them about that. Oh shit, there's a line."

They bought tickets for the second show and went to the pizza parlor. "What?" asked Janet, as they sat with their slices, "is Boyfriend dot-com?"

"What its name suggests. A place where you can buy boyfriends on-line."

"You mean a place where you can buy photographs of men who get paid to pose for a picture."

"It's not just the picture. Your start-up kit comes with a five by seven photograph, suitable for framing, a wallet-sized snapshot, some background information, and three telephone message memos you can leave on your desk at work."

"Start-up kit?"

"Yeah. There's no pressure to take it any further, but for an extra charge you can get him to phone you at the office, send flowers on important holidays, and even show up at key functions."

"So it's an escort service."

"Only if you want that. I have no intention of letting it go that far. I'm trotting Peter's picture out for the wedding, then retiring him for good."

"But you've got his picture on your mantle."

"Oh, that's just a goof. I did it for you. Hey, why don't you try it? I'd be curious to see who they hook you up with."

"No, thanks," said Janet. "My dream life is active enough. I don't need any more imaginary boyfriends."

"Oh, come on. It's a hoot. Besides, if you say I sent you, I get a discount."

"I thought you said you were retiring Peter after the wedding."

"Oh, I am. But I want to keep my options open, you know?"

On Monday, when Janet returned to her desk after a briefing from her boss about a client from Saudi Arabia, she checked her voice mail. Someone had left a message of a "personal nature." Just that and a phone number. Janet was about to push the erase button when the voice added that Kerry Casey had said she might be interested in their product. It took Janet a few seconds to think what that product might be. Then she remembered their conversation about Boyfriend dot-com and was furious. She called Kerry, and left a nasty message on her answering machine. She immediately regretted it. Kerry wasn't being malicious, after all, and Janet did have a tendency to take things too seriously. So, when a woman called at 4:15 pm, saying she was from Boyfriend dot-com, Janet was a little more receptive than she might ordinarily have been.

The woman explained that they would ask Janet a few questions, send her a boyfriend start-up kit, and bill her credit card. It was a no-risk offer, the woman added, guaranteed to please, or her money back.

"Fine," said Janet and gave the woman her MasterCard number. "What are the questions?"

"Actually, we already have a profile of you. I just need to make sure our information is accurate."

It was. Kerry must have given them the information. Now Janet was annoyed again.

The intercom buzzed. The receptionist informed her that the Saudi client was on the line. "I'm sorry," Janet said into the phone. I have to go now."

"That's fine," the woman said. "We have everything we need."

Janet forgot about Boyfriend dot-com until Thursday when Billy, from the mailroom, dropped a package on her desk. From the crooked little smile on his face, Janet knew he had seen the return address. Her face burned as she opened the package. The man in the five-by-seven photograph looked up at her expectantly. Janet felt her heart beating, and she blushed again. There was something familiar about this man. He was probably an out-of-work actor. She must have seen him in a TV movie. As she stared at the photograph, her nemesis, Ralph Findley, stuck his head in.

"Hi, Janet. I wanted to go over some points on this contract with that Saudi client. I'm not interrupting anything, am I? Hey, hey! Who's the lucky fellow? I always thought you were an all work, no play, kind of gal. Glad to see I was wrong."

Janet picked up the photograph and dumped it into the wastepaper basket. "Actually Ralph," she smiled at him, "you were right. I tried playing and realized that it doesn't suit me at all. Guess I'm just a dull girl. Now what did you want to ask me about?"

She knew what Ralph wanted. He wanted her to tell him what was in the contract, because it was 75 pages of legalese that he hadn't gotten around to reading, and he had to make a presentation the next day. Janet gave him just enough information to make him feel that he had he no idea what was going on, a not-too-difficult feat, and told him to call her if he had any more questions. "You know where to find me, any time, day or night," she chirped.

When Ralph left the room, looking worried, Janet fished the packing slip from the wastepaper basket. She had been billed for $12.95 plus shipping and handling. Fortunately there was an 800 number on the bill. Janet punched the numbers furiously.

"Boyfriend dot-com. How may I help you?" a man's voice purred.

"I want my money back," she said, preparing for a fight. She knew they'd try to weasel their way out of it, but she hadn't paid the bill yet. Just let them try. The voice on the phone sounded genuinely concerned.

"I'm so sorry your boyfriend didn't meet your expectations. Do you want to talk about it?"

Janet was not about to be charmed out of $12.95. "I tried taking him white-water rafting," she said nastily. "He got all wrinkly."

"I see," said the man. "You no doubt have our two-dimensional model."

"No doubt," said Janet. "Is there another kind?"

"Well, yes. Most of our business is now in our three-dimensional products, guaranteed not to wrinkle, except, of course, for attractive laugh lines."

Oh, this outfit was smooth.

"I'm not interested in your two- or three-dimensional products," Janet said firmly. "I want my money back."

"Of course," the man said. "Consider it done. There's just one more thing. I'm sorry, but I have to mention this to everyone who calls."

Janet reminded herself that this guy wasn't making the rules. He was just someone the company hired to handle the phones.

"Please make it quick," she said.

"Of course. I'm supposed to tell you that we have a new product, a four-dimensional boyfriend. It's still in the experimental stage, so, if you want to try him out, we're offering him free of charge."

It took Janet a second to realize the guy was joking.

"You almost had me going there."

"Is that a 'yes'?"

"Oh, sure. I've always wanted a four-dimensional boyfriend, ever since I was a little girl."

"Great. I'll credit your account for $12.95 plus shipping and handling. Have a nice day."

"Right," said Janet.

The next day, as she was on the Internet with the Saudi client, Janet got a flash message: *Meet me tonight at The Crescent Moon Café at 8:00 PM. Very important.*

Janet transferred the message to her day planner, but didn't respond. She was annoyed. It had to be Kerry, who knew she hated to be interrupted at work.

The next time Janet came up for air, she noticed that the office was deserted. Even the cleaning lady had gone home. She glanced at her watch. It was only 7:45. She often worked later than that. She walked over to the plate glass window that, from its 23rd story height, revealed a pink skyline straight ahead and whirl of activity below. People with friends, lovers, spouses, were greeting each other, and entertaining themselves with activities they somehow found time to plan for. How did they manage it? The weekend always caught her off-guard. She went back to her computer. Something tugged at her memory. She clicked on the day planner icon and realized that she was supposed to be at The Crescent Moon Cafe in ten minutes. Then she read something she hadn't remembered from the first message: *After you enter, go to the very back. You'll find a door. Go through it. I'll meet you on the other side. Speak to no one.*

Kerry was getting weird.

Janet looked up The Crescent Moon Cafe in the phone book. It was on Second Street in the East Village. She really wasn't in the mood to face the Friday night bar scene. All she wanted to do was go home, curl up on the couch, and dream about Tom. But she knew she had to break that habit. It was time to get a grip and get over this phantom lover.

The cab let her off on the corner of Second Street and Avenue A. None of the doors she passed had numbers on them, and there were no signs indicating a cafe. She noticed a blue crescent moon painted in the upper right-hand corner of a gray wooden door and figured that had to be the place. She didn't knock - this was a cafe, after all. Except for a heavy-set woman with long braids wiping down tables, the place was empty. Probably too early for the East Village scene. The place wouldn't fill up until midnight. Janet walked past the woman, who never looked up, to the back of the café. She looked around for a door, but all she saw was a wall. She turned around to see if she had missed Kerry in the café. When she turned back to the wall, it shimmered. She stepped back, or thought she had, but felt herself being pulled forward, right up to the wall, then through it.

She was standing on a boardwalk that paralleled the ocean. She took a deep breath of the salt air and watched the seagulls as they spun in the air and cried out, looking for fish, or popcorn, or cotton candy. Men in straw hats strolled arm in arm with women, who had large chests and impossibly tiny waists. Janet looked down and found that her own waist looked daintier than usual. Her feet had somehow been squeezed into narrow pointed leather boots with buttons on the side. Feeling restless she left the boardwalk and headed down the beach away from the crowds enjoying the fine summer evening. After walking a few yards, she took off her boots and stockings. She wandered by the water and let the waves wash over her toes and stain the hem of her dress. But something compelled her to keep moving. In fact she lifted her skirt and broke into a run until she reached a deserted section of the beach where the sand dunes rose up like sentinels guarding the beach. A sense of urgency pushed her farther into the dunes. She spotted a bicycle lying on its side, stalks of beach grass sprouting out between the spokes. She bent down to touch the bicycle. A pair of arms encircled her. Tom, bareheaded and barefoot, spun her around. He pulled her into his chest and whispered in her ear. "This is better. No one can disturb us here."

Janet wondered where she was. Not the Janet embracing Tom, but her sleeping self. She didn't remember going home from the office.

Tom took off his striped jacket and spread it on the ground. He knelt on it, and pulled Janet towards him. She tumbled onto the sand and began fumbling with the buttons on her blouse. Tom helped her, and she helped him; but they were both trembling from excitement and were soon tearing at each other's clothes, kissing each other everywhere. She and Tom made love fiercely and quickly. Then they spent a long time stroking each other as the sky darkened. Tom wrapped his jacket around Janet, and they watched the stars come out. Then he made love to her again, slowly, tenderly, cradling her head in his hands so she wouldn't get sand in her hair. When he was spent, he rested his head on her stomach. She stroked his hair and tried to think of the question she needed to ask him; but she kept drifting off to sleep.

Janet awoke on a cot in a strange room. She was alone, dressed in the beige suit she had worn to work. She got up, opened the door, and found herself in a larger room that smelled of smoke and stale beer. It was empty. She walked past tables that now supported upside-down chairs and let herself out the front door. She got on the subway headed uptown. She was mystified. She didn't remember drinking that much at the cafe. In fact, she didn't remember drinking anything at all. Maybe that's what happens when you're out of practice, she thought. Then she remembered her dream and felt very happy.

Janet thought she was well prepared for the presentation to the Saudi client, but she didn't feel well that morning. She couldn't understand why she was nervous. She knew that Ralph Findley and some of the older men resented her position in the company and wanted her to fail, but that was nothing new. She had nothing to prove to those bozos. She made it through her part of the presentation, but at the luncheon she excused herself. She barely made it to the ladies' room, where she threw up. When she came back, Ralph sidled up to her. "You're looking kind of green. Sure you're not pregnant?"

Janet smiled sweetly and murmured, "Since there's no way in hell that you're the father, I don't think it's really any of your business."

His smirking comment kept coming back to her, especially when the nausea didn't go away. Finally, knowing it was absolutely ridiculous, she bought a pregnancy test. It came out positive. In desperation she called Kerry.

"Hi," she said. "It's Janet. I haven't heard from you in a while. What's going on?"

"Actually," Kerry said. "I've been dating Peter."

"I figured as much. How's it going?"

"Horribly. I just found out that he's dating at least three other women."

"Have plane will travel."

"I guess," said Kerry. "What's going on with you?"

Janet told her everything. "The worst part is, I know I dreamt that encounter with Tom, but now I'm pregnant. How can that be?"

"Hold up," said Kerry. "It's time to get aggressively real. You told me your version of the story; this is how I read it: some sleazeball got hold of your E-mail address through Boyfriend dot-com and told you to meet him at a seedy bar. He got you drunk, screwed you, and now you're pregnant. Are you with me so far?"

"I guess so, but..."

"Please, Janet. We both know you have an active imagination, but you need a reality check. How pregnant are you?"

"Let's see, it's June 21st. That would make it a little less than two months."

"Good. Now here's what you have to do. Go back to that bar and find out the guy's name and number. Threaten to press charges for rape if he doesn't pay for the abortion. In fact, I'll come over there now and drive you down. He's not getting away with this."

"It's Sunday," Janet protested. "I doubt the place will even be open."

"If not, we'll go to the local precinct. I'll be there in fifteen minutes."

Kerry waited in the car as Janet pushed opened the wooden door and went to the back of the cafe. The wall shimmered. She went through it and found herself on a windy hill overlooking limestone cliffs. Waves crashed on the shore below. A World War I bi-plane was parked nearby. Tom, wearing a leather helmet and bomber jacket, rose out of the cockpit and jumped down.

"Why don't you want to have our child?" he asked, taking her hand.

"I don't know. I guess I don't like the idea of being a single mother."

Tom looked out over the cliffs. "I'm trying to join you in your dimension. Would you like that? The child would have a father and we could be together on a more consistent basis."

"I would love that. Is that possible?" Janet asked.

"It is if you follow the instructions I give you very carefully."

"What happens if I don't?"

"I'll be forced to stay in the fourth dimension."

"Are you sure you want to leave?"

"It's very pleasant here," Tom admitted. "But something terrible is about to happen. I never told you this, because I didn't want to upset you, but... I have another lover."

Janet nodded slowly. "Go on," she said softly.

"She's a kind of leader over here. I always assumed that she had all the power, but there's someone she answers to, someone who requires a blood sacrifice every seven years. The sacrifice is always performed at midnight on Halloween. This year, I have it on good authority that I am to be offered up. Will you help me?"

Janet swallowed and nodded. Tom gave her the instructions.

"My fate is in your hands," Tom said, getting back into the biplane, "I hope to see you on Halloween."

The plane bumped along comically, then sailed off the cliff into the sky. Janet watched it disappear from sight, and then she made way down the cliff. When she got to the bottom, she found a pub with a thatched roof. She entered the pub, walked to the front and came out into the small room at the back of the Crescent Moon Cafe.

Kerry had fallen asleep. Janet banged on the car window. Kerry woke up looking terrified. "Don't do that! I thought you were going to drag me out of my car and kill me. Did you find who knocked you up?"

"Yes," said Janet.

"What's he going to do?"

"If everything goes according to plan, he's going to marry me."

"I've heard that one before," said Kerry. "I should have gone in with you."

Halloween was cold and rainy. Janet decided to drive into Manhattan, because she couldn't imagine Tom riding the subway.

She wore a voluminous black wool cape that made her look as if she were wearing a costume and hid her five-and-a-half month pregnancy. She parked in a lot and merged with the crowd who had come to watch the parade in Greenwich Village. Despite the gloomy weather, people were decked out in elaborate costumes, from Marie Antoinette, with a six foot hair-do, to the usual black leather, body piercings, and magenta and blue hair.

At a little after midnight, as the parade was winding down, Janet heard the mechanical roar of motorcycles. She pushed her way to the front of the crowd. A gang riding black motorcycles sped by. Their leader was a woman with greenish white skin, green hair, and long red fingernails. Janet couldn't decide if she was the ugliest woman she had ever seen or the most beautiful. She was certainly one of the scariest. As soon as they passed, another troop followed on brown motorcycles, then one figure on a white one. Janet leaped onto the white motorcycle and pulled the rider to the ground. The motorcycle spun out of control and careened onto the sidewalk, sending people screaming and running in all directions. It crashed through the window of a bar and fell over.

Janet held onto Tom as tightly as she could. He turned into an iguana, then a poisonous snake. Janet tried to turn its head towards the ground so it couldn't strike her, but as she did she found herself wrestling with an enormous grizzly. As it dug its claws into her back, she heard a roar and the stench of raw meat assaulted her nostrils. She found herself staring into the mouth of a lion. She thought she was going to pass out from fear and nausea, when something made her extremely alert. She was grasping a red-hot iron. Janet ran eight blocks to the Hudson River. She flung the iron into the water and started to cry. Her hands throbbed and huge red blisters were forming. Tom hoisted himself up onto a rotting pier. He was naked. Janet wriggled out of her cape and kicked it over to him. He wrapped himself in it as a woman on a black motorcycle pulled up. The woman with the greenish skin scowled at them. "Outsmarted by a mortal," she said bitterly. "May a thousand curses be visited upon you!" she snarled at Janet. She turned to Tom. "I should have plucked out your eyes and replaced them with wooden ones, as is customary," she spat, and drove away.

Janet's hands had healed nicely by the time the baby was born, but something was worrying her. "Tom," she asked. "What about that woman's curse? Does she have power in this dimension?"

Tom looked up from the *New York Times*. "I don't know," he said. "I guess we'll just have to wait and see."

Boyfriend dot-com sent Janet an e-mail:

> *Dear Valued Customer:*
>
> *Please take a few moments to complete a brief survey.*
>
> *How would you rate your satisfaction with our product? Very satisfied, Satisfied, Not Very Satisfied, Unsatisfied.*

Janet thought about her husband. Since coming to the third dimension, his thick, black hair had begun to thin and turn gray. He had a slight paunch. Her thoughts turned to her beautiful and brilliant baby. She considered the curse hanging over her head.

She clicked the "reply" icon and typed, *All of the above.*

Wolf Dreams

by Gary McMahon

1

"The Dreamtime, of course, contains a multitude of parts: It is the story of things that have happened and will happen, how the universe came to be, how human beings were created and how the Creator intended for human beings to function within the cosmos. But above it, it is a story; and that story is forever being told."

 - *Faces of the First Day: Awakening in the Aboriginal Dreamtime by Robert Lawlor*

2

Wolf Dreams
By Milo Banzak
A synopsis:

by Gary McMahon

A boy is raised as feral by his loutish father, kept locked up in a garden shed and treat as little more than an animal. Living in the gaps between dream and reality, he finds solace in the conceptual place that is the Dreaming Quarter.

Aged sixteen, he is freed by a social worker when his father dies of a coronary. After moving between several foster homes, he eventually ends up on the streets of New York City, barely able to communicate except with the stray dogs that subsequently adopt him into their pack.

Gradually, the boy accepts his identity as an outcast, and begins to move back and forth between dreams and reality. Soon he finds that by watching people, he can view their dreams. Some of them are dark and troubling; he takes it upon himself to root out these dark dreamers before they can act out their fantasies.

The boy becomes an urban legend, a latter-day superhero. Wolf Dreams chronicles his adventures as he struggles to master his own demons and become in life the man that he is in his deepest dreams.

3

As far as I can tell, the first rumours began as early as January 2003, with the appearance of the following item on Ebay, the Internet trading community:

Item # (Unknown)
"Lost" Banzak illo
Original, signed.
Description:
This item is a 100% genuine original from artist Milo Banzak's infamous "lost" comic book Wolf Dreams. The page consists of the final series of panels from the epilogue of this legendary work.

Anyone acquainted with Banzak's unique style will recognise the blunt lines and subtle colouring, the use of deep shade alongside sparse colours, the trademark almost blank features of each individual character.

Note:
The illustration comes framed and protected under glass, and is signed by the artist. Slight fire damage to the lower left-hand corner of the page, but otherwise in fine condition.

The seller's name was listed as *Wolfbloke01*, his email address being Wolfy01@hotmail.com. When the eventual successful bidder failed to receive the item - and his prompt payment was refused - an investigation by Ebay revealed that no such seller had ever registered with their service; his details could not be retrieved from their database. Indeed, there seemed to be no trace of Wolfbloke01 at all.

The bidder was content, if ever so slightly disgruntled, with his refund; no criminal or fraudulent act was deemed to have been committed. The entire episode was put down to experience.

But the rumours caught fire.

4

Milo Banzak died in New York City during the catastrophic events of what is now commonly referred to as 9/11. During a publicity trip to drum up interest in his latest project (*KillGirl*: a graphic novel about a female serial killer's battle against the possibly incestuous ghost of her dead father), he paid a quick sightseeing visit to the famous Twin Towers of the World Trade Center.

Born in poverty-stricken rural Brazil, Banzak had always dreamed of visiting the USA, and due to the recent American interest in his distinctive brand of dark artwork, his dream had come true. Dreams in fact were the subject of his comics: the connection between dreaming and reality the theme running through his entire body of work. Banzak saw his art as an examination of the notion of what the Australian Aborigines call Dreamtime. According to Banzak's philosophy, it is a physical place that exists deep within the human psyche, and in times of violent psychological trauma it is possible to physically access and derive strength from the Dreamtime – a place he preferred to call the

Dreaming Quarter (which was also the title of his first major crossover hit in the American market).

When the hijacked plane hit the side of the building, Banzak was somewhere on the floors above, signing books and chatting about his ideas. Winning over corporate bodies to fund his stay in the land he'd always wanted to explore in both his life and his art.

His fans insist that Milo Banzak never really died. Instead, they say to anyone still interested enough to listen, he crossed over the boundary and into the Dreaming Quarter, where he watches and he waits, creating more stories to tell.

My own interest in the artist came about when an ex girlfriend showed me a tattered copy of *The Dreaming Quarter*. The book consisted of a series of interlinked stories, illustrated to perfection by a man at the peak of his powers, which attempted to hypothesise on what would happen if dreams started bleeding over into waking life. The main character was a troubled artist whose brother was a psychiatrist. His dead brother. Banzak's work always embraced the supernatural; he believed that this was the common ground between the dreaming and waking states.

Despite being unable to translate the text, I was stunned by both the originality of the piece and by the exquisite artwork, and convinced my boss at the time to buy the rights to release the book in the UK and the United States.

So, I was ultimately responsible for Banzak's death. It is something I cannot easily reconcile. Yes, I made him famous, and I realised one of his life's ambitions…but I was also partly responsible for his annihilation.

5

Wolf Dreams was to be his masterpiece. He'd been working on it for years, ever since he learned how to draw. You could even say that it was his life's work. He carried his original sketches everywhere, wherever he traveled in the world. He kept them in a battered leather satchel, an ancient shoulder bag that he'd bought with the fee from his first professional sale at the age of fifteen. He'd been carrying it when he died, buried under a million tons of steel and concrete, and burned to a cinder in the screaming air.

So when this so-called original turned up on Ebay, the fanboys and collectors, the cultists and comic book freaks, all pricked up their ears. None of them were at all surprised to discover that the whole thing was a sham; even the most ardent Banzak fans realised that Wolf Dreams was nothing but a dream within a dream of death and fiery destruction.

6

Okay: now to the rumours.

There are many, but the most persistent one involves the Ebay panels, the solitary page from the epilogue of Wolf Dreams. It is said that whoever possesses the page only has to hang it on the wall or place it under the bed where they sleep, and once they begin to dream something miraculous will occur.

Now, this miraculous happening could be one of several things:

a-   the death of a friend/enemy/family member

b-   the warning of the death of a friend/family member

c-   the acquisition of great riches

d-   a tear in the veil between dreaming and waking that will reveal the Dreaming Quarter.

This last option – option d – seems to be the favourite. Underground magazines and low-tech websites have been set up to discuss the very notion. Many believe that this is what happened at the point of Banzak's death; that the page acted as a kind of doorway, guiding him through into that other realm, the place where he drew upon to create his art.

7

Here's another part of the mythology, an important addendum: before the age of fourteen, Banzak was unable to draw. He was born with severe deformities in his hands; his fingers were crippled and arthritic, and curled into obscene claws. Some blame a congenital defect, others bad diet, and some even put it down to divine intervention.

Anyway, on the night of his fourteenth birthday, Banzak fell asleep as usual on his packing-crate bed. When he woke, his hands were cured. He picked up a pencil and a piece of paper, and before breakfast he'd drawn a beautiful unicorn with a woman's face.

The reality is no doubt far less romantic, but Banzak came from such a poor part of Brazil that the legend has become fact: his people rely on their dreams; they are sustained by them. I'm starting to believe that they have the right idea.

8

It was a muggy Friday morning in London when I jumped off the tube at Embankment and walked to the office. Some obnoxious homeless guy was selling copies of The Big Issue from his usual corner, and despite having no interest in either the magazine or its noble charitable intentions, I was badgered into buying a copy.

I hate that guy; he always gets me.

I entered the building and rode the elevator up to the 4th floor, wishing that we could afford to move to a more spacious building. We shared the floor with the head office of a shelter group for battered wives, and required a special pass to stop the lift at our floor. On more than one occasion recently I'd stepped out of the metal box to find a woman weeping in the corridor, the attendant comforters staring at me with unguarded hostility purely because I'm a man.

Thankfully, I encountered no such scene this morning, and I hurried to open the outer door to Coyote Publishing, the small independent company I'd set up with an old college friend on the strength of a hit we'd had with our first release, a lewd and satirical comic called Sexy Bitz. Neither of us believed passionately in that particular title, but its runaway success and the subsequent line of popular merchandising – everything from T Shirts to lunch boxes - funded other, more worthy projects.

My partner, Barry Wiley, was out of the country with his family, so it was just me and our secretary, Katie, left to our own devices. If I was honest, I preferred it that way; Barry was a great bloke, but sometimes his grinning Family Man persona irked me in a way that made me feel intensely ashamed.

When I went through into the main office I picked up the post. Katie wasn't due in for another hour, so if I was in early I always took over that part of her job – as a small company, we didn't stand on convention. We stamped on it.

Flicking through the usual round of bills, circulars and submissions, I came upon a package that looked and felt different from the rest. For a start, the envelope was old and dog-eared, looking like it had been "round the houses" before arriving on our doormat. Also, there was no return address carefully hand-written on the back – something always present on the many unsolicited manuscripts we received. It also had Honk Kong postage stamps stuck to the top right corner.

I took the slim package to my desk and set it down next to my morning paper. After filing my newly acquired copy of The Big Issue in the wastepaper basket, I filled the kettle and waited for it to boil.

Sitting down at my desk, I fingered the strange package; then, unable to contain my curiosity, I tore it open.

I knew what it was immediately: the mythic lost page, Banzak's final masterwork. The page was carefully sealed into a thick plastic sheath, the illustrations clearly on display. The outlines were messy, the colours minimal. Oh, I could tell it was a Banzak within thirty seconds of setting eyes on the page, I was so familiar with his technique.

A slip of notepaper had fluttered out of the dusty envelope; I picked it up off the floor and unfolded it. The note was from Harry Devon, a good friend of mine based in Hong Kong. It was simple and straight to the point, much like Harry himself.

Dave,
I think this might be what you've been looking for.
Call me.
H.

I held the page up to the window, marveling at it in the blades of dusty light that spilled between the vertical blinds. It was amazing: those passionate pen strokes, that chalky use of colour palette, the way the faces of the two characters depicted were vague and so ghostly, lacking in discernible human features. Like people from a dream you'd once had, but whose identities remained tantalizingly out of reach.

There were four panels in total, and the sequence showed the main character finally having his revenge on the ghost of his abusive father. It represented both his acceptance of who he really was, and his severing of the links to reality to fully enter the waiting world of the Dreaming Quarter. It was powerful stuff, and even with the tiniest hint of facial expressions, the characters came alive on the page.

Regrettably, I'd never actually met Banzak, and in the few photographs of him in existence he looks small and remarkable only in the fact that he was distinctly unremarkable...but when I imagined him it was always like this: one of his own characters brought to life.

The time difference was such that it would have been a waste of time trying to telephone Harry, so I sent him a brief email demanding to know where he had obtained such a piece. And also asking why the hell he had entrusted it to normal postage instead of treating it like the solid gold it was. I didn't expect a reply for some time; Harry was a carouser, and spent his sober days dodging in and out of whorehouses and opium dens, looking for the next hedonistic buzz.

But I didn't care how he'd put his hands on it; all I cared about was the fact that it existed. And it was mine.

9

That evening I closed up the office earlier than usual, feigning a headache. Katie was pleased with the early finish, but slightly put out that the dinner date I'd promised her earlier in the week would not transpire. We'd been an item for just over a year; I wanted to keep it free and easy, but she wanted to move things along, get serious. It was hardly a match made in Heaven, more like one forged from convenience.

"Tomorrow night?" she asked, blue eyes growing wider, lips parting. She was beautiful, and knew how to use it to her advantage.

"Okay. Maybe." It killed me to be so noncommittal. I kissed her cheek, smelled her hair, and just about managed to turn away.

She gazed at me with those laser eyes, pinning me to the spot. "What would you say if I told you that you're the man of my dreams?" Her tone was playful, but with an edge.

"I'd tell you to wake up," I said, feeling smug and incredibly glib.

"But it's dangerous to wake sleepwalkers."

I backed up against the desk, banging the back of my knees against the hard wood. "Then maybe I'd just gently guide you back into bed."

"Whose?"

I smiled; she was getting to me, and she knew it.

"You know I'm falling for you, don't you?" Those eyes again: like knives through my brain.

"If you experience the sensation of falling when you're asleep, they say not to panic. But if you feel yourself hit the ground, you never wake up."

"Then maybe this is all a dream," she said, putting on her coat. "And we'll wake up married."

"Now that, my dear," I said, sensing victory. "Would be a nightmare."

Katie went home sporting a pout on her pretty little face, going for the pity vote. It almost worked – in fact, had it not been for the Banzak, I would have taken her to dinner then back to my flat, and spent a sweaty few hours dictating sweet nothings in her perfect little shell of an ear. Instead, I gave her my spare key and asked her to call round early the following evening, when I would make it up to her by treating us to dinner from my favourite Thai takeaway.

The Underground was less crowded at that early hour and I managed to snag a seat. As the train rattled and hummed, darting like a burrowing beast beneath the surging city streets, I took pleasure in the contents of my briefcase. The journey was endless, and it passed in no time. My head was full of dreams, and time became a notion that was merely part of the whole dream aspect. I could feel Banzak's influence working on me through his art, leading me somewhere that I dearly wanted to see, to experience, to be.

I disembarked at my usual stop, shuffling through the streets of North London. It was growing dark, the streetlights sputtering reluctantly to life, shop fronts spewing light onto the cracked pavements. As I passed the numerous off licenses and fast food joints, I let down my guard and became unaware of my surroundings, walking the route on autopilot.

Big mistake.

Lost in a reverie of all things dreaming, I veered off course and entered an unfamiliar estate. Streetlamps were shattered, the shells of cars sat up on bricks, and gutters were lined with empty beer cans.

Two figures approached me from the shadow of a chip shop doorway with steel shutters drawn down over the glass. Their small porcine eyes were bright, faces narrow and feral. One wore a greasy baseball cap, the other a hooded sweater pulled up to conceal his ratty features.

London: step outside the usual perimeters, stumble an inch off your normal route, and you always end up somewhere like this: a hostile zone, populated by creatures who mean you only harm. Forget the guidebooks and the holiday channels, behind the glittering façade the place is nasty, venal, and filled with malice.

"What's in the briefcase?"

I slumped inwardly, my chest caving in like a deflated balloon. This was a bad situation, and I realised what a damn fool I'd been. These dark nights bred fear and violence; the only way was to follow the beaten path, to stay in the dream and skirt the nightmare.

"Nothing. Just work stuff."

The youth wasn't convinced; he narrowed his eyes and stared at the briefcase I held tightly in my hand.

"Give it to us," said the other – the one in the hood. He stepped forward and casually raised a hand to waist height; just enough to show me the knife.

"Listen lads, I don't want any trouble."

"Tough shit," said the same youth, the nominated mouthpiece of the duo. "You've already got it."

The suitcase stirred in my hand; something inside twitched. It could have been me shaking with fear, but I know now that it wasn't. It was Banzak's artwork trying to get out, fighting to leave the Dreaming Quarter and rush to the aid of its new owner. A surge of power crawled up my arm, originating from the briefcase. It felt like static electricity, or gooseflesh. My shoulder throbbed with energy, then the side of my neck bulged as whatever power I now held exerted its influence, flexed its muscles.

I felt my features liquefy, becoming vague, like those of Banzak's people.

"Fucking hell," said the formerly speechless boy. "His face! Look at his face!"

They ran, the knife dropping from spasming hands, hood flying loose, cap spilling from shaven head. Screams echoed into the night, and thankfully they were not my own.

I felt the bones of my face reassert themselves, contorting into the usual formation. I was myself again, but altered. Changed by the suddenly undeniable power of the Dreaming Quarter that Banzak had transmitted into the page.

10

Back at my flat I drew the curtains and turned out the lights. Darkness was the breeding ground of dreams, and I wanted to nurture them, to bring them slowly and carefully to the surface of a reality I no longer recognised as my own.

Everything was different now, the walls that encased me, the roof over my head, the body that I had been born into. Nothing was definite; everything was malleable. Especially in and around the Dreaming Quarter.

I took out the page and laid it flat on the floor, smoothing the edges with the palm of my hand. Even through its sturdy plastic covering, I could feel the heat of something generating, some power building between the atoms of pulped wood and ink extraction. As I watched, the page began to unpack itself, bloating like a sponge collecting water, swelling until the plastic burst and curled away. I helped it with quick but hesitant fingers, like a mother bird cleaning bits of discarded shell and birth liquors off a hatching chick.

The paper breathed like skin; under my fingertips it felt like the belly of a lover, the hot breast of a woman eager for my touch. Desire built up inside me and I felt myself taking flight. I hallucinated for an instant, becoming the Wolf of the story – the shape-shifting fictional entity that skipped between worlds, between dreams. When I came to my senses I was kneeling on the floor, howling at the moon barely seen through a shaded window.

Without hesitation, I took the artwork into my bedroom and placed it under the bed, clearing a space among the dirty socks and forgotten condoms, the empty biscuit wrappers and mouldy dishes.

I didn't retire right then; instead, I prepared myself for the journey by taking a long, hot shower and anointing myself as best I could in perfumes and aftershaves. I felt stupid, but there was a need in me to ritualise the moment, to mark it in sublime rites and gestures. It didn't matter that I made these up, improvising my preparations for the divine: Wolf Dreams was, after all, a work of fiction.

When I did go to bed I fell into sleep without hindrance. But I did not dream. Certainly not in the traditional sense. I rolled through waves of euphoria, surfing the ridges of the One Great Dream, the single sleeping image generated by a slumbering consciousness. I saw stars exploding off the shoulders of great solar systems, black holes collapsing in on themselves, weird creatures with entire universes contained within the single blind spot of an opening eye.

Then I emerged into a city street, a strange grey district with leaning buildings and stepped sidewalks. People who passed me by all knew me by name, and their oval faces were soft and almost featureless, all blending into what I realised was a single very vague likeness of the same man. And that man was Milo Banzak, the artist, the creator, the adventurer who had discovered the Dreaming Quarter.

In my hand was the page I'd stashed beneath my bed, but here – in this weird place – it had become a key. A skeleton key, with separate jointed parts; possibly made from the finger bone of a large man with hands the size of shovels. I trusted the magic, and held on tightly to the key, certain that I'd know exactly when to use it.

The pavement shifted beneath my feet, forming funhouse steps and steeply angled walkways. I stepped softly, afraid of what might happen if I was to fall. Would I plummet forever, entering that reoccurring childhood dream of an endless fall without the promise impact?

I was led by the faintest suggestion of a magnetic pull through streets that bent and twisted like living things, my body being pulled out of true by the opposing forces that warred constantly in this place. Through barely lighted windows, I saw into the dreams of the masses. I viewed the cold, pale bodies of dead children reanimated, the warm smiles of lost mothers returned, the agony of absent fathers murdered by their resentful offspring. Huge shuffling creatures nuzzled against stained glass; I backed away from their probing eyes, unsure of what they might do if they smelled me on the air.

Some houses contained wonders: the bright-lit fantasies of sleeping children; yet others contained the diseased nightmares of damaged minds. And I saw it all, forgetting the images as soon as they passed before my aching eyes. These dreams were not mine, so I was unable to take any part of them, to store even the most slender particle of their matter in my mind. But still they hounded me, eager to be seen; insistent as hungry babies crying for a mother's tit.

Perhaps, I mused, here was where humanity played out their perfect moments, the lives they could have led where it not for the petty constraints of the nagging flesh. And if that were so, would I also find my own dream self? The being that I could be, in a perfect world; the prototype, the blueprint from which I could begin to shape my own existence when I returned to the dour waking hours?

I toured the area for hours, the city changing around me like an intricate Oriental puzzle box. My eyes ached at the sights they devoured; my mind reeled under the pressure of so much unreality.

Eventually I reached a small tower that lay at what appeared to be the heart of the district, and entered by an open door at its base. The structure was short, squat – only a few storeys high – but it was the place that housed the artist. In the Dreaming Quarter, Banzak did not reach for the sky; instead, he reached for the waking, the flickering open of rested eyes. From here, atop this stunted structure, he could see into the world he had left behind.

The internal walls of the tower were blackened as if by some great fire; scorch marks decorated the high ceilings; the floors were torn and contained huge dark-rimmed fissures.

At the top of a dark spiral staircase that rose through the stories like a mutated spinal column, lay a glistening black door, and beyond that door was the answer to everything that was happening, the great revelation, the coming together of sleeping and waking worlds. When I awoke, my name would become legend. I would be considered a pioneer: the man who returned from the Dreaming Quarter, bringing with him the artist who had christened it.

I looked at the key that was clenched so tightly in my fist, closed my eyes, and reached out a hand to unlock the black onyx door…

11

…and opened my eyes to see a face staring down at me. Short blonde hair. Pale blue eyes, thick red lips.

"What? Banzak?" I struggled to fight against the pull of the waking world, trying to hold onto the beautiful frosted dream but gathering up only bedclothes in my clawed hands. The face loomed into focus: it was one I knew. The features were bold, pretty. I had kissed those lips, stroked those gently rouged cheeks.

"Katie?"

She smiled.

"What-?"

"I have your spare key, remember? Thought you might like a late-night visit? Someone to cuddle up with in the dark; early morning medicine for that headache."

"What the hell have you done?" My arms and legs felt heavy as lead; my mind fell to earth with an audible crash (audible to me, anyway), sending shelves toppling in the bedroom, books and CDs tumbling to the floor.

"You were having a bad dream," she said; and I closed my eyes with dread, with despair, feeling tears fill them and wash down across my cold, smooth cheeks.

"You were moaning in your sleep, tossing and turning, so I thought I'd best wake you up."

Despite the futility of my actions, I rolled and spilled from the mattress, scurrying around on the floor, pushing my hands under the bed. I found nothing but dirty plates, sweaty socks: the bland detritus of a single man. No page. No Wolf Dreams.

Due to my rude awakening, I'd lost hold of Banzak's final page, and in doing so the page had been left behind…

"Oh my God," said Katie, stepping away from me as she turned on the bedside lamp. "Your face. Your fucking face!"

I shambled to the full-length dressing mirror in the corner of the room, peering out from behind the protective visor of my cupped hands. I left them there, covering what I knew I would see if I dared look.

A basic, almost blank, egg-shaped face, crudely sketched and sporting only the merest suggestion of features. A haunted dreamer staring back at me from deep inside someone else's dream.

You Snooze, You Lose

by Jane Gwaltney

7:16 AM. The ritual; Kyle could neither escape, nor explain it.
Sleep would evade—

"*Damn*." He could hear Skip Tate firing up that monster truck.
Concentrating harder, he finished surveying the bedroom. The throw-
rug lay unbuckled, centered between dresser and bed-- the pillows were
fluffed. He drained his teacup of bitter Skullcap, ready to perform the
final act. Succumbing fostered guilt, but refusing would leave him
wide open to nightmares. *Or worse*. Studies revealed the effects of long
term sleep deprivation. Hallucinations, paranoia...
He did the deed—

His face contorted. Tate's heap of junk had died, and its
resuscitation was violating the dawn. Kyle envisioned the blue-gray
smoke wafting into the cab to seek revenge on Tate's lungs...his fists
reluctantly unclenched as the truck roared out. He'd yet to even lay
eyes on the son of a bitch. One month prior, he'd awakened to the
clamor of a moving van...

He *hated* Tate. This he acknowledged as he drew back the
bedspread. Indeed, he *loved* watching Tate's wife Melinda prance
across the parking lot en-route to her morning jog. The corners of his
mouth crinkled as he drifted off.

"Don't you think you should answer the phone?" Melinda purred.

The ringing was infuriating--

Kyle snorted awake, hand grasping air. It curled into a fist and dropped onto the alarm button.

The house was black as pitch, but he maneuvered with the finesse of a man born blind. He flipped a switch and started the shower. Laughter amplified within the steamy echo chamber. "You're lookin' good--a real killer, y'know?" The shout bounced off his reflection as it dissolved into the fog.

*   *   *

Glancing over his shoulder, he yanked his shoelaces into knots. *Better wait and call Claudia from work.* The deadbolt rammed into its sheath.

Dusk had thrown a blanket of shade over the lot, but halogen streetlights glittered in Tate's bumper. The outline of a sticker titillated. Kyle loped across the blacktop...close enough to make out the words: *Fuck The World. I Wanna Get Off!*

"Figures." Within seconds he was unlocking his jeep, refreshing his disdain for the word Cherokee. Determined to afford bigots no fodder, he'd never owned a pickup truck. But wasn't the "bargain" jeep an equal sell-out?

The engine hummed. As he dropped his gaze, hair cascaded, and he groped for the elastic band in his pocket—

He *sensed* her approach and lifted his head. She was inanimate in the headlights' beam.

Incredible...the submissive, liquid eyes of a doe.

He'd yearned for this moment. Sunlight had flaunted her lithe, powerful legs, skin as smooth as stretched deer-hide.

Headlights showcased eyes illuminated by tears.

He jerked the door open as she turned--"Melinda!"

She did a half-pirouette.

Kyle found *himself* caught in the spotlight.

"You're the guy who brought our mail yesterday morning." Shielded by the sanctity of darkness, the heat from her flushed face closed the distance between them. "I looked out the peephole just as you walked away."

"No point in disturbing postal workers. Why are you crying?"

He heard her breath catch. As he stepped closer his shadow spooked, betraying her cover. She was exposed in the headlights again.

Her lips denied anything "serious." Her eyes darted to her apartment.

Her scent tantalized. Musky, addling as smoke from an opium pipe. Those Emerald eyes—

The steering wheel groaned under Kyle's grip. He'd overheard Tate, been jolted from slumber by the one-sided attacks outside his fortressed bedroom. Melinda's jeweled eyes, crystallized by fear of that bastard! He swung into Employee Parking.

The jeep's door slammed; --he had Tate pinpointed: typical redneck. Muscle bound arms, undersized flannel shirt, pendulous beer belly peeking out front and half his ass wavin' the flag. Greasy hair tucked into a ball-cap graffitied with obscenities. Lastly, a pair of big stompin' boots. And Skip! Skipper? A *dog's* name—

"Jesus!" Sam exhaled a strand of oaths as his hand slid off his holster.

Kyle's eyelashes flickered.

"Sh-shit...never see y'comin'. Somebody busted in 'cross the street; killed the guard. Christ. Didn't y'hear?"

"Nope. Looks like you're going to blow me away one of these nights if I don't learn to whistle." Kyle raised a handful of keys, giving them a lusty shake.

The twitch beneath Sam's eye responded before *he* did. "Aw...don't know how t'figger you. *Christ.*"

The pneumatic hinge hissed, the steel door pushing out Sam. Kyle sized up tonight's workload.

"Fat-assed pigs." The "crime scene" featured a popcorn fight. His foot transformed a nest of popcorn into airborne projectiles--he yanked a banner off his shoe, then sat to peel tape adhering to the sole. Glaring at the rolled strip of taffeta, he unfurled it across his lap: HAPPY...OVER...THE...HILL...DAY!

Viciously, he wadded it. *Thwack!* It skimmed the edge of a trash can, plummeting into a bag of Micro-Pop. A fireworks display poofed, then sprinkled the carpet like spent artillery.

Kyle's jaw dropped. He laughed until tears squeezed from his eyes. Then he slouched, head dropping into his hands. A tear doused the tip of a finger; he examined it antiseptically. Months back, he'd shed more tears in twenty-four hours than in all the days of his life...and *none*, since.

A phone came into focus. Claudia would be waiting.

*   *   *

The vacuum cleaner snuffed the remnants of stilted conversation. Actress, Claudia was *not*...

The hose coiled and snaked, slurping the day's leavings.

He kicked the OFF lever, and silence enveloped. Like a friend's handshake...*if* he could label any living soul as such.

"Any *human* soul," he amended. Cece's nose probed. He ran both hands through her silvery layers of fur.

The job met his needs. No one to answer to, no one to talk to but himself...and Cece. The biggest advantage was being able to sneak her inside. They were a team. "The perfect couple!"

She'd rolled onto her back, offering her belly. Obediently, he scratched her pleasure spots. Cece was content, her eyes slits, her paws criss-crossing her chest.

Kyle winced--her bony body had cowered on first meeting ...but months of gentle persistence healed the terror and scarring from metal cages. The Takers' attempts to profit from inter-breeding wolves with

German Shepherds backfired. Puppy-mill disassembled, Cece would live out her days in peace.

Cece's eyelids unrolled. An amber hue warmed her irises, her docile side taking over...*given* over. She would die for Kyle, if need be, employing the prowess of her wolf ancestors to shred his enemies in her steel-trap jaws.

For now, she regarded him through the eyes of a German Shepherd. He sensed her confusion during *other* times. Neither dog nor wolf, she didn't quite belong in either world.

Kyle understood too well...

The way so many people eyed him--especially women-- obviously stereotyping; fantasizing about "mystical powers." The term Native American tumbled end over end. So did genocide. The sterile gauze of political correctness couldn't sop up the vomit. In defiance, he referred to himself as an American Indian.

Cece was snoozing. Kyle tiptoed throughout the cubicles, enjoying the voyeuristic intrigue in sifting among workers' belongings. Sweaters bearing traces of perfume draped secretary chairs, "comfy" shoes were stashed beneath desks, and preschoolers' scribblings thumb-tacked at eye level. Scraps of home-lives...

Kyle noted the time on the buzzing monstrosity on the wall. No wonder his stomach was growling.

*   *   *

In the break-room, he corralled a sandwich and TV remote.

Faces filled the screen, mouthing "bleeps" of rage. Kyle propped his feet up. "Low-life cretins." A pimply kid's nose ring bounced as he spewed accusations at his petulant gum-snapping counterpart...

A commercial intervened. Pensive, Kyle observed the sleeping city through partially opened blinds. Rain sprinkled the window, turning passing cars' headlights into sparkly specters. His mind strayed to his gun cabinet—

A TV voice encroached. New "guests" were introduced. The woman sat, tears coursing down her cheeks. A semi-literate oaf shook his fist. He was "tradin' the old broad in on a new model."

Tate. This slob was his *clone*. Tate would break Melinda, use her up--Kyle jabbed OFF, and the screen extinguished, with a gluttonous pop.

Melinda and the shivery delight of their meeting kept him company throughout the remainder of his shift.

She'd begun to dominate his dreams, even that compartment of consciousness that held him limb-locked, paralyzed by impending slumber. The hypnogogic state had been a misery since childhood, rendering him captive witness to night terrors, mocking his attempts to rouse himself. Now he welcomed it with open arms...*filled with Melinda.*

His hands warmed as he returned to the store-room. The compact space hummed with the hot water heater's rhythmic gurgling *--if Melinda were here right now...*

He smiled wryly. Claudia would turn up her nose at the greasy concrete floor--and the idea of having sex standing up, propped against the shimmying water heater--horrors!

Reverie dissipated, he tossed scavengings into a bag: expensive equipment, cast off instead of repaired. He had no qualms about lugging it home. There was virtue in "stealing" what others misused.

Cece crouched on her haunches next to the exit. There she stayed, until Kyle assured himself Sam was at the far end of the lot. A signal and she bounded forth, flashing into the rear of the jeep.

The compactor gobbled as fast as Kyle could feed it. He entertained the thought of Tate's truck mangling inside its jaws--and the screams' metallic echoes.

*   *   *

A tangerine glow swelled the horizon. Tires swished, birds twittered, conducive to pleasant rumination or the total lack of it. Kyle's mind stretched in the expanse. Even the sight of Tate's truck couldn't deter his bliss--he strode into the house, Cece at his heels.

Opening the windows, he peeled off his clothing and stepped into a brisk and brief shower.

Sunshine had yet to scorch the rooftop. Kyle allowed a breeze to exhilarate his wet skin before tying a towel around his waist. Through fluttering curtains, he caught glances of Melinda's apartment. Her drapes were discreetly drawn.

He sank into mama's velvet couch cushions. Her record player was within reach, a vinyl disk suspended above the turntable. Time to lift its burden of dust and let it spin freely. He no longer feared being swept away on the wings of Hendrix' Stratocaster. *He would join mama.*

148

His heart pounded as he raised the dust cover. Incredibly, the record was immaculate. The sound of his sigh mixed with the rustle from her sleeve. *His heartbeat quieted with her touch.*

Her hand on his shoulder had numbed his pain one afternoon long ago, when he'd returned from school to find her sitting in the kitchen--a note on the table. Daddy was gone. He'd driven away to another wife, another family. Kyle would always hate pick-up trucks- -even more, the smell of stale beer.

"Electric Ladyland" elicited a shiver. He smiled, as tears flowed at last...

A tapping noise was breaking in, growing insistent--he bolted upright. Seconds passed. Then ...knocking. He stared at the door.

It was his policy to ignore visitors. But his hand was turning the knob—

Melinda.

Holy shit, she was beautiful. What was she holding in her hand?

"I-I, um, this is..."

"An envelope," Kyle finished.

She seemed elated. "Yes!"

Curiously, he could make no eye contact. He took the envelope, the brush of her fingers clearing his tongue of all but an automatic "Uh...thanks." He felt a draft--

The wind gust snatched Melinda's hair, and it fluttered wildly as she wrangled it away from her face. "Your mail--left in my box..." She blushed.

Suddenly, Kyle knew why. The letter hit the floor instead of his towel, which he hastily re-wrapped. "I'll pick up the later, *letter.*" An eternity passed. "*Letter*, I mean...*later*, uh..." He shook his head, unable to wrench his eyes from her shoes. "Yeah, what can I say?"

Then came eye contact. "Fate's playing tricks on us?"

"I think so." Shared laughter broke the tension. It was only right to offer her a cold drink at this point.

*　　*　　*

Melinda was more than he'd even imagined. Their tastes in music, art, and literature were parallel. Thus, the timing was perfect. "Are you ready to tell me what *really* made you cry last night?"

For an instant, she lost animation--freeze-framed in headlights--as before. She jumped to her feet. "That's none of your business."

He caught her hand. "I just thought--"

"*Assumed* what? Let go, Kyle."

He wanted to keep her hand.... ...He wanted to--

She was closing the door behind her.

Alone. Drowsiness took claim. Not the siren song of a nap, but the leaden anchor lifted only by the full repertoire of sleep cycles; that circadian journey averting the cliff-fall into madness.

He blinked. He'd sleep-walked into mama's room. If only he could curl up in her bed and drift away. Maybe *Melinda* would drift away, and there'd be no score to settle with Tate.

Mama's room was as she'd left it, her departure as graceful as her everyday existence. He'd enclosed one frail hand in two of his own as her pulse ebbed.

But he couldn't part with her, *ever*. Turning from her bed, he searched for the un-named. The bookcase beckoned.

A volume stood out from the rest. He smiled. How many times had he fought sleep, begging mama to read one more chapter from *Alice in Wonderland?* The pages had yellowed. Mama's cherished "flea market find". Her voice still highlighted each word as his eyes glided.

He yawned. One hand slid the book into its niche as the other saluted two posters. Yes, Jimi Hendrix would've been proud to share space with an American Indian Movement activist.

Leonard Peltier's eyes glinted.

*   *   *

The alarm jostled Kyle from his favorite dream. Three years had passed since he'd last experienced it; he dawdled amid its freshness, dissecting each detail.

The dream was the embodiment of waking control. He could voluntarily interrupt, then return to sleep, continuing where he'd left off. In this twilight world, he inhabited a life-form midpoint between man and beast. In joyful pursuit, he ran through ageless forests, bare feet leathered, reflexes diamond-honed, bounding from cavernous ledges to gnarled tree boughs.

He grinned, almost emitting a ferocious growl.

Then, he remembered. Claudia.

"Fuck." He stumbled out of bed.

*   *   *

Claudia fastened her seatbelt, scowling. Kyle played with the thought of finding her hopelessly ensnared, begging him to free her. He would stall, studying her without expression. Her pulse would quicken, and a flush ripen her cheeks—

"Kyle!"

"Huh?"

She was glaring, in a *puzzled* way. "I asked where we're going."

What a contradiction. Stiff, but sedate. Irritated as hell.

"What's funny?"

"Sorry, Claudia, just haven't been gettin' enough sleep. Movies make me drowsy."

"Just the ones I pick."

"I liked the movie," Kyle soothed. "Oh yeah, got a surprise; somewhere we've never been before."

*   *   *

"The only place left with traditional curb service; came here often when I was a kid."

Claudia gawked. A teenager-on-wheels was approaching.

Kyle's nostalgia dimmed. "Rollerblades?"

152

"Yeah." The girl's ponytail dipped as she checked out her feet. "You ready t'order?"

"Uhh...they used to wear those regular skates with...I mean the 'old fashioned' kind." He cleared his throat. "Still have poodle skirts and cashmere sweaters, I see."

"Hah, yeah. They force us to wear this funny shit. I feel like a frickin' moron."

Kyle swallowed hard. "Two chili dogs, no onions...and two medium root beers."

He watched the skirt's appliqués flounce to the order-window. What had become of the scratchy "Fifties" tunes blasting from the P.A. system? "I don't get it," he muttered to the back of Claudia's head.

The response was a snuffle.

"Claudia?"

"You sure don't."

* * *

"Careful. It's *hot*."

"...Oh--thanks." The carhop's sultry twang had startled him. *And the wink.* She couldn't be more than seventeen. Kyle's smile was time-delayed by obligatory guilt. He reached for a blurry object on the tray, refusing to allow himself to enjoy the view this time as she skated off..."Ow, son of a--"

"She *told* you it was hot," Claudia huffed.

"I guess it's worth it. You're *talking* to me." He sucked his singed finger, then offered it. "Here, taste--best chili in town."

She shook her head.

He plunged the throbbing digit into his root beer. "You know how to hurt a guy." No point in fretting; she would talk when she was ready. He perched her chili-dog on the glove compartment lid and nestled her root beer into the drink holder. "There you go, Ilse," he said softly.

Her expression stabbed him. "I h-haven't called you 'Ilse' in a long time."

She receded into a shadow.

Kyle knew how far he dared venture. German by birth, adoption had stripped Claudia of the identity bestowed by her natural mother. But she was truly Ilse...if only he could convince her.

The radio helped fill an awkward pocket of silence. What luck! KMGG was launching into Focus Fifties Hour. "Strange, eh?" Kyle mused. "This place is in a time warp, but nothing survives intact."

"Hmm." Claudia emerged, halfway.

"You're pouting."

"I'm not."

"You're not eating."

"It's too hot."

He shifted. *If she would just direct that icy stare at that steaming chili-dog...*

"What's funny now?"

"Nothin'." He blew the heat off a forkful of chili.

"The windshield's dirty," she said. "A bird must've bombed it."

"Hmmph. I'll get revenge next hunting season."

A flurry of motion resulted in a shriek! Kyle battled the emergency with napkins and water, but it was too late. The toppled chili-dog had defiled Claudia's linen skirt.

"Stop it! Just...*stop*!" she yelled.

He felt the sting of a slap.

"Wh-why?" she stuttered. "Why did you bring me here? You know I'm on a diet."

"Diet? You don't need--"

"*You* are deciding that for me? You *want* me to be fat, don't you? So no other man--"

"Now, wait!"

The sodden thud of napkins hitting aluminum snipped her tirade. *The shadow tugged, nearly eclipsing. Her eyes protruded...*

"We've known each other since we were kids, Claudia. You *know* me--better than anyone, except..." His hand tippled his cheek, re-tracing the poker hot "brand" of fingerprints. "You slapped me before, once. Remember?"

A nod.

The windshield. He considered turning on the wipers, squirting it with fluid; just wash the crap away. "How many times since, do you reckon you felt like slapping me?"

He heard a hollow laugh--then recognized it as his own, surprised it had squeezed past the lump in his throat. "Dozens. Hundreds?"

Her eyes betrayed her. And her scent. People's bodies revealed secrets, especially their eyes. Liquid remorse, naïve innocence, tawdry sleaze. Claudia reeked with ennui.—

"Were we meant only to be friends?" He'd finally said it. Rapid fire images were zinging through his head. He wanted to be sorry--he wasn't.

Claudia exploded; as raw as it was in her to be.

Coldly, he watched her unravel. She simply had no passion.

*   *   *

Claudia's plaintive whine still ricocheted off the jeep's interior: *I'll never be what you want me to be.* Their relationship had ended with that death rattle. Kyle felt nothing.

Headlights--he recoiled at his pin dot pupils in the rear-view mirror. A vehicle sped around, painting stripes of rubber. An insult of exhaust stung Kyle's nostrils...mixed with a *familiar* scent. His foot bore down.

Miraculously, the truck executed a hairpin turn, hurtling onto the ramp--the stop-light's red reflection swabbed Kyle's windshield as he clung doggedly to the bumper. There, Tate's *sticker* taunted.

They merged as one entity, into highway traffic. Kyle followed until the swarm diminished and inky darkness overtook. He held steady, turning off his headlights and dropping back.

A twinge of regret seeped through. *Damned shame about Claudia*...the herd had to be thinned, but she'd never see that; so illogical about his hunting. But life and death was a system of checks and balances. How could he explain what he felt in his gut when he spotted his quarry? The excitement in knowing his presence was unperceived...

The truck was slowing. When it veered onto the exit, he closed the gap like liquid graphite. His horn blared—

After herding the truck into a field, he switched on his headlights. It came to a stop, engine sputtering. Kyle thrust his arm beneath the seat as he popped open the door.

"Get the fuck outta there, Tate!" The rifle barrel rested cozily on the window frame.

The target twitched, eyes squinting into his mirror. "Wh-who are you?"

"Where'd your 'eat shit' voice go, big man? The one you use to wish Melinda a nice day."

Tate moved. The steering wheel was wearing his hat, his head wedged underneath. "Is that a-a *gun*?"

Kyle roared with merriment. "A cowboy hat--it's a fuckin' *cowboy*! Yes ma'am, Mr. Custer, but she'd druther you call her a rifle. She resents the misnomer. By the way, y'all comin' out t'dance?"

A bullet sheared off the mirror, the cacophony and Tate's shrill yelp echoing through the cornfield—

"Don't kill me! G-God, are you insane? What do you want?"

A harsh *caw* blended into a menacing rumble of thunder.

"Your mirror fell off...*Skip*." Kyle shrugged. "But what can I say? You went'n bought a Ford. Cool bumper sticker, though. Out of the truck--*now*."

The sobbing occupant spilled to the ground. *Onto his knees...*

Kyle's stomach fluttered, re-experiencing a horror and exhilaration, *like that day of cliff climbing...when the branch detached from the crag and he dropped, still clutching as he tumbled. Then--the pulse pounding in his ears as he dangled over a gaping precipice, another branch jutting through his pierced jacket-*

He erupted in gales of laughter, and his rehearsed speech crumbled. "No wonder you need that power over Melinda."

Tate's thin-lipped mouth bargained. "My wallet, take it-- I'll be good to Melinda, I *swear*." His glasses clouded, and his owl-eyes peered overtop. The stiff business suit was too large for his puny frame. "My watch." His tie jerked, Adam's apple bobbing like a yo-yo. "It's expensive--"

"Shut up! You still don't *get it*, do you?" Kyle was no longer amused. "Stand right there..."

*   *   *

Kyle lit candles, and *paced*. Sleep was out of the question.

He backtracked, jamming square blocks into square holes, round into round. Around and around, full circle. Yes, his uncertainty had begun with Claudia, and there it would end.

The knot on the back of his neck tightened into a noose--no, it was *Tate*. Claudia had begun to emerge--and he'd waited so long--his fist pounded the kitchen counter.

He'd *owed* her his patience...

The slap in the schoolyard that chilly morning was deserved. His new neighbor had entrusted him with her secret. Cementing a bond, they'd shared the summer fending off mosquitoes from his porch swing. One night their lips met...*then, school started*.

He'd seethed as Claudia cultivated friends. The boys ogled the precocious eighth grade girls. Undersized boys, with oversized hands--but Kyle hung back, smug in his role as "redskin savage", although no one dared taunt him anymore. The last to sneer "Geronimo" would forever wear scars from the concrete playground.

Pride eventually sealed his debt to Claudia...

Humidity chafed like a wool blanket--perspiration oozed. The candles usurped oxygen and vibrato rolls of thunder mocked. He shook his head frantically, lacing his fingers across his skull to counteract the building pressure. *Unbearable*--he considered shaving his head.

Mama had cut her hair during a traditional period of bereavement, ending the dance of its feathery ends brushing the backs of her knees...

A slam and the patter of rain on asphalt converged in a sensory clash as Kyle bolted from the house, going *somewhere*—-

Cece's growl tickled his spine.

"Kyle--"

The sound of his name was strangely foreign. He gripped a steel handle, mentally *squeezing off a shot*, and spun around—

"Oh!" Melinda's eyes were huge.

"*Back!*" Kyle raised his hand, and Cece skidded to a stop, reversing into the jeep.

Melinda's knees visibly buckled. "Wh-what?" Her head swiveled, rag-doll fashion.

The door closed. Kyle ignored the pain the handle's edge had creased into his skin and evened his breaths. "Whatever's wrong, I can make it go away."

The snuffing of the dome light had brought blackness, except for mushy gray flickers volleying through the clouds. *But he didn't even have to squint...*

"The outage," she sighed. "Too hot to sleep; I was on my doorstep, dozing. Do you have an extra flashlight?"

"I was about to go for a ride, outside the city, where it's cool...any reason you shouldn't come along?"

*   *   *

"I'm not dressed for an outing." Melinda wriggled her toes in front of the AC vent.

Kyle grinned. *Ah, spontaneity.* Her fear scent was diminishing with each turn of the odometer. He needed no further proof--she was The One.

"3:30 AM." She basked in the lime-green illumination from the dash. "I'm sleep deprived and giddy. Next stop: *insanity*."

"Hmmm, yeah...just saw the sign go past." Kyle swung onto the highway, switched off the AC, and popped the ceiling hatch. His voice floated above the rush of air. "Sleep's a bitch, isn't it? Oops--sorry."

The high beams delineated a long snake of open road. "Sorry for what?" She drew up her legs and folded them...sitting on one heel, hugging a knee.

"The 'B' word. I was taught respect." He noted her mute surprise. "I haven't been sleeping well," Kyle went on. "The lines, they sometimes...blur." A self-conscious smirk appeared as his eyes returned to the road. "As long as those *painted* lines stay clear, we're okay."

Miles zipped by, Melinda the first to break the silence. "I rarely see an empty highway--you were right. It's cool. I can smell the rain...uh oh, here it comes!"

"It" fell like a curtain, pelting them with mammoth drops. Jagged blue streaks split the sky, and by the time the hatch snapped shut, Melinda's laughter had given way to hiccups.

Kyle guffawed. "Ever try the 'breathing into a paper bag' method? Or I could try scarin' you."

"This always happens when I laugh too mu--*oh*!"

"Well, I'm turning on this exit. Whew...need a safe place 'til this blows over."

He navigated the narrow side road, startled by *a significance*--abruptly, he jerked into a driveway. "Auto-pilot," he said, killing the engine.

"Huh?" Melinda craned her neck.

"Nothing. Rough ride, eh?"

She broke into a wide grin. "Just what the doctor ordered. 'Bout time I took my own advice."

"So you advise people to chase tornados?" Cece nuzzled the side of his neck. He patted her head, then gave her an admonishing push...

"Hey, my hiccups are gone." Melinda pressed her face to the window. "I can't see a thing." Her head turned. "Did I tell you I'm a doctor?"

Hail drummed the roof and played a lively game of ping pong across the windshield. "Doctor?"

"Psychologist."

"I don't think I'd forget *that*." His mind was outlining a small building, like dot-to-dot drawing. He crossed the creaky threshold--"So, you probe people's minds? Tell 'em why they do those things they do?"

"If only I had that gift...no, I *advise* clients, assess options--"

"Clients? Thought the term was *patients*."

"Personally, I reserve that term for psychotics...ehh, beyond my expertise. I refer that category to someone qualified."

"Mmm. Good idea." His toes were cramping. He tried stretching his legs--a knee rammed the dash. "But...sounds risky. I mean, is there a tactful way to say 'Hey, you're fuckin' *nuts*--oh...sorry."

Damn, his knee was throbbing...and Melinda's skin had the delicate finish of the china figurines on mama's dresser—

"Kyle, stop apologizing. I'm not made of fine china."

He did a double take.

"I can't recall the last time a man took back his 'naughty' words." She severed the thread before he could reply. "Look, the rain slowed. I still have no idea where we are. Hope *you* do."

"...I know this place inside and out. Each blade of grass. The exact position the sun takes on the horizon when the red winged blackbirds sing their first notes...and *nothing* keeps the crows out of the cornfields."

"...I've heard that about crows."

Kyle drifted. *Moist yellow cornsilk between his fingers, the sun parching his scalp...microscopic scissor jaws of red ants. Sweet juice from tender kernels exploding on his tongue--* "Even gunfire," he said glumly. "The crows come back."

"So do memories. The disturbing ones...is that what we're talking about, Kyle?"

"*I was still hoping you'd confide in me.*" Turning, he settled his elbow on top of his seat, placing his hand on Melinda's headrest. *Her hair had the texture of moist cornsilk...*

"Funny," he said. "We talked so long in my living room, but never mentioned our ages. You out past curfew?"

"Not at thirty-three." Her hand found his, but didn't reprimand.

"How 'bout that? We're the same age. I have *another* surprise. I'm a 'Sanitation Engineer'." He paused..."You use a shampoo with chamomile, don't you?"

She tensed. "Y-yes."

"As I was about to say, I didn't finish college...been thinking, though. I made some changes recently. Might go back. Got a knack for computers."

"Yes, that's where the future lies." Her voice crimped. "My...husband is a Systems Analyst."

"You don't wear any rings--pretty amethyst earrings, by the way."

"Wow, you must have eyes like an eagle." Her smile was covert. "It's obvious how you can tell I have no rings on the hand you're inspecting, but it's too dark to--well, you're amazing...and *direct*."

He grimaced. "Directness can be cruel. I once got slapped when I called a German girl a fraud for concealing her birth name. It was in a schoolyard. Her "friends" dumped her, called her a Nazi. I was a hypocrite--'Kyle' isn't *my* real name. I'm Oglala Sioux, grew up on Pine Ridge. My mother named me 'Blind eyes see'."

"Bl-blind?"

"The doctor thought so. The hospital insisted on a birth certificate with a 'Christian' name. 'Kyle' means *blind* in Celtic. *Victory*, in Latin...anyway, mama knew I could see. And a re-examination pronounced me 'sighted'. But enough about my eyes, Melinda. *Yours* told a story when we met. The tears tell me why you run. They're there again."

"I'm not cry--"

164

"Yes, you are." His hand stroked her cheek, thumb gathering the evidence.

The shocker came when her hand found *his* cheek, sliding further, through his hair--until it wrapped around the back of his head. She pulled, her mouth crashing hungrily into his...

His "urgent" question disappeared, and his hands couldn't decide where they were needed most. He groaned as one found an exquisitely formed bare breast. He groaned again. Loudly.

"Mmm...what?" She'd managed to wrestle his shirt halfway off—

"Damn, that hurts." The location of the emergency brake was a major interference. Melinda's head jerked, colliding with his nose. "This isn't working," he whimpered.

"The rain's stopped, baby." Fingernails raked his back. "Plenty of room *outside*..." Her door opened. "Coming? Believe me, you *will*." She yanked her shirt over her head, and the dome light bathed her breasts.

His mouth opened, just one second before her wadded shirt hit his face...

It was no contest, even if she hadn't lost her footing. Kyle caught her in mid-fall, and having casually dispensed of his own shirt, tumbled and pinned her to the ground. His hands regained purpose, stripping the remainder of her clothing. Her protracted moans and choppy gasps became the roadmap for his siege...

Finally, grabbing his hair, she paused the delirious torture--"What are you waiting for?" She groped at his waistband.

"Not here," he said, scooping her into his arms. He carried her through the blackness. *Toward the one rightful place to consummate their union; the act would banish his accumulated guilts and restore the balm of untroubled sleep.*

His thick soles snapped twigs and mashed rocks into the muddy path. Melinda's arms tightened at the yipping of wolves-- "You're safe," he told her. "I'll carry you back, too. Don't want you to cut your feet."

"But where--"

"We're *here*."

A spray of raindrops christened them as he lowered her onto a plush grassy mound. He savored the aroma of damp earth wicking moisture through a sieve of foliage.

"Those animals," Melinda whispered.

"Wolves. Harmless...Cece is half wolf, and she'll love you as much as I do." He unzipped his pants.

"Cece?"

Melinda's skills put fantasy to shame, and with the co-joining of their essences came flight from Kyle's netherworld...

He felt the tips of Cece's mischievous claws skim his back. Her tongue flicked his cheek, her melodic whine tweaking the quiet. Playfully, he pushed at her muzzle--she began digging.

"Woodstock," Melinda said. "Mud and rain...and I hear music!" A hint of melancholy softened her zeal. "Dawn is breaking through the clouds."

166

"I'll get a day job. My face is what you'll see each time you open your eyes in the morning." He placed his palm just beside her left breast. Her heartbeat quickened—

"...Kyle, I..." The corners of her mouth twitched, in a losing effort to preserve a smile.

He watched the blood course from chamber to chamber, the thin walls shuddering as her heart pumped. Beautiful on the inside. So rare. "Cece set us *both* free." He patted the ground adjacent to Melinda's body. Then he repeated the ritual on the opposite side.

"What do you mean?"

Cradling her head, he stretched out on top of her again. "Cece is here...*underneath us.*"

Melinda stiffened—

He rolled, pulling Melinda onto her stomach. "I'll show you her name."

Propped on his elbows, he yanked and tossed aside handfuls of weeds. Daylight threaded through the trees, casting lacy patterns-in-motion across his shoulders. A translucent beam lit the spot where he busied his hands. Melinda inched closer...

She gasped--"A gravestone."

"Stay...*please*. She won't hurt you."

"Wh-who *is* Cece? She's buried here?"

"Yeah--this is a wolf sanctuary. She was a German Shepherd-wolf hybrid. Mama and I were volunteers. Cece was rescued in a puppy mill raid. My closest ally, *always*...mama's too."

167

Mama had pitied Claudia, but Melinda would've pleased her. He watched her crawl forward again, this time to trace Cece's graceful inscription with a fingertip.

"I've been a selfish son. I have to let go."

Tears had etched muddy trails, transforming Melinda's face into a charcoal portrait. "I-I got the feeling yesterday--is your mother..."

"Passed on, yes. 'Bout a year ago." His eyes became scopes, penetrating the dense forest. *Experience reminded him he could scale the fence surrounding the enclosure in less than a minute--*"Lupus...'wolf', in Latin. You might say she *literally* gave her life to them." A sigh sealed his anguish. "The place was re-named, in mama's honor. It's 'The Raven Corbin Sanctuary' now."

He swallowed a gulp of air. "Since she died, I...have a ritual, several things I do before I can sleep. One I save for last. I can't fall asleep, unless...*unless I kiss her photograph.*" It was as if he were rotating a brightly colored balloon in his hands, testing its buoyancy...suddenly, a thunderclap implosion--"I've never told anyone."

So much to tell. Later, Melinda would hear about that night, three years of eternity ago...when dad showed up to re-claim his Raven. Drunken cursing. Fists bashing the door--Cece's lunge at his throat.

A wolf's precision, a jugular tapped. Blood coagulating in her silvery tipped fur. Kyle could still smell the discharge from the cop's gun...

"Kyle, we all have compulsions. Even in sleep, the psyche must have order...*control.* She shook her head. "Mirrors and photographs. Contradictory symbolism--ever stare into a mirror so long, your image disappears? I've shattered that slick, polished surface of mine. Long overdue," she added. "Been ages since I stayed up all night. College 'pajama parties' come to mind...secrets crumbled by dawn--"

"I have the advantage here," Kyle gloated. "I'm *always* up past dawn--and your 'pajamas' are somewhere between here and the jeep...while I managed to keep my pants within reach."

"Except when you answer your door!"

"Fresh out of the shower does *not* count."

She made a face and collapsed. "I hope you meant it when you promised to carry me back. I'm wasted..."

"Can't move a muscle, huh?"

"...I don't believe this." She smiled feebly, as he planted kisses along her shoulder.

"Nothing like having the advantage," he whispered into her ear.

*   *   *

Fresh from the shower, Melinda lay on Kyle's beige sheets. He chortled, convinced nothing quieter than a jet take-off could awaken her...and he anticipated her surprise in eventually waking to find her hair arranged in two prim braids! After lowering the thermostat, he covered her with a light blanket.

The sight of mama's face immobilized him—

First came the usual sear of anxiety...then he perceived a 180 degree turn, followed by a Great Quiet. He closed his hands around her cowl shell frame.

His bare feet padded into mama's room, to the bookcase. Sunlight slit the curtains, welding the window to the top shelf...setting the incense burner aglow. Mama's portrait was a perfect fit.

How wrong he'd been to capture her soul with the camera lens as she lay in death's repose. The curse of insomnia and garish visions had begun that night. The kiss had allowed mama a temporary passage into the Afterworld as he slept, *fitfully*...fearing if sleep were prolonged, she might not return.

Cruelty for *both*--finally ending--as ashes plummeted to the base of the picture frame.

*   *   *

Melinda's muffled sobs opened Kyle's eyes, his arms clutching her cold pillow. The phone cord led him to the hallway.

She cringed as he opened the bedroom door, eyes apologetic. *Her braids were undone*...he snatched the phone from her hand—

"Skip? Ah, thought so. Do we need to talk?"...Kyle smiled, replacing the receiver. "He said he smelled something burning."

Melinda's jaw clenched, then unlocked, releasing an incomplete series of phrases with all the makings of a linguistic car crash. She began again--"I know you mean well, Kyle, but isn't this the *last* thing I need?" She tugged at the hem of his borrowed tee shirt.

"It's the last thing you'll *ever* need. You realized that last night. I'll take care of you--"

"T-take? You're presuming again; confusing the issues--"

"I'm not one of your patients--um, *clients*--"

"And I'm not one of *yours*!"

"No problem, then."

She crossed her arms, then undid the gesture. "We're supposed to have a...talk? Like *this*? Ridiculous. You're naked."

"Take off my shirt and we're on even ground," he laughed. "The ground...muddy, wasn't it? Let's talk about *Skipper*."

Melinda paled.

Kyle caught the scent of her rage--"I'm sorry. I was wrong to assume."

Her backstep faltered.

"Let's get dressed. Let's *talk*, Melinda."

*   *   *

The phone would ring. If not today, surely tomorrow...

The story was big, and newscasters shook their heads while directing queries to on-the-scene reporters. Kyle had diverted Melinda's attention *so far*--not difficult, considering the choices to be made, the options to be assessed. *She'd be driving home now...*

Late-breaking details unfolded. The next of kin had been notified, so they could now divulge the identity of the victim...

Kyle flinched--"*Ilse*! Her name was Ilse."

171

They garbled on, with "shocking" revelations about the "grisly" discovery: no forced entry. The victim had died of blood loss, her throat ripped open by an animal--initially assumed to be a large dog. Sketchy reports from the coroner's office hinted at something far more sinister. The incisor wounds were characteristic of a different variety of canine...*a wolf.*

Kyle lunged for the remote control—

Melinda looked over her shoulder, then shut the door in a hurry. Her eyes questioned.

"I...dropped the remote." He got to his feet. "So used to living by myself, I don't expect the door to open. Uh, how'd work go?"

Her silence was alarming. He held out his arms..."I know it all feels upside down, your first day back." He kissed her temple. "I'm calling in sick."

"No..."

"Did Tate bother you? You did have his calls forwarded to your lawyer, didn't you?" He was content to be her protector--like Cece had been, for mama...and for him.

Melinda relented. Kyle made the call, and the night was free to erase her doubts. He closed out the world and they made love...

As Melinda slept, he sipped tea and read Alice *in Wonderland.* She would know about Claudia when the time was right. But only what she was *meant* to know.

*   *   *

The call came not more than one hour after Melinda left for work.

"Yeah, that's my name. What's this about?" Kyle pursed his lips, anticipating the moment he would interrupt...

"Claudia? N-no...no, she *can't* be!"

A badge was displayed. "You look like you haven't slept a wink," the lieutenant commented.

"I work nights. *Graveyard.*" Kyle rubbed his puffy eyes. "Have a seat--and get to the stuff you wouldn't talk about on the phone. You...said she'd been killed by a *wolf?* What the fuck--"

"That's part of it. There's an even stranger element."

"What's stranger than a wolf coming into the city to hunt down a woman? Wolves don't attack people; they run from 'em."

"We figure it must've attacked on command, been *trained.* An animal didn't wrap a bumper sticker around her throat after tearing it open--"

"What...this is a *joke?*"

"I wish. I've seen a shit-load of weird crimes, but this is in a class of its own. If...*when* we find the owner of that sticker, we've got that killer nailed. A real *stupid* bastard-- It says 'Fuck the World. I wanna get off'. I can just picture that type, can't you? Pity we have a major glitch..."

Kyle braced.

"Very little mess on the scene. *Tidy* psycho. No prints so far, except the woman's, and what's sure to be yours. On the TV remote, things like that...*expected*, since you two were dating. Her family's suspicious, but that's to be expected, too. So, I'll stay in touch. Your input's vital." The lieutenant headed for the door. "Don't sweat it, though, pal. Nothin' to lose sleep over, okay?"

"Dinner's ready, Melinda. Then...there's something I have to tell you."

"Tell me now, Kyle. You're upset." She touched his cheek. "See? I know you so well, already. I'm *so* glad your Cece brought us together. I love you, baby."

His arms surrounded her.

Yes, they'd always be a team, he and Cece. The perfect couple.

Dreams, Wholesale

by A.C. Wise

3:52 a.m. burns ruby-bright from the bed stand. It's been 3:52 a.m. for hours. He can't sleep. He can never sleep these days, no matter how tired he is. Streetlights wash through the window, broken by the blinds, throwing bars across the tangled mess of blankets on the bed.

He gets up. Karen is still sleeping. He watches her for a moment and frowns. She starts to wake, blinking sleep from her eyes. Her skin is blue with night and yellow with the streetlights - the color of a bruise. Her hair is a mess.

"Go back to sleep." He tells her before she can speak. She blinks again – still half caught in dreams – and obliges. Smudged with shadows, her eyes look like bruises as well.

He goes into the kitchen and sits under the halogen glare; it burns his eyes and buzzes in his head, a faint sound that follows him even after he turns off the light. He wonders what Karen is dreaming. He wishes he could dream too.

He opens the refrigerator – more light – a whole wash of it; artic cold and steaming when he breathes. He gets milk and then a box of cereal. In a bathrobe and slippers and boxer shorts he sits at the table and eats breakfast at 3:52 a.m. In the broken light from the kitchen

175

window he reads the back of the cereal box and notices something he has never seen before. It is an advertisement and it makes him think of x-ray goggles and secret decoder rings.

It says: *Dreams, wholesale or specialty — we have what you need! Insomnia got you down? Can't get a good night's rest? Send proof of purchase from any of these fine products (he skips the list) and $5.00 shipping and handling and we'll send you our finest. Not convinced? We'll give you a full refund if you're not completely satisfied. Ask about our bulk packages and specialty subscription services. Supplies unlimited. We have what you need.*

He blinks. He can't believe his eyes; they ache anyways, they have for days. It must be a joke. He reads it again. He glances at the clock and suddenly he feels like laughing, but he can't remember why.

"Okay, what the hell?" he tells the cereal box. "I'll be the sucker, I'll bite. Joke's on me."

He finds an envelope and a stamp. He carefully cuts the proof of purchase from the box and drops it in with a five dollar bill from Karen's purse. He licks and seals the envelope and carefully copies the address from the advertisement onto the front. Still wearing his slippers and bathrobe, he slips outside and pads down to the mailbox on the corner. He smiles at an early morning dog-walker and chuckles as he lets himself back inside. He sits down at the table and eats another bowl of cereal and waits.

It's 3:52 a.m. He has forgotten all about the cereal box and the advertisement. He can't sleep. Karen is snoring lightly beside him and he wishes she would stop. It reminds him of the halogen light in the kitchen. He wonders if he's left it on. He can't stop thinking about it. He gets up. Karen doesn't even stir. He goes downstairs.

Everything is dark and quiet. The house looks strange. The blocky furniture looks alien. For a moment he wonders if he's in the right house, but he can still hear Karen snoring upstairs. For a moment – irrationally – he hates her. He sits in the dark and after an hour or two, he watches the sun rise.

Karen leaves for work at 7:00 a.m. He is still in his bathrobe and slippers. When she's gone, he eats a bowl of cereal and scans the help wanted section. Nothing catches his eye. He puts the paper down and goes to the door. Like precognition, he meets the postman at the door. There are a pile of bills (to go on Karen's desk) and a circular from the local grocery store.

There's a strange look on the postman's face. Almost hesitating, as if he's unsure, he pulls a slim envelope out of his bag that he's been holding in reserve and hands it over. There's no return address, no real delivery address either – just a name.

"You might want to have this one tonight, or right now even." The postman tells him, still smiling his queer smile. "You look like you need it."

He is looking at the man in the bathrobe out of the corner of his eyes. The man in the bathrobe wonders if he has ever seen the postman before. He can't remember.

He closes the door and takes the envelope to the couch and sits down. He looks at it from every angle before opening it. Sometimes it looks translucent. If he turns it on his side, he thinks, it will disappear.

There is a single sheet of paper inside, neatly typed.

It is a bill – itemized.

Dream – Qty. 1- Discount applied – $0.00

S & H – Standard next day service - $5.00 (paid)

Applicable taxes - $0.00

Total - $5.00 (paid)

Thank you for your order.

There is nothing else on the paper. He turns it over and over. Now he knows it is a joke. He is annoyed at himself for being taken in. He almost crumples the paper, but then he has a better idea. He takes the paper into the kitchen and lights the front burner on the stove. He holds the paper to the flame and the edges begin to crisp. There is a certain satisfaction in watching the paper turn black – chasing an angry line of red as thin as a thread across the creamy white.

The flames are blue and gold. He holds the letter over the sink, letting it burn up to his fingertips. He watches the ash dropping off the paper and drifting down into the basin. The flakes remind him of something. Snow, he thinks at first, but no, something else – moths maybe? No, something bigger…

He gasps. The room is filled with birds. All this time, the ashes have been turning into birds, bright yellow canaries and they are filling the kitchen silently – perching on top of the refrigerator, the cabinets, the tables and the backs of the chairs. There are even four hopping in and out of the flames on the stove as if it was a birdbath. Yellow feathers clog the drain in the sink. If he turns the tap, it will pour out canaries. If he opens the drawers, he knows the cutlery will be avian – all the forks and knives now feathers and beaks and birdsong.

All at once, they notice him. Their bright eyes turn to him and they open their beaks in song. The song is a meadow. He can see it. He can feel the sunshine on his skin and the faint hush of long grasses swaying like the sea. There are yellow flowers everywhere, but he knows they are just canaries in disguise. He is dizzy. The birds are flying all around him and there is something faintly unsettling in the ceaseless whir of their wings.

He wakes up trying to bat the birds away. He is in bed. It is 9:36 in the morning. Karen's side of the bed is empty, but he can still see the dimple in the sheets where she was. His head aches and feels heavy and dull and full. His mouth tastes like the inside of a garbage can.

He gets up slowly and when he doesn't fall, he goes into the bathroom. He pisses and flushes and takes a shower. He is feeling less dizzy now. In the kitchen he eats a bowl of cereal over the sink. Outside the window, he sees four birds in a line on the telephone wire. They are starlings and grackles, spotted and shimmering like oil slicks in a parking lot, but they all look pitch-black against the sun. He finds them disturbing. He can't help thinking that they are watching him.

He picks up the cereal box and examines it. There is a phone number printed at the bottom of the advertisement. He can see the place where he cut out the proof or purchase. That, at least, he is not imagining. He glances at the phone.

It is an old model – off white, stained dirty beige by the previous inhabitants who smoked. It clings to the wall like an insect. Its buttons are square and ugly and gray. He feels like a fool.

He chews and swallows and crosses the room to the phone. He lifts the receiver and listens to the dial tone, as though he expects a coded message or someone breathing on the other end. His hands are shaking as he dials. He holds his breath as he listens to it ring.

"Hello, customer service, this is Mary speaking, how may I help you?"

She sounds bright and chipper. She sounds like she has blonde hair curled and a little frizzy and flattened where she is wearing a headset to speak to him. She sounds like she has blue eyes and a white sweater. Under her sweater, she sounds like she has perky breasts. She sounds like she really cares. She sounds like she really does want to help him.

His throat has suddenly gone dry. He croaks and wheezes; a terrible sound like a perverted prank call. He blushes, even though she can't see him and that makes him blush even more.

"Are you calling about one of our dreams?" She suggests helpfully.

"Yes!" He gasps gratefully, clutching the phone.

"What seems to be the problem?"

He closes his eyes. He feels dizzy again. The phone in his hands is the only thing that is real and his palms are sweating, threatening to drop it on the floor. He clings to Mary and her voice, she will keep him safe; she will keep him sane.

"There were birds…" He whispers and falters, swaying again.

"Oh yes! That's a lovely one, isn't it?" Mary coos enthusiastically.

"I didn't…" He begins.

"Most people find our bird dreams very soothing." He hears a faint note of disapproval in her voice as if she knows he doesn't agree. He feels he has let her down.

"A refund?" He croaks quickly. It is almost an apology.

"Oh, of course, sir! If you're not fully satisfied with any of our products or services, we do offer a full refund, but might I make a suggestion, sir?"

He finds himself nodding, even though she can't see him. It doesn't matter, because she keeps talking anyway.

"You see, sir, not every dream will suit every person. We do offer a wide range of dreams, varying in price depending on length and complexity. We take special pride in having something to suit everyone. Of course, if you aren't specific when you place your order, our warehouse will ship you something generic and those dreams aren't tailor-made.

"If you'd care to try again, sir, we have a promotion running right now on some of our made-to-order items. They're a little more expensive, of course, but it comes with the same guarantee, shipping and handling is free and you get exactly what you need for a good night's sleep.

"Is that something you'd be interested in, sir? I can take your order right now and we do accept all major credit cards as well as personal checks and money orders."

"I...I..." He sways, clutching the phone, eyes squeezed tightly closed.

"I want a dream about super models!" He bursts out, suddenly, surprising himself. "The way they used to look in the old Sports Illustrated swimsuit editions that my dad used to read and didn't know I looked at." He babbles. He doesn't know why. He's still blushing, clutching the phone. He's starting to get an erection. He feels like an idiot.

"Of course, sir, we can do that for you. Would you like to pay by credit card? It speeds the process up and we can do it right over the phone."

Her voice is so encouraging. He thinks about her perky breasts. He feels that he will start hyperventilating or crying soon. Karen's purse is on the table. He finds her credit card and breathing rapidly and shallowly, he reads the number desperately into the phone, where Mary receives it calmly on the other end.

He is shaking when he hangs up. He feels like a junkie, de-toxing. He paces. He is sweating. The air is buzzing. He is going insane. He knows he *must* be going insane. If he could only sleep, everything would be okay. His mind wouldn't be filled with crazy thoughts, his head wouldn't ache, his eyes wouldn't burn.

The doorbell rings and he nearly jumps out of his skin. He glances at the clock. It's nearly noon. He's still wearing his bathrobe and slippers. He hurries to the door and wrenches it open. The postman is standing there with a package in his hands.

"Special delivery." He holds it out. This time he doesn't smile.

He takes the package and the postman goes away. He closes the door. His hands are trembling so he can barely get the box open. What should he do? Should he burn it? Eat it? He *is* going mad; he *must* be.

He holds the piece of paper in his hands. They're shaking so badly that the neatly typed words blur in front of his eyes. Or maybe he is crying. He can't tell. He can't read what the paper says. He's almost frantic in his desire to read it. He has to know. He has to dream.

He forces himself to sit down on the couch and take a deep breath. He closes his eyes. He tries to think about super models in bikinis. He wants to help the dream along. He wants it so badly it hurts. He's still clutching the piece of paper in one hand. He starts to masturbate with the other. He can almost see a woman coming out of the water, glistening with suntan lotion and drops of water.

The door opens. He starts up. Karen is standing there, wide-eyed, staring at him. Her keys are still in the lock and they jingle slightly. Her briefcase is in one hand. She has a paper bag in the other. She begins to stammer.

"I came home for lunch. I just thought I would come home, a nice surprise. I brought bagels."

He crosses the room towards her. The piece of paper falls out of his hand.

"Karen…" He reaches for her.

"No." She turns her face away. She can't look at him. "It's okay. Don't." She backs up a step.

"Karen." He tries again.

The door is still open. The sunlight coming in is terribly bright and it hurts his eyes. They burn. He needs to get some sleep.

"Karen." A third time.

She backs away from him. Her heel catches on the step and she stumbles back and falls against the stairs.

"Karen." He reaches for her. She's screaming. He has to stop her from screaming. The door is open and the neighbors will hear.

"Shhh, Karen. Shut up, Karen."

He hits her and her face goes white and still. Her eyes are wide. She's terrified. He hates the look in her eyes. He hates her. There is blood at the corner of her mouth. She is quiet now, but hitting her once isn't good enough. He knows that. He puts his hands around her throat. She's struggling. He can hear children on bicycles going by outside. The sunlight hurts his eyes. He's choking her. He's whispering her name, over and over again.

"Karen. Karen. Karen."

He opens his eyes. The alarm clock is glaring at him. 3:52 a.m. He throws back the covers and jumps out of bed. He stumbles downstairs in the dark, he fumbles for the phone. With shaking fingers, he dials. It doesn't ring. Silence breaths out on him. He clutches the phone and listens. He is sweating.

A recorded message comes on the line.

"Thank you for calling customer service. Our hours are nine to five, Monday through Friday, except for holidays. If you have a question or complaint, or would like to place an order, please leave a detailed message with your name, mailing address and phone number and the nature of your request or complaint and someone will get back to you as soon as possible. For all other inquiries, please call back during our business hours and one of our customer services representatives will be happy to assist you."

He lets the phone fall. It buzzes hollowly, echoing a thousand miles away. He can't help thinking that behind the hum someone is listening. He climbs the stairs. His limbs are heavy. He stops in the bedroom door and looks at Karen sleeping.

The light is falling in through the windows, throwing bars of shadow across her form. The covers are pulled up around her and above them he can see her nightgown. She used to sleep naked. He wishes she would sleep naked again. He thinks about picking up a pillow, holding it over her face while she sleeps. It seems like it would be so easy. She would never wake up and then he could sleep again.

Instead, he gets quietly into bed and lies down. He stares up at the ceiling. He watches the shadows moving on the walls. He watches the darkness fade and the light rise. Reflected in the ceiling and the walls, he watches the sun rise.

There is a letter waiting for him outside the door. He doesn't want to open it. He's afraid of what is inside. He doesn't remember placing another order, but there are a lot of things he doesn't remember these days. He's so tired; it's hard to think. His head aches. His eyes feel like cotton balls being pushed out of his skull. His lids feel like sandpaper and it hurts every time he blinks. If only he could sleep. If only he could dream.

He picks up the envelope and turns it every which way. What is in it this time? Will he push Karen down a long dark well and lean over the edge to watch her fall? Will he take a knife from the kitchen and stab her in the back as she's standing at the stove? Or maybe it will be like a fairy tale, maybe he'll push her into the oven and roast her alive? Or something more elaborate? A gigantic iron cage, which he can hang up in the narrow little yard, where she will simultaneously starve to death while the birds pick her bones clean?

He laughs. It is mad unstable laughter. He lets the envelope fall. He doesn't open it. He walks away. He can't forget it though. And the next day another envelope arrives.

And every day after that, there is another envelope, waiting for him at the door. He tries hiding them, tearing them up, throwing them away. He doesn't dare burn them though. It doesn't matter. They keep arriving, just the same.

He tries to keep himself awake. He makes pot after pot of coffee. He doesn't fight the insomnia – he embraces it. He's afraid of sleep, afraid of dreams. They lurk behind every corner. He jumps at every sound. He looks suspiciously at the coffee machine as it burbles to itself, twenty-four hours a day. He looks at Karen's hair. There are strange things hiding there. He wants to pick them out and crush

them like bugs, but he's afraid to touch them. They might bite him
and he might dream.

He's seen Karen die a thousand times. It doesn't matter if he's
asleep or not. He dreams anyway. There are birds in his kitchen.
They fill every room. Their feathers rustle softly and they watch him
with their beady eyes. He sees other things too – a field where
dreamers are laid out row upon row, their bodies spun tight in spider
webs, like cocoons. They dream and men and women in white coats
with clipboards walk up and down and rows and make notations.
They check tubes and machines that beep softly. Every now and then,
one of them stoops down and harvests a dream.

He pushed Karen down an elevator shaft yesterday. He is sure of
it. He sits at the kitchen table with his head in his hands; his eyes
aching and wide. The cereal box is staring at him. Or maybe he
chopped her up into a thousand little pieces and ate her for dinner. He
can't remember.

He gets up and walks through the empty house. The front door is
open and sunlight is coming in. It hurts his eyes. The windows in the
bedroom are open too and the breeze stirs the curtains, but there is
still a stench in the room. It smells like meat rotting. He walks
downstairs again. He walks into the kitchen and he picks up the
phone. He can't remember dialing, but there is a voice on the other
end. It might be Mary from customer service; it might be a policeman.

He is laughing hysterically. He is crying at the same time. He babbles into the phone, clutching it for dear life. Whoever is on the other end will keep him safe; keep him sane.

"I think I killed my wife." He tells the listener on the other end. He can't stop laughing. It's the funniest thing he's ever heard.

They take him to an institution. Doctors ask him questions. They prod him and poke him for what seems like hours on end. The walls are white, the floors are white; the lighting is white as well. The doctors and technicians and nurses and aides all dress in white. It is supposed to be calming. There are no clocks on the walls. It is always bright inside and it hurts his eyes. It is never night here and he is relieved. He doesn't want to dream.

But he does. He aches with it. He wants it more badly than anything he has ever wanted in the world. He wants to dream and dream and never stop.

"Can I make a phone call?" He asks, hoarse and parched to the doctor who has been asking him questions for hours.

"Of course."

A phone is brought. It is white, just like everything else, except the buttons, which are square and ugly and gray. He dials a number by heart and listens. He can't remember if it rings.

"Hello, this is Mary in customer service, how can I help you?"

"I'd like to place an order," he whispers. "A bulk order."

A box arrives the next day.

He never gives the doctors any trouble. He's in his room all the time - sleeping. Every now and then an aide dressed in white comes in with a clipboard to check on him and makes a notation and goes away again. Every now and the aide bends down and almost touches him, as though picking something out of the air near his head. But it doesn't wake him. He sleeps very deeply these days. And he always dreams.

Roadkill

by Christa Faust

Lucy flew along the 5, raw, humpbacked silhouette of the San Gabriel Mountains already in the Nova's rearview and ahead flat endless nothing as dark and hopeless as she felt. She pushed the protesting automobile up to 120, hot dusty wind pulling bleachy-green strands of hair loose from her sloppy ponytail and whipping them across her face. Her lower lip was chapped and she chewed at it till it bled, scraping her teeth across the ragged edges over and over. The cute sparkle blue lipstick was long gone.

The Nova had no stereo so she kept a shitty boombox in the back seat, tinny old punkrock tape, Dead Kennedys or some shit, getting their ass kicked by the wind and the straining engine and it didn't matter anyway since all she heard was Joey.

"So leave then," casual shrug and deep drag of his cigarette, not even looking up from his canvas, angry red and black slashes across sickly fishscale shapes. "I've had it with this clingy shit."

And Lucy feeling more and more lonely inside her own skin, more and more useless, as if the more he ignored her the more pastel, the more translucent she became. Like a ghost in their little Hollywood apartment, leaving behind a half-full coffee cup, a teal green blob of Manic Panic hairdye on the edge of the sink, desperate to leave some kind of spoor, some small proof that she was still here, only to find everything cleaned up and pristine the next day.

In the darkness up ahead somewhere was San Francisco. A new city, a new life. A place where someone might look right into her eyes, might ask her if she wanted anything, if she was hungry or cold. A place to reinvent herself, if only she could believe in it. Out here in this dull dusty no-mans-land her fantasy of San Francisco seemed about as realistic as the Emerald City of Oz.

A black fluttery shape sprang into road in in front of her - a bat? an umbrella? - and she slammed on the breaks, her heart whiplashing in her chest as the car skewed off in a cloud of bone-colored dust, tire squeal replaced by the grating crunch of gravel and then silence, ticking of the engine weirdly in sync with her pounding pulse.

She was shaking so badly that it took a full minute to unfasten her seatbelt. Suddenly in a panic to get out, gasping and fingers scrabbling around the doorhandle Lucy whispered fuckfuckfuck until the door finally popped open and she tumbled out.

The road was near deserted, only an occasional shuddering semi roaring past and enveloping Lucy in dust and diesel stink. On the other side of the freeway was a featureless wall of rock. Her side was some kind of orchard, endless rows of identical, leafless trees like Halloween cutouts as far as she could see. The Nova steamed on two flat tires and she kicked it spitefully, sending up a spray of grit.

The thing she had hit was about 25 feet up ahead, semi-collapsed amidst winking cubes of safetyglass on the shoulder. It looked like a broken umbrella skeleton festooned with shredded plastic bags and scraps of rusty foil and it's crooked winglike crest flapped in the hot desert wind.

"Fuck you," she told it, spitting a wad of gritty saliva onto the yellow line that divided the questionable safety of the shoulder from the speeding death of the freeway. Watching her spit dry almost instantly on the tarmac, Lucy found herself noticing the detritus around her thrift store boots. There were all kinds of things, weird things like a cracked plastic letter H with prongs along it's center bar, a watch with no hands, a can of soda she had never heard of, it's size slightly smaller than normal, emblazoned with a pale and anachronistic logo. There was a flattened stuffed toy of some sort, a greenish thing sort of like a cat with no ears and an old porno magazine folded open to a spread of a shopworn blonde getting it in both ends from headless goons with bad tattoos. A Polaroid that hadn't come out, just a gray green blob bisected by a streak of red like a wound. Bits of metal and shards of glass, crumpled paper and cigarette butts. And Lucy, just another scrap of unwanted flotsam, stuck here for fuck knows how long with no cellphone and no one to call anyway, no AAA and worthless Joey about as likely to come out and save her as Superman or Mother Theresa or Bruce fucking Willis.

"So what are you gonna do Lucy?" she said out loud, her own name lost in the rumble of a tanker truck going the other way. She spat again, dry dusty flavor shriveling her tongue. "Walk I guess."

She grabbed her knobby vinyl purse from the passenger seat and locked the Nova's doors - like someone's gonna steal the damn thing on two flat shoes but urban habits die hard. Standing for a moment, toeing the Polaroid, she was struck with sudden inexplicable anxiety about leaving the familiar comfort of her car. Which way should she go? It seemed ages since she'd seen a gas station and it seemed a reasonable assumption that there ought to be one up ahead fairly soon. But she was quite preoccupied and she could have passed one without noticing.

Nevermind the fact that thing was up ahead, that dark flapping thing that had caused all this trouble. Wrapping her arms around her skinny ribs, Lucy set out in the direction she had come without looking back. She walked forever, or so it felt, one foot in front of the other and chewing her lip, humming tunelessly. The orchard never seemed to end and it's relentless sameness gave her no hint of how far she'd gone. Two cars and a truck passed but none even slowed as they blew by and Lucy felt sure that Joey had finally won, that she really was invisible now and she'd just keep walking until she died of thirst here in this dry unchanging wasteland while fat unseeing tourists and sleepy truckdrivers drove by sucking their Big Gulps and singing along with top 40 radio. Finally something different up ahead, just a lump by the side of the road. Probably some dead bloated animal and Lucy found herself breathing more shallowly in anticipation of the stink. But the closer she got, the less sure she was. It seemed too skinny, too lopsided. When she got within 10 feet she started to notice metal struts poking up out of it and was hit with a plunging elevator realization in her gut. It looked a lot like that thing she had hit. She slowed as she approached it, realizing at the last second that she had chewed her lip bloody again. That copper flavor mingled with dust and carbon monoxide on her tongue as she bent to peer cautiously at the twisted shape at her feet. It was a dead animal or part of one, here a row of yellow dog teeth set in mummified black gums like beef jerky, here a broken stub of bone protruding from a nest of snarled wire and hair. Clusters of dirty pigeon feathers and patches of matted fur along with the familiar umbrella struts and shreds of plastic all tangled together. It made her uneasy and sick, just a stupid heap of trash but there was something about way the wind made it flutter and seem almost ready to leap at her just like it had leapt at her car...

It couldn't be the same thing. She had left that thing miles behind her back with her car and her scratchy punkrock tape and that shitty boombox that someone probably smashed the window to steal by now.

Looking back over her shoulder she saw nothing but endless road and skeleton trees and found herself struck by an awful vision of that scrawny thing flapping awkwardly up into the sky and winging raptor-quick to plunge down up ahead and wait for her all sharp rusty points and predator patience. She sidled past the ragged heap, almost expecting it to snake out and snag her pant leg. Maybe there was a whole flock of these things strewn all along the road, whispering to each other in their secret plastic-crinkle language about the strange lonely girl with the green hair and the bloody lip. She hurried away, afraid to take her eyes off it, in case she looked away and back again to find it closer. When she was finally far enough away to safely turn her head, she spotted another car parked on the shoulder. Someone with a cellphone maybe? Someone waiting for her with his lights off and a hard-on and a gun in the glovebox. Or maybe just another empty car, owner gone on down the road looking for help. Maybe she'd find the owner a few miles down, dried bones tangled up in wire and torn plastic.

Ok now she was just freaking herself out. She made herself breathe slowly and resisted an urge to check on the thing behind her.

You're acting just like a girl, Joey's sardonic voice told her. Grow up already.

"Fuck you," she said to Joey, to the garbage bag monster, to her own stupid self. "Just keep moving and pray for a goddam SpeedyMart."

The car up ahead was a Nova. A black Nova. What are the chances of that? she thought Two Novas broken down on the same stretch of road. More likely than the truth, the terrible slow-dawning truth that it was her Nova, familiar battered warhorse she had bought from her old boss for 500 bucks and driven nearly into the ground, sitting forlornly on two flat tires, just like she left it. As she approached it, she felt a twist of nausea in her gut, hands shaking as she gripped her key and of course it slid into the lock like she knew it would and there's her boombox with the tape popped out, half-ejected in her sudden panicked stop. Paper coffee cups with chewed edges smeared with blue lipstick. Her things. So what the fuck happened?

How did she get so turned around? She'd heard about people lost in the woods going in circles but how the fuck could she have been following the road in the same direction the whole way and still wound up back here. She backed away from the car, keys jingling in her hand.

OK fine, however it happened, she's here. Now what? Wait here? Yes that was the only sensible thing to do. Just wait and eventually somebody, some cop or something, somebody would have to stop. You weren't allowed to just lounge around by the side of the road. A cop was always there ready to bust her for speeding, so where was Dudley Do Right when she needed him? She would wait. Anyway there was no way in hell she was gonna venture back out into the night and get herself even more lost. From here she could keep an eye on that thing, make sure it wasn't sneaking up on her. Throwing a glance back at the flapping heap, she got back into the car. After a moment, she reached over and locked the door.

Lucy was getting thirsty. Her tape had repeated more than 3 times, and she had turned it off for a few minutes before the silence started to drive her buggy and she turned it back on again. No one stopped.

There was a bottle of Evian that had maybe a half inch left in the bottom on the floor by the passenger seat but she was saving it for a just-in-case she really didn't want to think about. There was nothing to eat but the fuzzy butt-end of a package of cherry Rolaids and four mint flavored toothpicks. The thing that was really starting to get to her was the fact that she had no idea what time it was. It had been around midnight when she had left L.A. and she had to be at least an hour into the flats plus the hour through the mountains would make it 2ish when she'd hit that thing. Then add at least an hour of walking and at least three rounds of an hour-long tape so why wasn't the sun starting to come up yet? And she was really very thirsty. She reached down and picked up the Evian bottle and set it up on the dashboard. The umbrella thing was still there and didn't it seem a little closer?

Christ, Lucy you wanna nip that kinda shit in the bud right fucking now.

Lucy turned the bottle so the label faced her. You want mindgames why don't you just go move back in with Joey. But it was closer. It had turned a little too so that two winglike struts stuck up in the air like horns. OK so the wind blew the thing over, big deal. Probably weighed about as much as a pigeon or a paper bag. It got blown out in front her car once too, no reason it wouldn't get moved by the wind again. Except the trees were still as charcoal sketches against the black sky. There was no wind at all.

A car then, Lucy told herself. The breeze from a truck passing. But she couldn't remember a car or truck passing at all within the last tape round. She curled up against the seat, cheek pressed to the cracked vinyl. She closed her eyes and tried to will herself to nod off, anything to kill time till the sun came up, bland yellow sunlight making everything mundane and non-threatening. Morning commuters with go-cups of bad coffee and hey Marge that gal looks like she could use a little help and no more shadows, no more garbage bag monster.

She found herself thinking of all the things scattered along the side of the road, things that must have meant something to someone once. Things that had been tossed or fallen from the windows of speeding cars and disappeared, become invisible. She made up stories in her mind about where the things came from. The magazine was found in the glovebox by a religious wife and tossed in a fit of holy fury. The once cute stuffed animal was an unwanted gift from an unforgiven lover, jettisoned during a high speed argument. The H had been part of a sign in the back of a truck - HARDWARE maybe or HOTDOGS or ever HOT GIRLS XXX jostled loose by bad shocks and blasting, bass heavy music. The Polaroid was an attempt by a driver to shoot down into his own lap at a 90 mph blowjob. She wanted all these things to have history, to mean something but she knew that even she never really noticed anything by the side of the road. It all meant about as much as the bad rear-projection in a cheesy TV show. What was that old black and white show, Outer Limits or Twilight Zone maybe, where the people were stuck in time, moving too fast while everything around them was slowed to an almost indiscernible crawl. The one with the little girl on her tricycle heading slowly and inevitably towards the truck. Well for Lucy and the things strewn around her it was the opposite. All round her people were speeding by with no awareness of her molasses-slow, neverchanging existence. Nothing ever changed. Nothing except...

Lucy sat up sucking air, mouth dry as a dustrag and her eyes wide - - that thing where was it now? Was it closer? It was still dark but it had to be getting lighter... was that a hint of dawn in the distance or just the yellow fever glow of the sodium lamps. She squinted down the road, looking out for the thing, the garbage bag monster, but she couldn't see it anywhere. Could it have finally blown away for good or was it out there just out of sight waiting for her...

"For fuck sake Lucy," she said. "You really have lost it."

Her body felt cramped and stiff and the air inside the car was stale, redolent of old coffee and burnt brakes. She felt sure she would die if she didn't get out and stretch her legs. The thing was nowhere. Maybe it got bored and flew down the road to the Dennys for a Grand Slam and a big fat slice of cherry pie. She laughed out loud and popped the lock, swung the door open.

Christ the last thing she wanted to do was start thinking about food. She got out of the car, chewing her lip and concentrating on not thinking about food. Not thinking about garlic pepper squid from her favorite Thai place or molasses cookies or lasagna or her dad's banana bread or summer barbecues with a cut-in-half 50 gallon drum and sticky-sweet spareribs and corn on the cob and cold beer and...

The thing was on the roof of the car.

This weird little shriek slipped out between her teeth as she flailed out against it with both hands, wire and ragged metal ripping her sleeve and the skin beneath and she stumbled away, brushing at her arm like it had touched fire or something contaminated. The thing tottered and fell in nearly hypnotic slow motion landing with a wet snapping plastic sound between her and the open car door. She turned and ran, breath ragged in her parched throat. She had no idea which direction she was headed but she didn't care as long as it was away. The scrawny trees flew past and the road unrolled beside her and paring knives dug into her calves and gut and she kept running, kept running until she tripped and nearly fell, dry heaving with her palms pressed against her thighs and her heart close to bursting in her chest. She ventured a look behind her. Nothing. No car, no garbage bag monster, nothing.

Nothing but road and trees and broken glass and bottlecaps and cigarette butts and her, shaking and near tears andfeeling stupid and angry and sick.

Her arm really hurt. It throbbed resentfully and the scratches looked dark and puffy in the sodium light. Her mind whirled with thoughts of tetanus and infection and she made herself start walking again, just keep walking no matter what and what fucking time is it, the night can't just go on and on forever, can it?

She was thirstier and thirster and she couldn't stop thinking about the water bottle left behind in her car, the water she had been saving - should have drank it dammit then I'd be less thirsty now - and how people really did die of thirst out in the desert, how happy she was gonna be to see that SpeedyMart. She would just go right in and put her mouth under the Mountain Dew spigot and let em call the cops. Where were you when I needed you pig-fuck? she'd say and she laughed out loud, a rough grating sound like her feet against the gravel.

Every step she took thumped like an extra heartbeat in her arm and she stopped to roll up her sleeve. The skin was hot and swollen and the lips of the cuts had peeled up and blackened, shiny like...

...like plastic.

She started trying to signal cars, waving her good arm hysterically but no one stopped. They just sped by, spraying her with grit, silvered windshields as blank and blind as cataract covered eyes.

Leaping up and waving at a passing SUV, Lucy fell, landing heavily on her injured arm. She screamed, pain blaring up through her arm bones, shooting up the side of her neck and she rolled onto her back, sobbing and holding her wounded limb out away from her body like a dead thing. Her broiler-hot forearm was now studded with gravel and shards of dirty glass and the shiny black splits had widened, sprouting curls of wire like newborn ferns. It was beginning to stink, a curious blend of burnt rubber, sun-dried roadkill and rust.

She scrambled to her feet, shaking her head, eyes squeezed closed and started to run again. She ran until she was tired, stopped gasping and then started again, stopped and started, laughing and sobbing until she could not go another step and she collapsed in the dirt, half hallucinating flickering bits of plastic brushing against her cheeks and eyelids and a sound like a thousand crackling garbage bags and she lay there drifting in and out of consciousness as the black-edged cracks crept across her chest and back. When she swatted at the imaginary tickle of plastic on her face and felt gritty, quivering feathers bristling from a thick split that had formed behind her ear she yelped and wrenched herself back to her feet.

There was a car coming, blinding light and engine shrieking like a hoard of angry wasps. A kind of desperate fury coursed through her, obliterating everything as she flung herself towards the speeding car, overwhelmed by this mad desire to smash the windshield with her bare hands, to drag the clueless occupant out through the broken glass and shriek into their bloody face "I'm real you fucker I'M REAL". The moment elongated into a lifetime as she tottered in the yellow wash of the headlights, a single word over and over in her mouth like the dry click of insects.

"Stop." she said. "Stopstopstopstop..."

The car hit her, and for an instant there was no pain, only a curious hot weightlessness as she spun up over the dented black hood . The bug-splattered windshield filled her vision and the driver's face on the other side seemed huge and distorted, so pale, green hair like chemical fire and bloody chapped lips skinned back in terror and then blank nothing like cold black plastic smothering her, obliterating everything.

Madness

by James S. Dorr

She dreamed that she was running on snow. She didn't know where to. Around her, in darkness, the shapes of trees -- jagged, triangular evergreen shapes. Ahead?

She heard howling. She felt the sting of snow on her face.

The cold biting in blackness.

She woke. The sting on her face persisted. She hugged her pillow, trying to drive the pain into its smooth cloth.

She woke up crying.

She thought of the day before. Mary, her friend at the office, introducing the new manager around. "Mr. Armbruster," she said, "this is Kerri -- Kerrilea Stava. She does accounting in our sales division."

Accounting, sure, she thought. She had a degree in business and marketing, but what she did was operate a computer station. A glorified typist. But, with a recession. And being a woman. . .

She smiled. She said, "I'm glad to meet you, Mr. Armbruster." In his mid-forties, to her twenty-three. Slightly graying, his body still trim, though.

"Just call me Robert," he said as he smiled back. "At the branch I used to run, we found that a certain informality helped everyone work better together."

Uh huh, she thought. She smiled again as he turned his back, being led by Mary to the next work station.

After lunch, he made a pass at her. The girl at the next station was on her break and Mary was off doing some errand when Robert Armbruster came up behind her. She smelled his cologne first -- sweet, like a woman's. But then she felt his hand on her breast.

She didn't think. She just reacted. She grabbed his hand in hers and bit it. In his surprise, he swung back and slapped her. Then slapped her again, hard.

Just as Mary came back from her errand.

"Uh, just a sort of misunderstanding," Armbruster said, the glare in his eyes adding that it had better be *just* a misunderstanding and nothing more. "We'll, uh, we'll talk tomorrow, Kerri. Thank you, Mary."

After he left, and Kerri and Mary were on their own break, Mary asked, "Just exactly what *did* happen?"

"You saw, didn't you. What did you see?"

"Just the two of you with your backs to me. Your face red when you turned around. Him looking sheepish."

"He slapped me, Mary. He tried to grab me, then when I . . . I tried to stop him he hit me."

Are you sure, Kerri?" Mary smiled, but sympathetically. "That is, he *is* a married man and . . . well . . . you know, if you're sure, you could file a complaint, but. . . ."

Kerri nodded, mouthing the unspoken words herself. There is a recession. Then: "Maybe, tomorrow, when he wants to talk to me, do you think maybe I ought to apologize to him, Mary?" She wasn't sure she meant the question to be sarcastic.

"I don't know, really. I didn't see it. Maybe it *was* just a misunderstanding."

Kerri nodded again. Maybe so, she thought -- Mary was her superior. She knew the ropes of the company better. But Kerri had trouble the rest of the afternoon concentrating on her work. The pain on her cheek, where he'd slapped her, persisted. She went to the women's room, looked in the mirror, and saw a small bruise beginning to form. She applied makeup to it.

Even at five, when she left the building, stepping out into the wind and a just starting snow that was blowing in from the lake, the pain persisted.

She walked through the snow to her bus, got on, got off at her stop and walked to her apartment. A thin, gritty snow, early for the season, already blackened with soot from the air by the time it melted on the sidewalk. It stung, like the pain, when it blew in her eyes.

And that night, she dreamed of snow.

Kerri looked in the mirror long and hard when she got up the next morning. She looked at her body, her breasts, her thighs, still shiny

205

with redness after she'd toweled off from her shower. She sighed as she got dressed. Thank God it's a Friday, she thought as she prepared her breakfast -- just cocoa and toast, not very nutritious, she thought as she ate it. But neither was it very expensive.

She thought about Armbruster as she got off the bus at her stop and walked the block and a half to her office. Ahead, on the corner, she saw a beggar, a man, not that badly dressed, selling something.

She thought about wolves for some reason. Her dream.

The distant howling.

The snow that was still coming off the lake in flat, spurting flurries.

She ducked in the lobby of her building almost furtively, took the elevator to her floor, and waved to Mary as she hung her coat up.

"Kerri," Mary said, once they had settled in at their stations, "Mr. Armbruster left a message. Something about having to clear up a few final matters at his old office. Anyhow, he won't be in till Monday."

Kerri nodded and turned on her screen, trying, she hoped, to look casual about it. Thank God, she thought. Thank someone -- she wasn't sure she believed in God, really, at least not since she'd stopped going to Mass when she was in college, after her mother had passed away. But at least the confrontation was put off. She had made her mind up she would have to apologize, even if what had happened had hardly been *her* fault. Seeing the beggar -- now that she thought of it, that was what had made up her mind for her. There *was* a recession. And she was a woman, over-trained for what she was doing, but lucky to have a job at all.

Sometimes, she thought. . . .

"Kerri, you okay?" Mary's voice broke in.

"Huh?"

"I'm sorry, Kerri. You looked kind of funny."

"Uh, yeah," Kerri said. "I guess I was just daydreaming or something. You know, it's been a kind of a hard week."

Mary replied with a knowing smile and they both went back to work. Figures. Spreadsheets. Balancing totals. Kerri *did* daydream. She added a column -- she punched the one key that added it for her. She thought about wolves. She multiplied sums, subtracting the products from earlier sums -- two more keys punched without having to even look at what she was doing. She saw snow and darkness.

She smelled the evergreens she was running through. That and something else.

Whiteness on whiteness, gleaming in moonlight. The moon had risen now. Whiteness and something else.

She saw the rabbit, lying, its throat torn, its blood already congealed from the coldness. . . .

"Hey, Kerri," Mary said after lunch, when they were on their afternoon break, "you got any plans for this evening?"

"Uh, what do you mean?" Kerri asked.

"Well, you know, you look kind of down. And I'm feeling pretty dragged out myself. But there's this new club that's opened near the lake. I understand they have really great music -- sort of like jazz, but kind of punk too. I thought, maybe -- you know, if you'd like to --

we might get a bite to eat someplace after work, then go down and give it a try."

"Gee, I don't know, Mary," Kerri said. "I mean, if it's expensive. . . ."

"I guess there's *some* cover charge," Mary answered. "But, because it's new, not that many people know about it yet, so it can't be too expensive. Anyhow, it's Friday night and, if you're like me, you probably just stay home by yourself half the time, watching TV. So -- unless you have other plans. . . ."

Kerri laughed. When was the last time she'd had a date? The damn recession -- working overtime when she was asked to, getting home too tired sometimes to even fix dinner. She thought, why not?

"What's the club called?" she asked.

"Uh . . . the Underground, I think. Something like that. Not all that much imagination, but they say the music is good."

Kerri laughed again. "Yeah, sure, why not? I mean, if we decide we don't like it we can always get up and leave. . . ."

"Yeah." Mary laughed too. "If we really don't like it, we can demand our money back. You know, threaten to make a scene. Either way, it'll be fun, huh?"

"Yeah," Kerri said, "but I guess we'd better get done with our work first." She turned back to her computer screen and thought about rabbits. White, furry, red blood against the snow. And afterward when they left the building, she thought she heard howling.

The club, though, was everything Mary had said. It was in a basement, which wasn't surprising given the name -- it was doubly apt, in fact, since they'd ended up having to take the subway to get there. Outside, the building was unprepossessing. The whole neighborhood was one that was run down. But once inside the painted red doors, and down the stairs, Kerri was greeted first by a smell of sweat and incense, then, through the haze as they turned the corner from the coat check, a flash of color.

A stage, neon outlined. Flashing. Spotlights.

A wave of sound.

On the stage, a man singing, a woman behind him -- behind them both a second man, tall and blond, shirt-off and muscular, playing bass guitar. Driving rhythm.

"Hey Kerri, let's sit here," Mary shouted. They sat at a small table, almost in front. The music washed over them. After a moment a waitress came and they ordered beer.

"Just two dollars a bottle? That's not so bad, is it?" Kerri shouted after they'd gotten served. Feeling wicked, she took her first sip straight from the bottle.

"Not for a place like this," Mary answered, pouring her own beer into the glass that had been brought with it. "Still, I don't know about you, but I'm nursing mine."

Kerri laughed. "Maybe that new Armbruster guy'll give us both raises."

They both started laughing, just as the drummer on his throne at the back of the stage took off on a solo. Sound throbbed, crashing, causing the floor to shake. -- Kerri took another sip of beer straight from the bottle, her lips caressing its long hard neck. Afraid to try pouring it into its glass now for fear she would spill it.

A chord from the bass guitar. Wailing. Rising. Answering the drummer, banging out into a broad counter-rhythm.

Then the low squeal of a tenor saxophone. Then the lead guitar, spitting out grace notes. A second singer. Sucked in the vortex of bass and drums.

Kerri looked up -- caught the bassist's eyes suddenly. Just as a swinging spot passed over them.

Saw they were ice blue.

Sucked another sip from her beer, then turned to Mary. "Wow!" she shouted.

Mary sat, glass-eyed, not touching her own drink. She started at Kerri's shout. "Yeah," she shouted back. "Didn't I tell you it'd be terrific?" She started to clap -- to answer the main rhythm of the drummer, while Kerri nodded in time to the bass.

The smoke. The incense. The lights. The air swirled.

Deafening silence.

A man in a dark suit came on stage to announce the band was taking a break while Kerri, Mary, the whole club applauded.

Somewhere, in the distance, a jukebox started up.

Kerri sipped again from her bottle then drew back, suddenly, when a second bottle thumped down on the table next to it. She looked up. The waitress.

"I didn't order . . ," she started to say.

"A gentleman, Honey," the waitress answered and gave her a wink.

"I . . ."

Mary giggled. "Here he comes now, Kerri. Uh," -- her face took a serious expression, just for a moment. -- "Uh if, you know, it turns out I start being in the way, just give a signal. Okay, Kerri?"

Kerri took Mary's hand and squeezed it. "Hey, don't worry, Mary. But thanks anyhow." Then she turned to see who was approaching their table.

She looked up -- up. Into ice blue eyes.

"Hope you don't mind, Ms.," the bass player said. "I couldn't help seeing you from the stage while I was playing that bit with the drummer." His voice had an accent, sort of English, or European.

"No, uh, please join us," Kerri answered, nodding as he pulled out a chair. His body was gleaming -- she smelled its sweat as he turned the chair's back to face the table and straddled its seat. She looked at his hair, almost silvery-white in the room's smoky dimness, the chain around his neck, heavy and gold, suspending an upside-down cross on his smooth chest.

She took a quick sip from her bottle, the new one, that he had bought her. She took a deep breath.

"Uh, this is Mary, my friend from work," she said. "My name's Kerrilea -- uh, Kerri."

"Kerri, is it?" the blond man said. She noticed he had a tattoo on his shoulder -- the head of a wolf. "I couldn't help seeing the way you drink. Straight from the bottle. I like that in women. It shows strength of character."

"Uh, thank you," Kerri said. "That is, I, uh, I really don't drink that much, but. . . ."

"Hey, I said I like that in women. So, here, I'll have the waitress get you another when you're finished with that one. Your friend as well. I've got to get back, but, maybe, you know, me and the guys play Tuesdays and weekends. They call me Gear."

"Uh, thank you then, Gear," Kerri said as he got up to leave. Feeling *quite* wicked, she picked up her bottle and licked its opening, then circled her lips around its neck and tipped it up in a kind of salute. The bass player answered by tipping his chin up, reflecting her motion, then weaved his way from her between filling tables as more people came down the stairs to the club. He tipped his chin up again as he lifted himself to the stage, then picked up his instrument as the other musicians joined him, bringing their heads together to retune.

"Gee, Kerri," Mary whispered, leaning across the table toward her. "Did you notice how tight his pants are?"

"Mary!" Kerri said, then started laughing. Mary laughed too. Kerri realized her friend was just joking. Nevertheless, she felt her blood rising. The warmth on her cheeks.

She reached in her purse to take out her compact, and gazed at the redness.

That night Kerri dreamed again. She *saw* the wolves this time -- just like Gear's tattoo -- but still far in the distance. She knew, when she looked down, she'd see the rabbit, its throat torn open. The red of its blood spreading over the snow like the pulsing lights in the club with Mary.

She woke up screaming -- no, not really screaming. She'd dreamed she was screaming. She didn't know why.

There was nothing, so far, in the dream that was hurting her. Not even threatening.

The wolves in the dream were running away.

Lying awake in the dark -- the half-darkness -- she thought of Gear suddenly, then started giggling. The boy was what? Eighteen? Twenty at most, with no kind of job, playing jazz in a nightclub, while she was twenty-three. Going on twenty-four -- and with a college degree in business.

She laughed out loud.

Still, as Mary had said just before they'd left. . . .

Kerri laughed again, then, on an impulse, reached under the covers and touched between her thighs. Drawing her hand back, she looked at it carefully, then at the clock. Not too early to get up.

She cleaned her apartment most of the day, not thinking of anything. Only humming.

It wasn't until it was nearly evening that she realized that what she was humming, over and over, was a riff line from Gear's bass guitar.

So okay, she thought, the guy fascinates me. Not as a person. Not even as a hunk, as he apparently fascinates Mary. But more for the background. The music. The milieu.

So, why not? she thought.

She took the bus downtown that evening. She passed the beggar she'd seen Friday morning, still selling something, as she walked the block to her transfer to the subway.

She got off where she and Mary had the night before and found the red doors, otherwise unmarked, that led to the Underground. Pulling her coat collar up around her, she walked down the dingy, smoke-stained stairs and, passing the coat check, she found a table, alone, in the back. She ordered a beer as the club filled up -- it was busier this night than it had been the night before -- and concentrated on watching the stage.

The musicians set up, Gear, the others, but he apparently didn't see her. She hoped that he wouldn't -- she didn't know why. She was careful to pour her beer in a glass as her eye lit on the group's sole female, the backup singer.

Could she be Gear's girlfriend? She wondered. The girl was not unattractive: Long yellow hair, in contrast to Kerri's, which was straighter and nearly raven-black. A slightly fuller figure than Kerri's, though hers was okay. Mr. Armbruster had certainly liked it, she suddenly thought, even if she herself thought of herself as slim and willowy. Lithe. Unlike Mary.

"Excuse me," a voice said, just loud enough for Kerri to hear it over the opening set.

"Huh?" she answered. The voice was a woman's. She looked up and saw a blonde -- platinum blonde, perhaps in her late thirties -- wearing a fox stole.

"I mean -- uh, I'm Tanya. Is this chair taken? You seemed to be by yourself, and it's so crowded. . . ."

Kerri looked around. It *was* crowded, much more so than Friday, and the extra chair at her table seemed to be the only one free.

"Uh, okay," she said. The set was just ending -- she watched as the blonde on the stage nuzzled up to the lead guitarist. *Not* Gear's girlfriend, she thought, unless, of course, she acted that way to all the musicians. Like Mary, busty Mary, did sometimes with men in the office.

"I asked, would you like another of those?" Tanya's voice broke in. She pointed at Kerri's half-finished beer, and then up at the waitress.

"Uh, yeah, sure, thank you," Kerri stammered. "Uh, Tanya? I'm sorry. My name's Kerri. I guess I'm sort of, uh, lost in my own thoughts."

"I understand, Kerri," the older woman said. "I'm sort of that way too tonight. The music *is* good, though."

Kerri nodded. She finished her glass and, just as a second set started on stage, a fresh beer appeared along with the Scotch sour Tanya had ordered.

This time she drank her beer from the bottle.

She'd left one set later. It wasn't the same, with the older woman, as she had expected. It wasn't as though Tanya had bothered her. Not exactly. The two had just sat, each woman on her own side of the table, scarcely speaking except when Tanya had asked if she might smoke.

Kerri didn't mind, not in *that* room, filled with smoke already. Still, she was uneasy. So, when the music had crashed to a close, she had smiled and nodded, then gathered her coat up and walked to the stairs, nearly taking a wrong turn through an arch she wasn't sure she had seen before.

She had opened the red doors into the night air, freezing, still blowing gritty snowflakes. That night she had dreamed again of the dark snowfields, running, screaming -- no, howling, as wolves howl.

She dreamed again Sunday night, realizing this time the wolves wouldn't harm her. As long as she followed them.

Monday morning she woke up early. She looked at her body, hard, in the mirror. She finished her breakfast with time to spare and took an earlier bus than usual.

"Excuse me, Ma'am," a voice said when she got off.

"Wh-what?" she asked. She looked around her.

It was the beggar.

"Would you like to help in the good work?" the beggar asked, thrusting a cardboard tray out toward her. In the tray she saw silver crosses -- well, not silver really, but silvery-colored. Some had mountings, to be used as pins, while others were on chains like Gear's in the nightclub.

Except his was upside down.

"What's this?" she asked, backing her way around the beggar.

"The Mission, Ma'am. It's help for the Mission. Help for the good work."

She *tried* to back away, but he was forcing her into the gutter. "Dammit," she muttered. Then: "How much for two of these?"

Why did she want them? She didn't know. But she watched her hand point to two spidery pin-backs. She heard as he answered, "Only five dollars -- and it's for a good cause."

She reached in her purse and found a five-dollar bill -- there went her lunch money! -- and took the pins from him. She looked at them in the morning light -- gleaming nearly two inches tall, from top to bottom -- and thrust them angrily in her coat pocket. She glared at the beggar and shoved her way past him, then ran the rest of the way to her office, afraid she'd be late now.

She cursed, softly, under her breath, as the elevator seemed to stop at every floor before it let her off at her level. At least, though, she wasn't late -- she'd checked her watch against the lobby clock, only then remembering that she had taken the early bus. But then she saw him. Mr. Armbruster! Talking with Mary, both of them smiling.

She'd almost forgotten about Thursday afternoon.

She wondered -- she thought of turning around. So much had happened, she'd almost forgotten. Of going back down. Of calling in sick from the lobby pay phone.

She wondered . . . she couldn't. She had to face him. If not today, then he'd still be there Tuesday -- after all, he *was* her new boss now.

She squared her shoulders and strode, carefully, toward the two of them, chatting together.

Mr. Armbruster suddenly turned. "Uh, Ms. Stava, isn't it?"

"Y-yes, sir," she answered.

"Excuse us, Mary." He gestured the other woman away, then brought his voice down. "Uh, Ms. Stava -- do you mind if I call you Kerrilea? What I want to say is, last Thursday, I guess I must have been tired or something. Long trip, you know, it gets on a person's nerves. Makes them act funny -- do things they'd never do. Anyway, about that afternoon, I wanted to apologize."

"I. . . ," Kerri began to say.

"Really, Ms. -- Kerrilea -- I acted terribly. And I *am* sorry. I really don't know what came over me. What I wanted, to make it up to you, I wondered if you'd be willing to let me meet you around noon. Let me buy lunch for you."

"I, uh, thank you, Mr. Armbruster, but. . . ."

"Please. Call me Robert. Did I mention -- the branch I ran before they called me here for that new vice president's spot, we found that everyone seems to work better if we let go of some of the formality. Uh -- not like Thursday, of course -- but, you know. First names and things like that. Anyway, please, may I make it up to you?"

She thought of the beggar. So much had happened. And then she remembered -- her five dollars lunch money. And the recession.

He was the boss, wasn't he?

Slowly, she nodded. "I, uh, I guess I sort of owe you an apology too. I guess I was startled. I, uh, bit, you, didn't I?"

She almost laughed then -- she had almost added, "I must have been hungry." She took a long, deep breath, feeling the heat of her blood rush upward.

She started again. "I. . . ." He *was* the new boss, and not that bad looking for his mid-forties. "I . . . as for lunch, uh, yes," she answered. "And, uh, thank you, Robert."

She couldn't believe it that night as she sat, alone, in her apartment watching TV. She'd gone out with Armbruster -- Robert -- halfway afraid that he'd paw her again, but then it turned out that he *was* a gentleman after all. That he *had* apparently been just tired or something Thursday. And, best of all, he'd said that when he had been talking to Mary, they'd been discussing personnel records, and Kerri's education had come up. And that he'd been thinking that maybe the department could use reorganizing, and that that could mean there might be some promotions.

She'd actually winked at the beggar that evening on her way home. She'd whistled a tune. One of Gear's? She tried to remember, but she had forgotten.

She didn't dream that night, at least not that she could remember. The next morning, on her way to work, she was humming. This tune she did know, it was from the TV. The program she had watched after dinner.

She passed the beggar at her bus stop, only dimly noticing that he now had a companion. She hunched her shoulders against the cold -- but it wasn't that cold. For the first time -- how many days had it been? -- the sun was shining.

She still hummed the tune from the TV as she rode the elevator up to her floor. She turned on her screen and started to work. Columns of figures. Bright, shiny figures.

The morning went quickly.

"My, we seem happy today," Mary said that afternoon when they shared their break time. Kerri nodded. She did feel happy.

She tried to remember -- how much she had worried last Thursday, last Friday. But Mr. Armbruster -- Robert -- had apologized to *her* yesterday morning. Her troubles were over. At least for the moment.

Tuesday. Wednesday. Wednesday night, she dreamed of her mother for the first time she could remember in years. She didn't see much of Mr. Armbruster, but, then, he *was* the boss. He had his own work in his office upstairs. Then, Thursday, as she was finishing her lunch in the basement break room, she saw him approach her.

"Uh, Kerrilea," he said. "Could I talk to you a few moments?"

"Uh, sure," she answered. She nodded to Mary as Mary got up and Mr. Armbruster sat down across from her.

"What I wanted to say," Mr. Armbruster whispered, keeping his voice down so no one else but her would hear, "is that this weekend I'm going to be doing some extra work, so I'm going to have to stay in the city. And anyway I was wondering, maybe Friday night, when I'm done in the office, if I could take you out to dinner."

"Uh, gee, uh. . . ."

"Robert. Remember -- first names? Anyway, after dinner, I could get tickets to the theatre. Or maybe dancing. . . ?"

Kerri nodded. Slowly, though, as if she were thinking. She didn't want to appear too nervous. And she *was* thinking. Last Thursday, to be sure, was almost forgotten. He was a gentleman -- that much she knew now. Nevertheless, he was the boss, too.

And wasn't he married?

Well, Mary had said that. And what did it matter? All he was asking was dinner and dancing. Like probably he and his wife had some expensive house way out in the suburbs -- she knew that much about company policy, that when it brought an executive in it made sure he would be comfortably settled -- and, naturally, *she* wouldn't want to spend her weekend cooped up in some hotel room.

So, he would be on his own. . . .

Why not? she wondered.

She nodded again, more forcefully this time. "Uh, sure, uh . . . Robert. Tomorrow night, then? About what time. . . ?"

"Sevenish, maybe?" he suggested. He went on to say that he could pick her up at her apartment -- he'd taken the liberty, he admitted, of looking her address up in the company's records. That she should dress nicely, but not too fancy. He realized, of course, that she didn't spend her whole salary on clothes.

But she did have some nice dresses from college, she thought as she got home that evening. And she hadn't put on a pound of weight since then. She went through her closet, then went to bed thinking she would wear the black one. The formal strapless.

She almost had second thoughts the next evening when she got home. The black *was* severe -- and it *was* a bit low cut. Nevertheless, she thought as she tried it on, then pirouetted in front of the mirror, she did want to give the impression she knew how to dress with elegance.

After all, a person like Robert was used to good clothing, even if he had tried to let her off the hook by saying she didn't have to be too fancy.

She looked in her jewel box -- something to set it off -- settling finally on a pair of plain, button earrings in burnished silver. Then, thinking of silver, she thought of the pendant -- a family heirloom her mother had given her. Rummaging through the lower level, she finally found it, a miniature crescent, fastened onto a finely-linked chain. She put it on, inspected herself again in the mirror, then, just as she was giving her hair a final touch-up, the doorbell rang.Exactly seven.

"Uh. . . ." Robert looked startled when she let him in. "Uh, I must say you look really beautiful. I mean, the way you've fixed your hair. And that dress, it sets it off so nicely. . . ."

"Thank you." Kerri smiled. "Do we have time for a drink or something, or do you think we should get going?"

"Uh, yes," Robert said. "The taxi is waiting."

She nodded and got her coat -- not the everyday coat she usually wore to work, but a dark, high-waisted coat with long skirts, perhaps just a tiny bit out of fashion, but one that also set her hair off nicely.

The dinner was heavenly. Shrimp cocktail. Rare steak. She joked about it -- the way she liked hers was practically bloody. Afterwards, a show. A supper club. Real champagne.

But then she felt it. Not her breast this time -- they were dancing so there was no room. But Robert's hand clutched on her bottom.

Her body stiffened. She twisted it off.

She pushed away from him, feeling her blood rush up to her shoulders, her throat, her face.

"Mister Armbruster!"

"Kerrilea, I . . . I'm sorry. Really." His hands resting gently now on her shoulders. "I, uh, I must have misunderstood. . . ."

She saw his face was as red as hers felt. Perhaps it was some kind of misunderstanding. Nevertheless she disengaged herself from him completely and went to their table to get her purse.

She checked her face in her compact mirror, then glanced toward the street door. "I think you'd better take me home now," she said.

He nodded, still blushing, then helped her into her coat. "I'm really sorry," he whispered as they got into the taxi. "I mean -- I just don't know what came over me. Y-you're so attractive, I. . . ."

Kerri turned from him. She looked out the window of their cab, noticing that it was snowing again. She scarcely heard him, although, deep inside her, she realized he did sound like he was at least trying to be sincere.

That maybe -- it could have been -- *maybe* an accident.

And, when they finally reached her apartment, when he asked her in front of the front door, she did let him give her a small kiss goodnight.

She dreamed about wolves again that night. She was running on snow, the moon a pale crescent above the horizon, the wolves all around her.

She ran with the wolves -- she felt blood in her jaws.

She felt wind and sleet whistle through her long hair, not piled on her head like it had been that evening, but loose and free. She felt the wind whip her thighs.

Her own blood pumping.

She felt. She sensed. She saw the black hillside. Looming ahead of her. Sensed the opening.

Smelled through the dim glow inside, the faint, acrid scent of resin. But meat and blood also. The wolves rushing with her, into the cave entrance, low arched, brick-lined, stained with torch smoke.

Grooved, as if from many feet, wolf paws as well as human, on the floor inside.

She woke up, shivering. No, not shivering -- feeling a warmness, not on her shoulders and face like before, in the dance club last evening, but lower down. More within.

She felt -- no, heard -- music. Felt its rhythm, though. Something she knew.

Something to grasp on to. Something she knew, not in a dream, but in the world she slept and worked in. Then she remembered where she had heard it.

She looked at the clock. It was nearly noon.

The music, she realized now, was from the Underground. Gear and the band -- how long had it been since she had last heard it? A week ago Saturday.

This was Saturday.

She got up. Showered. Had a late breakfast. Bacon and muffins, the bacon maybe not cooked quite as long as she ought to cook it, but she was hungry. Later she picked up her clothes where she'd left them -- the elegant strapless -- she *did* look good in black, now that she thought of it -- her mother's jewelry. The coat she'd worn last night.

Then she thought of her other coat, her workaday coat, where it hung in her closet. She reached in its pocket and pulled out two crosses.

Yes, the beggar. She'd gotten them Monday. She looked at their backs, their flimsy pin mountings, and prodded one with her fingers.

She felt the mounting slip and turn upside down.

Then she had an idea. She twisted the other pin upside down too, then found a nail file and dulled their points. She thought -- would they do as hangers? For earrings?

She tried them on.

Gear wore an upside-down cross on his chest. They sort of matched, didn't they? Earrings and pendant. Gear's cruciform pendant.

She got her own pendant, her mother's crescent, and put it on also, then looked at the clock. It was almost evening.

She had a quick supper, then thought about blackness. She changed into a pair of dark blue jeans, excitingly tight, and a velvet-soft, coal-dark blouse that she left halfway unbuttoned, to show off the whiteness of her chest and throat. She looked in the mirror, selected a pair of black leather boots to add to the impression, then picked up her purse and her workaday coat and left her apartment.

She took the bus downtown, then switched to the subway, feeling a sort of fascination as she strode down the stairs into the tunnel. She stood on the platform, feeling the weight of the earth above her until her train came. Then back to the surface, then stairs again, this time through the red doors into the Underground. This time, tipping the coat check girl, she asked for a table directly in front.

The stage lights pulsated, red, white, orange. The rhythm of blood. She leaned back, showing her chest to the stage. She ordered a beer and drank from the bottle.

But Gear wasn't there.

She asked the announcer during the band's break. "You his date, girly?" the suited-and-tied man asked back, looking her up and down with an air of apparent approval.

"Well, no . . . uh . . . not really," she admitted. "But I really did want to see him."

"Yeah, so who doesn't? I'll be honest, though. He called in sick. Flu or something -- left the band in a bit of a hole. He'll be back Tuesday, though, when they play then. At least he'd better be."

Kerri thanked him. She went back to her table and finished her beer, looking around the club as she did so. She thought for a moment that she saw Tanya, the woman she'd sat with the last time she'd been there, but then looked again and saw that she hadn't. When she finished her beer she got up -- there was no sense in staying. She retrieved her coat from the coat check, then started to walk to the stairs to the front door.

But then, to her right, she saw the arch. She remembered now -- the week before. How she'd almost taken a wrong turn.

But now she was curious. She looked around her, then ducked through the arch to the door inside. Carefully, she pushed it open.

She saw -- it was from her dream! Low-ceilinged, lined with brick, floor curving downward. Far in the distance, she saw a dim glow.

She took a step inside, first making sure there was no kind of catch that might fasten the door so she couldn't get back out. She took a few steps farther, slowly, carefully. Suddenly all around her she thought she heard the sounds of feet -- or paws? -- shuffling. She fumbled in her purse for matches. She found a packet, took one out, struck it, nearly burning her fingers.

In the dust of the floor she saw -- paw prints? No. Only the grime of years swirled in patterns. Swirled by the wind that she felt now, blowing down, blowing as if over empty snowfields, snuffing her match out.

She turned back, half frightened, half wanting to go on. Then shrugged -- maybe Tuesday. She slipped back through the rusted iron door, easing it soundlessly closed behind her. She caught her breath in the deep, shadowed archway, realizing no one could see her unless they turned to look straight at her. She felt her heart beating. Why? she wondered.

Why her excitement? Gear wasn't there. And, even if he had been there, what had she expected?

She shrugged again, then, pulling her coat more tightly around her, she climbed the stairs back to street level. Outside she saw shadowy figures, huddled together against the cold.

One turned to approach her -- beggars, she realized.

That night, in her dream, she entered the tunnel beneath the black hillside. She followed its winding, jagged passageways, discovering that it was more than just one cave, but a whole network of chambers and hollows. A city beneath the ground, reeking of smoke and blood.

When she woke, she remembered her own tunnel and how it smelled, not of blood, but of garbage. No, not even garbage. Of dust and ozone. Of ancient and modern. Of roots of the city.

She thought of her mother while she fixed her breakfast. The coat she had worn Friday evening with Robert had been her mother's, a gift for college. "Something nice to wear, daughter. For special nights." That's the way her mother had put it. Daughter, not Kerrilea. Like it was a title or something.

Or had it been the dress she'd said that about? Kerri thought back, to when her mother had helped her pick it out. Had helped her pay for it, even though Kerri had had her own money. "It's right to help this way," her mother had said.

She laughed. Her mother had been brought to America as an infant, but still she often spoke of the "old country" as if, in some ways, she had never left it. But this was America. This was the city -- a city currently suffering from the recession to be sure, but nevertheless one that looked toward the future.

But one with roots underneath. Tunnels, like in her dream?

Kerri was curious. The public library was open on Sundays, so she went downtown to look for books about the city and its understructure. She looked up histories first, then statistical books on utilities, then maps of streets and, beneath them, the subways and water mains and sewers and air shafts. The city's breathing and shitting and blood veins.

She took books home with her and studied them as she ate her dinner. Patterns emerged: the subways and air vents, at least, were connected. But air vents then often led to storm sewers -- to broad holding basins for extra water when the main system became over-filled.

And then the utility tunnels -- seemingly that was the kind that she had discovered -- led back to the subways, following cable trails often to the oldest sections. And sometimes these tunnels had since been abandoned, with parallel, more modern shafts drilled since.

She imagined what she would have seen had she gone farther in Saturday night -- it *was* like a city!

She made up her mind -- Monday, after work, she'd buy a flashlight. Then, Tuesday. . . .

She dreamed of the tunnels. Not the real tunnels, but rather the tunnels beneath the hill of her previous dreams, but one set of tunnels mapped over the other like streets that were mapped above the subways.

She ran with the wolves through whistling cave-ways, with snow still blowing in feathery patterns across the stone floor.

She ran toward figures, huddled in torch light -- the wolves ran ahead of her, oddly unafraid. Dark, hooded figures.

Monday, when she arrived at work, she found Robert and Mary huddled together in conversation. Their voices trailed off as she approached them and Mary nodded, but Robert ignored her. "Got to get going," he mumbled to Mary as Kerri sat down and switched on her computer.

The day went quickly enough for a Monday. When their afternoon break time came, Mary had to go off on some errand, so Kerri had coffee by herself. She thought her thoughts -- what she'd buy that evening. She didn't miss Mary.

When quitting time came, she thought first of going to a hardware store, but then ended up in an upscale outdoor equipment place. The prices were high, but she found a flashlight -- more of a searchlight, she thought, almost laughing -- that not only would do, but also was compact enough that she could fit it, if not in her regular purse, at least in her shoulder bag at home. And she bought a knife too.

She saw it as she was about to leave, a thin-bladed, slightly curved knife, like a grapefruit knife, only much sharper, with silver feathery patterns wrapped around its handle. "How much?" she asked a clerk.

Why? she wondered. Why would she want a knife?

She didn't even hear what the clerk said as she handed him her credit card. Maybe the beggars, she thought as she took it back. They might be dangerous. And they must live somewhere.

Maybe the beggars live in the tunnels.

And maybe Robert. . . .

Robert and Mary were talking again when she arrived at work the next morning. And later, at lunchtime, Mary said she'd be unable to join her. Kerri shrugged, "Okay." She thought her own thoughts.

After work she went straight home and changed her clothes, putting on her jeans and blouse, her earrings and pendant. She went to the Underground, taking a table again in front, and let the sound of the music wash over her. First a warmup group. Then. . . .

Then Gear and the others burst on stage, starting with an almost Dixieland number. The saxophone wailed -- an alto this time -- while Gear's bass pulled it downward, descending through blues to a punkish snarl.

Kerri ordered a beer and sucked on the bottle, staring upward, trying to catch Gear's eye when the set ended. But Gear ignored her.

She knew that he saw her -- she tilted her beer up, but he looked away.

She thought of Robert Monday morning, chatting with Mary. Looking away, too, as soon as she'd come in.

She thought about Friday night and started crying.

As soon as the next set was over she pushed her chair back and stalked out. Still crying, she turned right, into the alcove, and carefully pushed the iron door open. She thought -- she thought of Gear. What had she wanted? To lead him in here with her when his break came?

She wondered if he even knew that this place existed, behind the iron door. If anyone knew -- in the dimness of the archway it looked rusted shut. But now she was inside, with her shoulder bag and her flashlight and knife for protection and it was still early. Even if she had to work the next morning.

She turned on her flashlight and followed its beam, threading her way through a maze of cables and pipes and ductwork. She heard, far ahead, sounds. A shrieking of metal. She saw, above, sudden light, then once more darkness. The lights of the city a story or more above, filtering to her through sidewalk gratings.

She followed the passageway, twisting downward, careful to memorize her turnings so she could retrace her steps. Incongruously, she thought of Robert.

Then -- shrieking again. Metal on metal. To her left, an expanse of concrete, like a shallow arena. An overflow basin. To her right, sudden sparks.

A stink of ozone.

She stepped from one tunnel into another, and followed it, curving, into brightness. She climbed the ladder, three feet to the platform. The subway station.

She thought of her maps at home -- she was sure she remembered the turning, where tunnels converged. And now -- the subway station -- the Underground -- now she knew exactly how to relate it to the streets above her.

That night she dreamed of Gear, stretched out on an altar-like table, surrounded by beggars. Dark, hooded figures, like in her last dream, except now they disappeared, leaving only her and the wolves, lapping up blood from a large stone bowl. She dreamed the wolves then sped off, each on its own path, spiraling outward through diverging tunnels.

Leaving just her and Gear, he on the altar, his throat torn open. She straddled above him.

She thought she heard wolves the following day on her way to the office -- the howling of wind through the city's canyons. She did see beggars. Christmas was coming -- at least it was near enough that the city was starting to put up lights -- and Christmas brought them out.

Mary and Robert. Wednesday morning. Talking again, as if they were old friends. Avoiding Kerri.

She had a sudden thought -- it wasn't Gear who should be on the altar.

Then Thursday, silence. When she arrived at work, Mary was alone at her station.

"Where's Robert?" she asked. "I mean, doesn't he come down here sometimes? Talking with you about work, I guess."

She stared at Mary carefully as her one-time friend answered. "He had to go back to clear up some stuff at his old branch again. Like that last time, remember? He said he hoped that he'd be back Saturday -- not have to make a weekend of it as well -- but, in any event, he said he'd be back here Monday."

"Oh," she said. She tried to sound casual as she turned to switch on her computer. At lunch she pretended she had her own errand so she could be alone with her thoughts, but then, when afternoon break time came, she had an idea.

"You remember that place . . . the Underground, I think it was called?" she asked. "You know, that jazz club we went to that night?"

"Uh, yeah," Mary answered. "Yeah. It was fun, wasn't it?"

"I was thinking. Friday night, if you're not doing anything special, I was thinking we might go back there. I mean, that is, if you'd like to go too. . . ."

Mary agreed and the following night they had dinner together, then took the subway like they had before. When they got to the club, though, Kerri suddenly stopped at the bottom of the stairs.

"Mary," she whispered, "you know, it's still early. I wanted to tell you, I came back here the following night and I saw something real neat." She led Mary into the archway. "I wanted to show you. . . ."

"Uh, I don't know about this," Mary whispered back as Kerri eased open the iron door. "I mean, uh, what is this?"

"It's sort of a short cut back to the subway," Kerri said, leading Mary through by the hand, then closing the heavy door behind them. "Here, just a moment."

She reached in her handbag, the black, vinyl shoulder bag she had taken the Tuesday before, and took out her flashlight. She turned it on and gave it to Mary.

"Ooh, it's dirty here," Mary whispered, but, from the sound of her voice, Kerri knew she was curious too.

"This is part of an old subway air vent," Kerri whispered, guiding her forward. "Here, shine the light this way."

"You sure we won't get lost?"

Kerri nodded. She led her friend almost to the overflow basin, then rummaged in her handbag again.

"Here, just a moment."

"What is it, Kerri? Maybe . . . maybe we ought to go back now?"

"It's a surprise, Mary," Kerri said. She pulled out the curved knife she'd bought with the flashlight. "You've been going with Robert, haven't you?"

"No -- what do you mean? I. . . ."

Kerri's blade shot out, slashing at Mary's throat. Blood spurted onto her hand and wrist as Mary sagged, dropping the flashlight onto the concrete. Kerri slashed again, seeing well enough even without light, stabbing down, kneeling over her friend now, ripping open her chest and face.

When she was finished, she dragged the body into a niche where two tunnels angled off from each other, then heaped trash around it. Even if it were found, she thought, no one knew she had been here. But long before that, even if there weren't any wolves in a modern city, there would always be rats to lap up the blood. To strip the body.

She shuddered. She wiped her hands on Mary's clothing, then retrieved her flashlight. She put it back in her handbag, along with the knife, also wiped clean and shiny. She no longer needed it -- high above her through the nearest sidewalk grating, she saw the newly risen moon, its light allowing her to get by well enough in the darkness.

Well enough, in any event, to continue onward until she arrived at the subway station. Her coat was filthy, but who would notice in this kind of neighborhood? Next week she'd wear her other coat when she went in to work. Her mother's coat that she'd worn for Robert.

And that night she dreamed of Gear on the altar, but living, flushed with blood. Sitting next to her.

The following night she slept with Gear. She'd gone to the Underground, dressed as Tuesday in jeans and open blouse, wearing her earrings and her pendant, and this time he did notice. During his break, he sat at her table.

"I've seen you here before," he said. "But with your friend -- now I remember. Real prissy and proper. I'm glad you got rid of her."

"Wh-what?" Kerri asked. "I mean. . . ."

"You know, you came here alone this time. I think maybe Tuesday you were here too, but there was something about your friend that still hung around you. You know, like a downer. . . ."

"Well, yes, I suppose," Kerri had answered and later, when he had finished his final set, she accepted his invitation to his apartment. She found it exciting. True, he was clumsy, but then he more than made up for it with youth and vigor. And, for her, it had been a long time.

Afterward, they smoked marijuana on the mattress that served as a couch too. That had also been a long time for her, and she'd never cared that much for pot when she'd tried it a few times in college. Still, she tried to enjoy it now, because it was part of the world Gear lived in. She tried to relax as she leaned against him, her head on his shoulder, breathing the fumes in. Her hair spread over his wolf's-head tattoo.

"You want to do it again?" he asked later.

"I -- " Kerri could see that he wasn't that strong. "I, uh, maybe Tuesday," she suggested and kissed him softly. "Tuesday, you know, when I see you play again. And, uh, I promise" -- she suddenly giggled -- "I promise that I'll be alone."

He kissed her back, then helped her get dressed. "Promise you'll wear black?"

"I -- huh?"

"You know, like now. Your blouse, your black hair. You really look good that way."

"We'll see," she answered.

Sunday evening she went through her closet, thinking of how her mother had dressed when she'd been alive, in old world styles, and mostly in black. Black had looked good on her mother as well, she thought as she selected and laid out her darkest clothing. She thought of the funeral then, shaking her head -- free associating -- and how she'd received the call at college. The talk of the accident, when she had gotten home, sudden and fiery. The black, closed coffin.

Had she loved her mother? They hadn't been close, and her father had almost never been home. Nevertheless, he died two years later, seemingly no longer wanting to live without his wife. And she -- she'd gone on, a small inheritance giving her enough to finish up at college.

But then the recession -- its own kind of blackness. And she was twenty-three, too old to waste time on people like Gear.

Why had she thought that? She giggled nervously, suddenly thinking of last night's pot smoking. Well, she *was* too old. Too old to go back to that kind of nonsense.

Robert, however, forty-something, wealthy, successful. Married, of course, but weekends alone. . . .

She dressed for Robert Monday morning. Dark clothes, but sensible. Not quite a come on, but still more stylish than what her mother's generation might have thought proper for office attire. When she got in, she found him waiting by Mary's work station.

"Uh, you seen Mary?" he asked, looking up.

"Not since Friday," she answered -- she looked at his eyes, watched them roaming over her figure. Certainly not ignoring her now.

"Uh, let me know when she comes in, would you, Kerrilea?"

Kerri nodded and watched as he turned to leave. She saw he was blushing, ever so slightly. At ten o'clock, her normal break time, she called upstairs and asked for his office.

"M-Mr. Armbruster?" she asked when she reached him. She made her voice sound just a little bit frightened.

"Robert," he answered. "What is it, Kerrilea?"

"I . . . uh . . . it's Mary. It's been two hours and she still hasn't come in. I'm getting worried."

"Did she seem sick or anything Friday? Or say something, you know, about how maybe she was expecting to be in late today?"

"No, uh, Robert. I. . . ."

"Tell you what, Kerrilea. I'm sure she'll come in, but meanwhile there's some work I need to get done. Think you'd be free for lunch so we could talk it over?"

She told him yes, then went through her handbag -- the black, vinyl shoulder bag that she'd decided went with her "new look" -- and found her cosmetics. Just before lunch, she went to the ladies' room to freshen up. She tried a new perfume. And, by the time five o'clock came around, and Robert came down to see how the new work he'd given to her at lunch was progressing, she ended up with an invitation for dinner Tuesday.

The week went rapidly after that. On Tuesday, Robert was a gentleman, apologizing for ignoring her and swearing that he had meant nothing that past Friday. Kerri, however, could see in his eyes he had other ideas, suppressed for now, but never that far below the surface. So, when he took her home after dinner, she invited him up for a nightcap and, this time, she allowed him to do much more than just kiss her.

Wednesday, with Mary still not having shown up, Robert made a perfunctory call to the city police missing persons bureau. Then Thursday, at lunch, he mentioned that, what with the extra work that he and Kerri were having to do in Mary's absence, it looked like he would be in town again for the weekend. "So," he concluded, "do you think that you could join me at my townhouse? Mostly work, mind you, but maybe we could have some fun too. . . ."

Kerri blushed, just a little bit. Things *were* going quickly. And. . . .

"Townhouse?" she asked.

239

"Uh, yeah. Didn't you know? Uh, between you and me, my wife and I no longer get along that well together so, when the company called me here, I specified that I'd need a sort of a retreat for weekends. Something nicer than just a hotel room. Something just a few blocks from here, since, ostensibly, it's for weekends when I'm working on company business, but. . . ."

Kerri smiled. "But sometimes for more than *just* company business. . . .?"

Robert looked around to make sure no one else from work was in the restaurant, then brought his voice down to almost a whisper. "Really more a place to just get away. Honest, Kerrilea. You're the first I've ever invited" -- she saw he was blushing, redder than she was -- "I mean, the first person so special to me I'd think of inviting. . . ."

She smiled and took his hand in hers. So what if he was sometimes a little grabby, she thought. It wasn't as though there were any question she wouldn't accept. "I understand, Robert," she finally said. "And it is mostly work that has to be done. Without Mary to help out."

He nodded and smiled back. "Incidentally, I meant to tell you. The work you've been doing is really first rate and, well, you know, if Mary hasn't shown up by next Monday, it's company policy that she'll have to be off the payroll. I mean -- I realize that she's been your friend -- but, if you wouldn't feel too bad about it, I've been thinking of offering you her position."

The following Tuesday, Robert popped the question, sort of. He'd taken her on a mid-week ski trip, even though the work was still piled up at the office. "The slopes are less crowded this way," he'd told her, "and it'll help get your mind off, you know, Mary."

Kerri had nodded -- implied also, she knew, was that executives *could* do these things any time that they wished to, and those they were fond of were privileged too. And, like with his offer the previous Thursday, while she hesitated, she wasn't about to actually say no.

In fact, it did take her mind off Mary. Especially Tuesday night as they stood in each other's arms, gazing over the open fields of windswept snow, and he kissed her softly, nuzzling her jaw line.

"Kerrilea," he said, "I want you to move in."

"What?" she answered. She wondered now -- things, perhaps, were moving *too* fast -- but he kissed her again and hugged her gently.

"Now, hear me out first," he said. "You know I'm married, but that my wife and I don't get along. She has a key to the townhouse, of course. Ostensibly that's in case she wants to come in to the city to do some shopping, that sort of thing, though she never uses it. But what's important to the company, as well as to someone in my position, is that appearances always be kept up. So, before you say yes or no, let me ask you this. In your records, it says you took an art minor in college?"

"Yes," she said. "Art history, really. I thought maybe, some day, I might find myself in a position to do appraisals."

"Good enough. You'd know something about interior decorating then? Or at least . . . what I'm getting at . . . you'd at least be a person with good taste?"

"Well, uh, I suppose so," she answered.

"Good," he said. "This is the deal, then. Ostensibly, I want you to move in as a consultant. On Christmas Eve, the company president wants me to use the townhouse for a party. A really important one -- overseas guests and people like that. So I need to worry about decorations that will give an aura of taste. Will show our guests that we're sophisticated people, capable of handling anything they might need us to do as well or better than they could. You understand?"

"Uh, I think I do," she said.

"Good. Again it's really appearances, but it's important. And I'd rather put you on the payroll than some kind of pansy professional decorating firm. Now, you'd have a full expense account too, though there really isn't that much to be done. But the thing is you'd need to see what things look like in different sorts of light, evening and daytime, so it'll be twenty-four hours a day."

"Uh, sure," she said. "I understand that. But you said 'on the payroll?' And what about my time at the office?"

He smiled and looked at her. Behind them both, she could hear the wind whistle. "Race you down the slope to the lodge in a minute," he whispered, then went on in more businesslike tones. "You'll get vacation pay for the office. Let's face it, even with Mary's duties it's not that the job is so complicated that we can't find somebody else to do it. And then, after Christmas, we'll see about something opening upstairs."

"Robert!" she said. She hugged him, hard, then pushed away from him. "I'd love to, Robert. But first, that race downhill?"

He laughed and pushed off on his skis. "Hey, no fair!" she shouted, then pushed off too, following closely, feeling the wind ripple through her hair. She imagined, ahead, in the shadowed trees, the sound of wolves howling as they ran with her, coursing downward under a waxing moon.

"Robert," she laughed, and she heard him laugh too, still just ahead of her.

"Kerrilea, look, one more thing after Christmas. About my wife, Tanya."

Tanya? she thought. She'd heard that name somewhere. "Yes, Robert?" she shouted back.

"You know how things are. It could take some money. A lot of time, maybe. But I've already promised her that I'd spend next weekend at the country house with her -- mostly for planning for the kids' Christmas, when they get home from school -- and, while I'm there, I'm going to ask her for a divorce."

Things went very fast from that time on. Kerri, with her own key now, settled into Robert's townhouse. She spent the first weekend unpacking things from her old apartment, moving most of them into a spare room which, officially, would be her "office." She ran across the books she had taken out from the library -- how many weeks ago? -- books on the city's underground structure -- and spent the evenings when Robert was with his wife going through them.

They were her hobby now. Daytimes were filled with work -- work she found herself growing into. First she went over the entire townhouse, room by room, memorizing every detail, visualizing how accents would change things, how moving furniture to new positions might alter spaces. How colors and lights could define new patterns.

And then came the buying. Trips out in the jostling cold of the city, elbowing through crowds of holiday shoppers. Fending off beggars.

She saw more beggars this year than ever before, she thought. The regular beggars with cups or outstretched hands augmented by the Salvation Army, the Goodwill, the others with fur-trimmed costumes and bells. She heard the music, deafening sometimes, blasting the streets from department stores. The carols of Santa and presents and luxury -- all in the midst of the longest recession that she could remember.

She even saw dog packs. One late afternoon, when she took a shortcut across the park, she saw shapes running between the trees, howling like in her dreams -- how many weeks ago?

Most nights now, when Robert wasn't there to keep her busy until almost morning, she found herself going to bed too tired to dream. She'd read of the city a little -- the tunnels -- their windings and crossings -- their generally half-concealed exits and entries -- perhaps as a substitute for dreaming. Or maybe just to take her mind off the pre-Christmas chaos she found on street level.

What was Christmas? She laughed. A time of rest and renewal. A time of birth of a new religion. A virgin named "Mary."

Not in this city.

A city of beggars and dog packs and snow that turned black before it could hit the sidewalk. A city of record colds. This month, according to the TV, it had gotten so cold that even parts of the lake were frozen.

But she had a fur wrap that Robert had given her.

And she had the soundproofed quiet of the townhouse that she could retreat to. Most nights she had it all to herself, although occasionally, even if it was a weeknight, Robert was able to find some excuse to stay late at the office and, afterward, spend the night with her. Weekends he had to spend in the country -- the kids -- the divorce -- Tanya was making trouble, he said, which meant things might drag on well into the new year. But weeknights, sometimes, he'd check her progress.

"I'm really impressed," he told her once, when things had only begun to take shape. Other times he'd just stare, open mouthed, but Kerri could tell from the look in his eyes, the feel of his lips later when they made love that what she was doing continued to please him.

She worked with whites, first off. Muted whites that matched her own skin, and contrasted sharply with her black hair and the dark of the clothing that Robert liked on her. For accent colors, she used browns and greens in soft, earth-like patterns, creating a stillness much like an evergreen garden in winter.

In one room the focal point was the fireplace. She lit a fire once, when Robert was with her. "What do you think of the lighting?" she asked him as they sat on the couch together, surrounded by flickering, orange-toned shadows.

"I. . . ." Robert was speechless. He kissed her, not even waiting to go to the bedroom beyond, and they made love violently on the rug in front of the hearth.

She thought about the effect she'd created the morning after, when Robert had had to go back to the office, and found a way to reflect it with track lights -- reds and purples -- in the master bedroom proper and, in a toned-down version in yellows, build a similar kind of excitement into the dining room and kitchen. Earth and sex -- stillness in winter, yet mixed with a promise of springtime and rutting. In contrast to outside, artificial, garishly lit with neons and searchlights, washed in the noise of traffic and bell-ringing, piped-in music and people shouting.

Robert took pictures. The Friday before Christmas, Robert told her he'd shown them to the company president so he could see what she had accomplished.

"What did he say?" she asked.

"Well, you know how I was when you showed me the fireplace?"

"He kissed you?" she giggled.

"No," Robert said, laughing too. "I mean at first he couldn't say anything. Then he asked me to tell him your name again. Then he said, in a deep, booming voice, 'Kerrilea Stava? You keep that young woman with you, Armbruster. Mark my words, she's going to go far.'"

Kerri laughed, then her voice turned serious.

"I hope you told him it wasn't finished. Robert, there's so much left to do, and Christmas Eve is just four days away. I've still got to finish planning the menu. Hors d'oeuvres at nine -- at least set up then so, when people come in, they'll find them waiting. A sit-down supper at eleven-thirty. Liquor and glasses. And then the final decorations -- the finishing touches -- silver and place settings -- muted crimson, I think, for the tablecloth, with green and white -- but a soft green, like ivy -- "

Robert cut her off with a kiss. "You'll do fine, Kerrilea," he said. "Listen, though. I've got to be home again this weekend -- you know, the divorce thing -- at least we've gotten to the point where we're choosing lawyers. And then the kids -- they've gone off to spend Christmas with friends of theirs, so that they'll be out of the way. But Monday and Tuesday I've got to go back and forth to the airport, to make sure the overseas guests are settled, so I won't see you until Tuesday evening. Probably not until maybe seven or even later -- just time enough for a bite to eat and a change of clothing. You understand?"

"I understand," she said. She kissed him back. "I just wish that wife of yours. . . ."

"Shhh," Robert said. "I've just got an hour more, then I've got to go. Maybe just enough time to see what finishing touches you've put in the bedroom?"

That night Kerri dreamed again of the snowfields, the white under moonlight. She dreamed of dark shapes howling beneath green trees, dashing in curving paths out to the open ice, beckoning for her to follow after. She dreamed she was running now, one hand clutched across her breasts, the other swinging free, breathing the frozen air.

Searching for something -- a cave? -- a spot of red staining the pale ground?

She woke to a pale dawn. So much to do, but the dream, somehow, had refreshed her. Strengthened her. That night she thought she might go out to dinner, but finally decided to stay at home and cook for herself in Robert's kitchen.

Before bed that night, she found one of the books on the city's underground -- even these had been neglected in the frenzy of the past few days, but she made time to look at its pictures. She looked at the map of the lakefront section and thought back, a month ago? More than a month ago? Going to that jazz club, itself called the Underground. Sleeping with -- what was his name? -- that bass player. Finding the tunnels.

So much had changed since then. Still, the next day, out of curiosity, she found her jeans and her black vee-necked top, her inverted-cross earrings, and, wrapping her old cloth coat around her she went outside. She went down the stairs of the nearest subway, nearly deserted on a Sunday, and thought of the map of the downtown section. She crept down the ladder from the platform and entered the tunnel, looking left and right, letting her eyes adjust to the darkness. Sure enough -- a blacker section -- she eased her way through, ducking slightly to avoid an overhead pipe, then, turning a corner, she found herself in a shower of whiteness.

Tunnel winter! Above her she saw a grate to the sidewalk, snow sifting through it. Ahead in the dim light, she saw caverns branching and, this time, because of the books she'd been reading, she knew

248

exactly where each tunnel led to. For laughs, she took one to the city library, coming up narrow stairs to a maintenance shed in the small park across the street from it.

She dreamed again that night of the snowfields, knowing, this time, what had inspired her theme for decorating the townhouse. Stillness, yet violence. A crimson tablecloth -- due to be delivered Monday -- and blood on the snow.

Monday, she finalized her menu -- rich, red meats and white, snow-soft cheeses; crisp, dark salads -- and called the caterer.

Tuesday morning, she went to the liquor wholesaler in person, to inspect a wine he'd said he was expecting. She made her order: delivery at precisely eight-thirty, before the caterers, yet not so early the bowls of cracked ice would be already starting to melt when people arrived.

Tired, thankful that it had been snowing again that morning to keep the last-minute-shopping crowds down, she decided to stop off for lunch at a cafe. So much to do, she thought, but now it was almost completed. A final go-over of her checklist -- she did that while waiting for her sandwich -- then, finally, a chance to relax and be herself, just for a few hours, before the evening.

But something was wrong.

She knew, as she opened the door of the townhouse, that someone was there. An unfamiliar smell, perhaps -- a lingering of perfume that she didn't use herself. Not in the room where she was, exactly, but somewhere, beyond, a faint sound of breathing.

She strained her ears as she reached in her shoulder bag, searching for something to use to protect herself. Her fingers closed around a thin, curved knife.

She pulled it out, carefully, gazing at the feathery patterns around its handle as she eased its blade from its sheath. Carefully, silently, she put her bag down, then followed the sound to the master bedroom.

She eased the door open -- then stared at a wolf's head. Gear -- that was the bass player's name -- and Tanya. Robert's wife, recognized now from a picture he'd shown her of her and the children -- the woman she'd met in the Underground club. The one who drank Scotch sours. Twined, naked, around him.

And now she lay sleeping, her platinum blonde hair swirled in tangles around Gear's tattoo. Turning scarlet as Kerri's knife slashed down, first opening the throat of the young bass player. Then, as the older woman woke screaming, cutting through vocal cords, adding blood to blood, flesh to flesh. Adding breath to breath in the sacrifice of their final consummation.

Kerri sat, breathing hard, feeling the slick blood against her buttocks. She wiped off her knife on Tanya's hair, then leaned across her shoulders to Gear and gave him a last kiss. "You might have done better," she said as she stood up.

She looked at the clock. There would be no trouble that night, she thought, as long as she made sure the bedroom door stayed locked. And as for tomorrow -- well, Robert *was* wealthy. Money took care of things. Nevertheless, half the afternoon was wasted, leaving scarcely enough time to shower, to hide her blood-stained clothes in the hamper. Once she had done that, she brushed her hair, letting it hang long behind her back. She selected her black formal strapless gown and put it on, then took out her mother's necklace and placed it around her throat, letting its silver, waxing-moon pendant dangle against the white of her breasts.

She inspected herself in the master bedroom's full-length mirror, seeing, as well, the dead lovers' corpses still sprawled across the bed behind her. She thought of her earrings -- not the buttons she'd worn for Robert when they'd gone dancing that time so long ago -- when he'd first kissed her -- but, for more drama, the upside-down crosses. The ones from the beggar.

She found them and put them on. Then, closing the bedroom door behind her, she slipped down the hall and into the kitchen. She looked at the kitchen clock -- no time for dinner before Robert got there -- the afternoon wasted -- but still time enough to calm her nervousness. To plan her announcement -- her gift for Robert.

She opened the refrigerator and took out a beer. Robert didn't drink beer himself, but sometimes she found *she* still enjoyed one. She found an opener and cracked the bottle, drinking it straight from its long, hard neck.

She heard the doorbell ring. It was Robert.

The opened the front door and let him in, his arms filled with packages, snow falling off his head and shoulders. "Boy, it's rough out," he said as she took the brightly-wrapped presents from him, then took his hat and coat. "Beastly. People will probably be late, but" -- he stopped a moment and looked around him, drinking in the

fireplace, the tree, where Kerri had already set down the presents --
"but these are for you, to open later. It's beautiful, Kerrilea, what
you've done here. The presents are a sort of thank you."

"Hush," she said, kissing him softly. Hidden lights glinted off her
earrings. "I've got a little something for you too -- in just a minute."

He held her at arms length. "You're wonderful, Kerrilea. God,
how I love you. That dress. Those earrings -- I don't know about
them. I mean, some of the people we'll be having are kind of
conservative. Still, it is part of the new generation -- the kind of thing
people your age are wearing." He paused and chuckled. "If anyone
says something, I'll just tell them that people your age, and even
younger, are the new customers we've got to reach to."

Kerri giggled. "I love you, too, Robert," she whispered, leaning
into his arms again. Letting him kiss her, his hand rove behind her.
"But now, my surprise for you?"

"Yes, by all means," Robert said as he followed her into the
bedroom. He waited in darkness while she found the light switch.

"No!" he shouted the instant the bedroom lights flared into
brightness. "That's Tanya and -- God! -- who's *that*?" He staggered
forward, gazing at the bed with its blood-spattered occupants, then
turned and faced Kerri.

"What the hell happened here?" he whispered, as if afraid, if he
asked out loud, that something even worse might be revealed in
answer. Kerri leaned forward and put her lips over his.

"Don't you see, Robert?" she asked when his body stiffened against
her. "I did it for you. It solves all our problems -- your wife an

adulteress. She and her boyfriend found dead together. No more worries about her trying to fight your divorce."

"No!" he shouted. He reached out and slapped her, hard, across the face.

"Robert!" she screamed. Her mind snapped back to the first time she'd met him. The hand on her breast.

The slap then. The pain.

She felt her blood rush up -- red over fields of snow.

Snarling, she lunged forward, feeling a surge of strength as she pushed him back, sprawling, across the bed with its corpses. Legs spread wide, she jumped on top of him, pinning him down.

She tore at his throat, not needing the knife she had used on the others. She tore with her teeth.

She felt the blood gurgle, then spurt in her mouth, and she sucked it in greedily. Sating her hunger -- a hunger of spirit as well as of body. She felt his legs kick out, his hands claw her back, but she only drank deeper, reveling in the warmth of his blood as it splashed on her shoulders.

At last she could drink no more. Slowly she sat up, his body already cooling beneath her.

She howled as a wolf howls. . . .

And heard a bell answer!

The doorbell! The caterers -- or else the liquor. It scarcely mattered.

She scrambled off the bed to her feet.

She looked at herself in the full-length mirror.

The back door, she thought. *Wolves have to run free.*

Wolves and. . . .

She shook her head, forcing herself to turn from the mirror. Now, as well as the bell, she heard knocking.

Wolves' dams were witches -- why had she thought that? She crept, soundlessly, through the kitchen and let herself out the back way to the alley.

The snow was still falling, hard enough to cover any tracks she might leave. But more important, except for the beggars -- the desperate people who had to be outside -- the path in front of her was deserted.

She reached her hand up, still slick with blood, and clutched it across the front of her ruined dress. She ran with the beggars. She led them, howling, through blazing neon and jagged, kaleidoscopic shadows.

She found the subway and plunged down the dark stairs, closing her eyes to let them adjust faster to the blackness. Into the tunnel -- she knew the way without having to look. Into mazes of caverns. She ran, strangely warm herself, through pools of harsher chill -- bright, colored snow-showers -- the city's festive lights reflected through sidewalk gratings.

She ran, scarcely caring, until she crashed up against an iron door. The door to the Underground -- she recognized it -- but, when she tried it, she found it was rusted shut. Stopping, she glanced around. To her left, orange light.

Warm, peaceful orange -- these were the tunnels she'd seen in her dream. The ones under the hill. But, when she blinked her eyes, she also knew them from when she'd killed Mary.

She looked for the beggars, but she was alone now. Except, in the distance, she now heard the murmur of chanting voices.

She followed the voices, as in her dream, except that also she retraced the steps that she had taken with Mary.

She laughed out loud -- *the Virgin of Christmas!* What time was it now? Nine or nine-thirty when she'd heard the doorbell? The storm would have made the caterers late. At least three hours more down here in the tunnels.

She followed the voices, knowing now what she would find as she paced the air vent beneath the city. She came to the junction where she had left Mary, then turned left -- not right as she had before to return to the subway -- but left to the hollow, torch lit expanse of the overflow basin.

Putting her hand down, letting the front of her gown fall open, she walked slowly forward through the ranks of dark, hooded worshipers to the altar. Lying at full length, partly shadowed under the huge upside-down cross behind it, she saw Robert's body.

She bent down to kiss it, then looked up and smiled as the priestess came toward her.

The old woman smiled back -- a smile Kerri knew well. A smile and a whisper:

"We've missed you, Daughter."

255

Leaving Avalon

by Lisa Mantchev

The Wearyall Hill Bed and Breakfast looked perfectly ordinary from the outside. Gwen peered at it through a curtain of gray drizzle, while rivulets of moisture worked their way under the collar of her cloak and down the small of her back. A compact, comfortably overrun garden separated the façade from the street, and a cherry-red door waited for her at the end of the narrow path.

This looks like as good a place as any to run away from home.

"Are you lost, then?" The masculine voice in Gwen's ear made her jump. She turned around, and the stranger gave her a lopsided grin. "Perhaps I can point you in the right direction."

"No, thank you." Gwen got a better grip on her dripping suitcase and pointed at the house. "This is where I'm staying."

"Will Mrs. Heath be expecting you?" The stranger angled his head to get a better look at the scrap of paper in Gwen's hand. Gwen barely registered his mop of dark and laughing eyes before she stuffed the address in her pocket.

"I called and confirmed my reservation from the airport. Thank you, Mr.--"

"White. Byron White. And if you find yourself in need of a tour guide during your stay in Glastonbury, promise to look me up." He gave her a mocking salute and moved down the street, whistling. Shaking her head at his audacity, Gwen walked to the stoop. An angular woman she knew at once must be Mrs. Heath, proprietress, jerked the door open before she could so much as reach for the knocker.

"Lord bless me! We weren't expecting you for at least another month! Come in! Come in and dry yourself, dearie."

Within minutes, Gwen found herself ensconced in the parlor, a cup of tea in hand and her sodden suitcase drying out before the gas logs. A gummy-eyed falcon eyed her from the mantelpiece, talons extended towards a frozen, fleeing squirrel. Gwen repressed a shudder when she noticed the footstool near her knee balanced on three precarious clawed legs. Furry legs.

"Those are interesting," she managed as she balanced a delicate china cup in one hand and the plate of cake in the other. "They look very... lifelike."

"My dear Ernie, God-rest-his-soul, had a rare hand with the creatures. Nary an animal would cross his path that he didn't track, trap and stuff with cotton wool." Mrs. Heath measured out sugar and lemon with genteel abandon. She wielded the sugar tongs like a weapon of war. "A goddess worshipper, are you? One of those New Age pagans?"

"I am, but I promise I won't dance naked around your garden in the light of the moon." Gwen gave up trying to balance cup and cake and set the china on the morbid footstool. She hoped it wouldn't spring to life and scratch her eyes out.

"'Tisn't the right time o' the year for dancing under the moon unless you've a mind to take a chill and spend your holiday in bed," Mrs. Heath advised. "Later in the season, all of Glastonbury will be awash with tourists for the fire feasts and Midsummer's Eve. You're a bit early for all of that."

"I don't mind. I'm not particularly fond of crowds." Gwen shook her head and the beads on her dozens of thin, blond braids clacked together. "But what makes you think I'm not here to gawk at the Abbey ruins and search out the Holy Thorn?"

Mrs. Heath smiled into her teacup. "The Christian pilgrims wear good sturdy shoes and walking trousers, not that hemp fabric your dress is made of. And with all your charms and bangles, I heard you coming from three blocks away."

Gwen laughed. "I want to explore the Tor a bit. Get a feel for the regional pagan activity."

"Writing a book, are you?" Mrs. Heath leaned in eagerly. "We have quite of few writer folk pass through, looking for some new way to tell the legend of Arthur, sniffing about for the Holy Grail."

"Sorry, but I'm not a writer. I'm a professional nomad. I've always wanted to visit Avalon."

Avalon.

The very name conjured up a vicious thrill in her stomach. Arthurian legend, biblical tales and Pagan beliefs wove themselves around the three syllables and breathed new life into Gwen's travel-exhausted body. A clattering on the stoop jerked her back into Mrs.

Heath's parlor as a teenaged girl bounced into the parlor.

"Back from school, Mum!" the girl cried. She dropped her books and bag next to the hearth and reached for a biscuit. Mrs. Heath swatted at the newcomer and gestured to the clutter on the floor.

"Pick those up directly, young lady. No doubt you've a pile of homework to see to. Gwen, this is my daughter Charlotte."

"Hi," Gwen said, and lifted a hand in greeting.

"Pleased to meet you," Charlotte said, and grabbed another cookie before gathering up her maligned schoolbooks. "Have a heart, Mum! I'll starve before I get all this homework done."

Charlotte pounded up the front stairs, voice fading into the distance. Gwen smiled at Mrs. Heath.

"I don't suppose anyone in the village is looking to hire on some help? I'm a bit low on funds because I left earlier than I planned, and I want to be able to stay a month at least."

Mrs. Heath pursed her lips and considered the matter, no doubt running through her mental file of shops and services, friends and neighbors.

"Is there something special you can do? That massage maybe, with the oils?"

Gwen nodded. Some of the worry in her belly relaxed for the first time since her hurried exit from America. "I've done a bit with aromatherapy, actually."

"The New Age shop, Mum," Charlotte hollered down the stairs. "Bernadette's having her baby and wanting a bit of time off."

"Go do your homework," Mrs. Heath shouted back, then lowered her voice back to a speaking tone. "But that might just work and we'll see about it tomorrow. What you need right now is a good night's sleep. You're nodding off this blessed moment."

Mrs. Heath scattered crumbs as she grasped Gwen's suitcase and propelled her towards the stairs. Unblinking glass eyes witnessed their progress up to the second floor. It appeared that Mrs. Heath's Ernie, God-rest-his-soul, had made good use of every available wall to display his collection of furry friends.

"I've put you in the Rose room. The bathroom is down the hall. I'll hope you'll find it to your liking."

Gwen's eyes lingered on a snarling badger in a glass case as she moved past Mrs. Heath and into a quaint room, thankfully free of dead animals. She changed into the first nightgown she pulled from her suitcase and fell face-first into the fat feather bed.

She dreamed of the Tor. Apple trees, or the ghosts of apple trees, stretched out before her for miles. Enchanted boughs, laden with milk-white flowers, reached slim arms towards the heavens as though in prayer. Byron stood at her side.

"Before the Christians, before the Celts even, this was a sacred place." His eyes roamed over the fairyland. "The apples are a food of immortality and of knowledge. Eve knew. This was her Eden. That's why so many came afterwards. Arthur of Camelot. Joseph of Arimathea. They were drawn here by something old and holy. It was the Earth, calling them home."

Gwen shivered; the words poured music into her tired soul. She reached for his hand, warm and solid.

"In all the stories, it begins with an apple. And inside the apple are the seeds for all the other stories."

Ghosts drifted through the ancient orchard; the ghosts of goddesses and worshippers, knights and fair ladies. They wove in and out of the moonlight, called to each other, wended their way through the labyrinth of branches and boughs. Gwen longed to join them, to travel back through the layers of time and place. The legend's heart pulsed red with the blood of so many believers.

"Never fall asleep in the moonlight, or you'll be lost to the dream of it," he said, and bent to kiss her. The trees melted away, bits of spun sugar touched by the heat of their bodies. Tears moistened Gwen's eyes as she woke. The enchanted vista evaporated into the chill night air and left her with an emptiness that cried out to be filled.

She woke again sometime the next afternoon, and lay for a moment with her eyes tightly shut against a lengthening shaft of sunlight. Through the floorboards, the sounds of Charlotte and Mrs. Heath in the kitchen confirmed that reality, in whatever form it might choose to take, awaited her downstairs.

The Heath kitchen welcomed her in with the aroma of baking bread and spices. The yellow-papered walls suggested egg yolks and lemon custard while an enormous white gas range of a vintage year radiated heat.

"She's awake!" Charlotte greeted her with a wave and a cheeky grin. Gwen looked closely at the girl, wondering if she should mention their midnight excursion. Mrs. Heath plunked a blueberry-studded scone on the table.

"You slept right through supper last night, breakfast and lunch," Mrs. Heath said with motherly disapproval. She smoothed back a wisp of mouse-brown hair that had escaped the coil at the nape of her neck. "And how will you take your tea this fine afternoon, dearie?"

Before Gwen could answer, Charlotte flounced in her seat. "I want to take Gwen down the meet Bernadette."

Mrs. Heath nodded to a napkin-wrapped bundle on the table. "Take those to herself, and don't squeeze the life from them."

Holding the warm and fragrant bundle of scones, Gwen followed Charlotte's streaming scarf tails out the gate and to the left. The architecture of the town charmed her with an incongruent assortment of Georgian and Victorian structures. Shops were crammed cheek-and-jowl against small houses, posh hotels and smaller bed and breakfasts. Charlotte, blithely oblivious to Gwen's fatigue, towed her inexorably down the sidewalk.

"The girls at school will be just wild when they find out I have a Yank staying at our house," Charlotte said, and tucked her arm through Gwen's companionably. "Your clothes are wicked and so are those braids. Think you could do that to me?"

Gwen contemplated the thick masses of Charlotte's hair. "If you can hold still for a few hours, and your mother agrees, we can have a go at it after dinner."

"Jubilation!" Charlotte skipped a few steps, her cheeks pink with fresh air and their swift pace. Gwen couldn't stop the laugh that bubbled up.

Charlotte soon turned in at Bernadette's shop, housed in the front room of a two-story stone building. New Age accoutrements cluttered the shelves: handmade soaps next to crystals and leather pouches. Plastic beads in rainbow strands hung in the rain-smudged windows, and a small library of New Age reading material occupied the wall opposite. Gwen breathed in the cacophonous aroma of oils, candles and incense, and felt at home.

Bernadette greeted them, her belly heavy with pregnancy. "So who's your friend?"

"Gwen Tanner. She's from America," Charlotte announced with importance. "We thought maybe she could give you hand with things here in the shop, what with the baby coming next month and you not able to reach your zipper."

"Looking for work, are you?" Bernadette looked Gwen over from Birkenstocks to braids. "You've the look of the goddess about you, that's for certain."

"Not only that, but I come bearing gifts of baked goods," Gwen said, and handed her the cooling napkin-wrapped package.

"I thought I smelled Maeve's scones! Bless your mother, Charlotte." Bernadette raised her eyes skyward in thanks. Charlotte bobbed her head impatiently.

"So, can you use her, Bernie?"

"I think we can work something out so you needn't fuss about working papers and the like," Bernadette said with a wink, wiping her hands on a paper napkin. "If you come in tomorrow Gwen, you can familiarize yourself with the stock and I can go over the finer points of our tourist industry. We'll be holding Fledgling Witch seminars, starting next week. I think your arrival will prove to be a blessing."

"Fledgling Witch seminars?" Gwen asked with a grin.

"Beginners in the Craft. They bus in from London, looking for ways to make their men stay faithful and wanting spells for fortune and the like. Harmless, most of them. We give them a day course in herbs and rituals and then they buy their supplies through the store. Think you can handle that sort of thing?"

"Absolutely!" Gwen offered her new employer her right hand, and they shook on the deal. She breathed an inward sign of relief. "Thank you so much."

Back out on the street, Charlotte crowed with triumph.

"It's perfect. Now you can stay for months and months!" She took a leaping step, arms thrown out wide and landed on Byron White, who had just rounded the corner.

"Charlotte, what in the ruddy hell do you think you're doing?" He disentangled himself from the pinwheel of her arms and legs. Charlotte's crimson scarf fell like a burning banner onto the gray stones of the street and Gwen bent over to retrieve it. Byron had the same thought, and she cracked her head against his.

"Lord Almighty, you have the skull of an ox, woman!" Byron yelped, jumping back.

"I could say the same thing about you," Gwen answered with a scowl.

"Byron White, meet my friend Gwen," Charlotte said, assuming the duties of hostess. "She's from America, and she's going to work in Bernadette's shop."

"We've met," he said. "A Pagan, then are you, Miss Gwen? The last time I saw you, you were mostly covered up with a very damp cloak, if I recall correctly." He ran a hand through his hair and seemed to take comfort in putting his appearance to rights.

"You must be the local witch burner. I'm afraid I don't have any Bibles I want thumped today, but you can check back with me next week." Gwen smiled brightly at him, and pulled Charlotte away, incapacitated as her young companion was with a fit of giggles.

"I can't believe you said that to him!" Charlotte said with a whoop of laughter. "His brother's the vicar!"

"At least he's not the vicar." Gwen's cheeks burned in the darkness, as much over his words as her retort.

"No, he's a barrister. My dad used to say that was worse." Charlotte giggled and turned in at her gate.

Gwen knew without looking that Byron White's eyes followed them until they passed through the red front door. Absorbed by the pre-dinner preparations of setting out linen, china and silver, Gwen nearly managed to forget the look on his face when he recognized her.

Nearly.

Gwen made the trip up the Tor three more times in the following weeks, once in the daylight and twice at night. Neither of her trips revealed the fairy-vista that had appeared in her dream, but the rolling green view soothed the heartache and eased the troubles from her mind.

And so she passed the days in Bernadette's shop, dispensing incense and advice to the locals and Londoners. When Charlotte and Mrs. Heath departed for church on Sunday mornings, Gwen strolled the streets of the village with her hands in her pockets. Invariably, Byron White intercepted Gwen's roving gaze when she passed the church on those rambles. Wearing what Charlotte referred to as his "Sunday face," he stood framed in one of the stained glass windows and lifted a cheerful hand to her as she hurried by.

Gwen was acutely aware of his presence, both in church and around the town. When she went to buy a packet of biscuits for tea, he was in Enid's tiny grocery store buying cigarettes. When she joined Mrs. Heath at the pub for a gin and lemon, he was there paying for a pint.

She told herself it was to be expected; in a small town like this, people crossed paths more often than not. If only she didn't have the sneaking suspicion that Bernie and Charlotte were plotting something behind the counter of the New Age shop. If only he didn't look so good to her, with his dark eyes and easy laughter.

You're not attracted to him, she reminded herself when found Byron waiting on the stoop at Bernadette's. Yeah. Keep telling yourself that, Gwen.

"Good morning, Mr. White," she said, pleased by her own polite tone. She moved past him and reaching for the enrollment sheets. "Shouldn't you be at your office?"

"It's Saturday, remember?" Byron followed her inside. The

breadth of his shoulders looked out of place against the low ceilings and delicate crystal displays. With wandering fingers, he selected a glass vial of essential oil from the counter, removed the stopper and inhaled deeply. "And I figured it was about time to expand my horizons, considering this town is a hot bed of Pagan activity--" He sneezed violently, spraying droplets of orange and ylang-ylang over the counter. Gwen took the bottle away before he could break it. "So I'm here for the seminar."

"Oh, right. You're here for the seminar! And I'll be teaching a Sunday school class next week." Gwen replaced the cork and put the bottle back in the aromatherapy rack. So you can just toddle off to the pub and tell them how you put one over on the green Yankee Pagan.

Byron reached for the enrollment sheet and pointed to his name, third from the top. "There I am, right there. Signed up and paid for." His vivid blue eyes crinkled at the corners when he smiled at her. "So just point me in the direction of the tea caddy and I'll help you get ready for that busload of tourists that will be arriving any minute now."

She realized that her mouth was hanging ajar. Gwen closed it and pointed in the direction of the back room just as a very unwieldy Bernadette rounded the last turn of the stairs.

"Byron, whatever are you doing here?" She accepted a hearty kiss on the cheek from him as he headed towards the back room.

"He's here for the seminar," Gwen said, cutting open a box containing a new shipment of candles. She checked the inventory against the invoice and tried to ignore the heat creeping up her neck. "Don't pretend you don't know. You enrolled him."

"Can I stop the man from taking a class or two, especially when it puts money in your pocket and mine?" Bernadette began clearing merchandise off the heavy wooden table in the center of the room. "How many chairs do we need?"

"Eight." Gwen set out enough white candles for each participant, and followed it with a selection of herbs. The tang of lavender filled the room and calmed her ruffled spirits. She would lead the seminar the same way she always did, with enjoyment and professionalism. Even if Byron White's blue eyes followed her every move.

"I hope you got your money's worth," Gwen said as she locked the door to the shop. They'd eaten dinner with Bernadette and her husband, and it was now past eleven. Byron watched her, weighed down with a paper sack filled with candles, books and crystals. Gwen had seen to it that his wallet was considerably lighter than when he'd arrived that morning, heaping "essentials" on the counter and ringing him up before he could even protest.

Not that he had protested. He'd raised an eyebrow and paid the bill without saying a word. He'd also waited until the busload of tourists had departed to help her clear the chairs and sweep out the shop. Then he'd announced his intention of walking her home, and all the curt words she could summon would not dissuade him.

"I don't need an escort. I'm not a child."

"I know," he said, his tone agreeable even as he matched her swift pace.

"It's only a few blocks, and I can find my own way."

"No doubt you can."

"I hope you got your money's worth."

"I think I did. A few hours in your company are worth two hundred pounds, don't you think?"

Gwen came to a standstill and peered up at him with incredulity. "You didn't go through all of that just to spend time with me."

"Sure enough, I did. You wouldn't give me the time of day at the pub. I think if I caught on fire, you'd go searching for marshmallows and a good, sharp stick. And I couldn't go on sneaking peeks at you during church without the entire town knowing my business, so I had to come to you, didn't I?"

"That's the most ridiculous thing I ever heard." Gwen pushed past him and hurried down the street.

Byron kept pace with her. He caught her right hand in his left and tucked it under his arm. "What's so ridiculous about it?"

"Let go of my hand." Gwen skidded on a slick pavement stone and fell against him.

"Careful there." Byron ducked his head and pressed a warm and lingering kiss against her lips. Gwen felt the world drift away from her. The bottom fell out of her stomach and stars exploded behind her eyelids. When he pulled away, Gwen stared at him. Byron smiled down at her, and Gwen jerked back into herself by landing a well-placed kick on his shins.

"Argh!" He hopped back from her. "What the hell was that for?"

"That was for coming into the store and wasting my time and kissing me without asking!" Gwen pushed a handful of wayward braids off her face and tried to glare at him.

Byron didn't seem at all put off by her stern look. "You can't blame a man for trying, now can you? You've been here a month and I didn't know how much longer I could wait. I've been thinking about kissing you since the night you arrived."

"Four weeks today," Gwen said. She looked up at the sky, embarrassed by her recent assault on his person. Her lips burned where he'd kissed her, and she struggled to forget her body's response to him. Say something to him. Apologize for kicking him in the shin. If only the devilish part of her brain wasn't urging her to kick him again. She settled instead for a lame observation. "There's a full moon again."

As soon as the words left her lips, she wanted to bite her tongue.

"The full moons here are special." Byron ventured within range of her feet. When she made no sudden moves to hurt him, he reached for her hand and drew her down Chilkwell Street, past the Chalice Well and towards the Tor. "Even my brother says they're magical, and he's the most practical person I know."

"You have no idea just how magical." She let him tow her up the hill.

Byron stopped abruptly and Gwen crashed into him. He turned and leaned closer until Gwen could smell his soap and something innately masculine--cologne, perhaps, or aftershave. Gwen resisted the inexplicable urge to bury her nose in the front of his shirt even as he peered closely at her.

"What made you say that?"

"Say what?" Gwen found it hard to concentrate with him standing so close.

"That I have no idea how magical. What did you mean by that?" He held both her hands now. Gwen couldn't take her eyes from his face. There had been another face she'd wanted to see, one that had disappeared without fulfilling the promise made to her by moonlight. But Byron's face didn't waver and disappear into a passing cloud, like the man hidden in the trees. He was solid, and his eyes burned with a contagious fire.

"The first night I came here, there was a full moon. And I dreamed I came out on the Tor. There were apple trees, Byron."

"And why wouldn't there be? They used to grow here, a long time ago.

Gwen looked up at the moon, full and heavy. It shone down on the pregnant belly of the earth. "Apples are for fertility. Did you know that?"

"Too many children born in this town to disprove that theory."

"And what do you think children should be raised to believe?" Gwen leaned against him, tested his solid presence. "The Christian or the pagan beliefs?"

"A little of both, I think."

Byron reached for her hand and gave it a little squeeze. "Just say that you won't be leaving anytime soon."

"How could I leave?" Gwen looked up at the sky. "I think, without meaning to, that I've come home."

Biographies

At the age of thirteen, **Gill Ainsworth** was whisked away from her 'green and pleasant land' to spend three years living in darkest Africa. She fell instantly in love with the continent and has never since missed an opportunity to return. During one such visit, she and her husband sponsored a little girl, Neema, and this story is dedicated to her. Gill may be contacted either though Apex *Science Fiction and Horror Digest* (www.apexdigest.com) or through Murky Depths (www.murkydepths.com)."

Boyfriend.com is **Amy J. Benesch's** twelfth published short story. Check out her web site: www.talewaever.org. She lives and dreams in the wilds of Yonkers, NY.

Louise Bohmer writes dark and erotic fiction, for the most part, but her pen does tend to wander where it wants. The muse controls Louise--not the other way around. Ms. Bohmer works full-time as a writer and freelance editor. In 2007, she begins work as a writing instructor, as well, for the International Order of Horror Professional. Louise is also the Canadian Regional Representative for IOHP. She lives in New Brunswick Canada, with her tattoo artist husband and their two rattie children. You can visit Louise in her virtual forest at: http://www.louisebohmer.com

272

James Dorr's new book, *Darker Loves: Tales of Mystery and Regret*, is due out from Dark Regions Press www.darkregions.com as a companion to his current collection, *Strange Mistresses: Tales of Wonder and Romance* (Dark Regions, 2001), while other work has appeared in such venues as *Alfred Hitchcock's Mystery Magazine, New Mystery,* and numerous anthologies. Dorr is an active member of SFWA and HWA, an Anthony (mystery) and Darrell (fiction set in the US Mid-South) finalist, winner of Best of the Web 1998, a Pushcart Prize nominee, keeper of a gray and black cat named Wednesday and has had work listed in *The Year's Best Fantasy and Horror* eleven of the past fifteen years.

Jane Gwaltney, a member of the Midwestern Writers of Horror, has twice received Honorable Mention in the Year's Best Fantasy and Horror. Her poetry, fiction, and art appear in *Dreams and Nightmares, Wicked Hollow, Whispers From The Shattered Forum, deathlings.com, Redsine, Simulacrum, Champagne Shivers*, and more. Her novella "Darkness, Darkness" will soon be available from Sam's Dot Publishing.

On Halloween '75, the witching hour struck and **Peter Mihaichuk** was thrust into the world. These auspicious beginnings foreshadowed an affinity to dark art and Peter has lived up to these expectations. Beginning his babblings early, in grade school, he was brought before a child psychologist to discuss a disturbing piece that consisted of an all-consuming tornado wreaking havoc with human and animal captives. At present, he lives in Sudbury , Ontario , Canada with his extremely understanding wife, beautiful daughter and strapping son, whittling away the wee hours documenting things that go bump in the night.

Christa Faust in her biography says "I'm a writer, a cynical, hardboiled broad with a fetish for noir cinema, tattoos and seamed stockings. I'm older than you think and younger than I feel. I've got great gams and perfect size five feet, if you can handle the razor-edged tongue that goes with them."

Caitlin R. Kiernan was born near Dublin, Ireland, but has spent most of her life in the southeastern United States. In college, she studied zoology, geology, and palaeontology, and has been employed as a vertebrate palaeontologist and college-level biology instructor. Her published novels include, *Silk* (1998), *Threshold* (2001), *Low Red Moon* (2003), *Murder of Angels* (2004), and *Daughter of Hounds* (2007).   To date, she has published more than sixty short stories, which have been collected in *Tales of Pain and Wonder* (2000), *Wrong Things* (with Poppy Z. Brite; 2001), *From Weird and Distant Shores* (2002), and *To Charles Fort, With Love* (2005). She has also scripted comics for DC/Vertigo, including *The Dreaming* ('97-'01), *The Girl Who Would Be Death* ('98), and *Bast: Eternity Game* ('03).

Lisa Mantchev casts her spells from an ancient tree in the Pacific Northwest. When not scribbling, she is by turns an earth elemental, English professor, actress, artist, dog wrangler, mommy, and domestic goddess. Her stories have been published in places like *Strange Horizons and New Voices in Science Fiction*, and she has stories slated to appear in *Weird Tales, Fantasy, Electric Velocipede* and various anthologies. She has just completed her first novel, entitled Scrimshaw. You can Taste the Bad Candy at her website: www.lisamantchev.com

Gary McMahon has sold stories to various small press magazines and anthologies. Recent appearances of note include stories in the World Fantasy Award winning Acquainted with the *Night, Poe's Progeny, Midnight Street, Bare Bone, Nemonymous and Bernie Herrmann's Manic Sextet*. A 35,000-word novella called *Rough Cut* is currently available from Pendragon Press, and a collection of short fiction, *Dirty Prayers*, and a new novella, *All Your Gods Are Dead*, will follow late in early 2007 from Gray Friar Press and Humdrumming Books respectively. Gary was lucky enough to receive 2 Honorable Mentions in The Year's Best Fantasy & Horror 18, and will receive 4 more in YBF&H 19. His latest project is co-editing (with Gary Fry) the Gray Friar Press themed anthology *Paging Mr. Hitchcock*. Gary can be found at: www.garymcmahon.com

Bev Vincent is the author of over forty stories, including contributions to the Bram Stoker Award-winning anthology *From the Borderlands, Doctor Who/Destination: Prague, A Dark and Deadly Valley, Thou Shalt Not, Apex Digest, Cemetery Dance, Corpse Blossoms, Shivers IV*, and the upcoming MWA anthology *The Blue Religion*, edited by Michael Connelly. His first book, The *Road to the Dark Tower,* an authorized exploration of Stephen King's Dark Tower series, was nominated for a 2004 Bram Stoker Award. He co-edited *The Illustrated Stephen King Trivia Book* and is a contributing editor with *Cemetery Dance magazine*. Visit him on the web at www.BevVincent.com.

Larisa Walk lives and writes her "fiction from the other side" in California. She shares her home with her husband who always knew that she would some day be published and two spoiled cats. All three of them are the nearest thing that she has to her own personal writing muses.

A.C. Wise was born and raised in Montreal, Canada and currently lives just outside of Philadelphia. Wise's work has appeared, or is forthcoming, in publications such as, *Realms of Fantasy, Fantasy Magazine, Lone Star Stories*, and the anthologies, *Shadow Regions, The Undead 2* and *Read by Dawn Volume 2*, among others.

About the Editors

Jason Andrew lives in Seattle, Washington with his wife Lisa. By day, he works as a mild-mannered technical writer. By night, he writes stories of the fantastic and occasionally fights crime. As a child, Jason spent his Saturdays watching the Creature Feature classics and furiously scribbling down stories. His first short story, written at age six, titled "The Wolfman Eats Perry Mason" was rejected and caused his grandmother to watch him very closely for a few years. Jason has had stories appear in Nasty Snips, Time for Bedlam, Hell's Hangmen, Arkham Tales, and the upcoming horror anthology Raw Meat. In addition, Jason was one of the co-editors for the anthology Gods and Monsters, recently released from Simian Publishing.

Check out his blog at http://highway-west.livejournal.com/

Michael Dyer lives near Seattle with his wife and son. His full time job is his son, but he helps out Simian Publishing in his spare time. He is sometimes an editor and sometimes a sounding board for Simian Publishing and doesn't like to pad egos by saying garbage is steak. He continues to hope this encourages better writing rather than crushing fragile psyches. When he isn't covering stories in red marks, he creates a webcomic called Heroes of Audioland at http://www.heroesofaudioland.com which he knows is just good enough to keep a few readers and just bad enough for his criticisms to come back to haunt him. Naturally he welcomes this.

About Simian Publishing

Simian Publishing is a small press company devoted to primal dark fantasy and horror fiction. We're interested in seeing how the old gods, monsters, and Jungian archetypes work in the modern world. We want fiction that touches our souls.

With Print on Demand technology, Simian Publishing is able to take chances on a story or novel that might never see the light of day through a mainstream publisher. Currently, we looking for more direct distributors, but for now you can find our products on a variety of online stores.

www.simianpublishing.org